MW01241870

Sterling University

Love Under the Stars

RK Phillips

LOVE UNDER THE STARS
by RK PHILLIPS

Editing by:
Michelle Edits

Cover Art by:
Anya Kelleye Designs

Cover Images:
Adobe Stock Images
www.stock.adobe.com

DEDICATION

This book is dedicated to everyone who loved Peyton in my first ever novel. Hope you enjoy reading about the students as much as I loved writing them.

ACKNOWLEDGMENTS

Thank you to all my readers who continue to pick up my stories and read them. Without you, I wouldn't have anyone to keep pushing me for the next book.

Thank you to my friends and family that listen to me talk on and on about my ideas. Your enthusiasm and tolerance is noticed and valued.

Thank you to my writing group. We keep one another accountable, share encouragement, and celebrate all the victories whether they are small or large. Without you, this book would not have been done in time.

Last, but not least, thank you to my cover artist, Anya, who was able to help an author out when it was crunch time! I appreciate your dedication and support through all of my tweaks.

CHAPTER 1

EVE

Eve clutched her schedule in her hand as she wandered down the hallway. She was a little lost as to where her first class was. Most everyone had already been going to this school for at least a semester, but she was just beginning and felt like she was the new kid in the middle of a school year yet again.

She finally found the room for Freshman Comp 101 and took a seat on the second row so she could focus. There weren't very many students in the classroom yet as Eve wanted to ensure she arrived in plenty of time in case she got lost, which she obviously had. Another girl sat down to her left and smiled over at her.

"Hi, my name is Nori. How are you doing?"

Eve grinned back and held out her hand. "Hello. I'm Eve. I'm fine. What about yourself?"

Nori took her hand and shook it before groaning. Eve thought maybe she didn't like the handshake until Nori's next words let her in on what was going on. "I have been avoiding this class. All English classes to be honest. But, my advisor told me that I had to take them or else I couldn't graduate. So, here I am."

"You aren't a freshman?"

"No, I am finishing up my sophomore year. Are you a freshman?"

"Yeah, and this is my first semester."

The warmth of Nori's smile was radiating. "Well, welcome to Sterling University."

"Thanks." Eve looked around the room and it had filled up quickly in those few minutes she had spent introducing herself. "Looks like this is going to be a big class."

"Yeah, most of the gen ed ones are." Nori lowers her voice a little, "Mr. R is about to start. I have heard good things about him. If you don't have another class immediately after this one, let's go get some coffee and I will give you some pointers."

Eve wasn't sure what to make of this very forward girl, but she appreciated the offer and wasn't about to refuse any sort of assistance. "Thanks. I have a break until my next class."

Nori pulled out her notebook and Eve took the cue and opened her laptop.

Mr. Rodriguez took a big stack of papers and began handing stacks of them to the first person in each row as he spoke. "Good morning, class. I am Mr. Rodriguez and this is Freshman Comp 101. If for some reason that is not the class you are to be attending at this time, you may leave. I once sat in a class for two weeks before I realized that I wasn't even signed up for it."

The whole class laughed and Eve relaxed, knowing while this might not be her favorite topic, at least her teacher appeared to be friendly and relaxed. Or, it could simply be the first day's good impressions. She hoped it was the former and not the latter.

He continued on with his story. "Luckily, I was still able to change my schedule. I ended up enrolling in the class and eventually switched what I wanted to pursue. This is why I stand before you now. Lesson one for my class. Embrace your mistakes, you never know where they might take you. Now for routine stuff of the class. You each have a syllabus in front of you. You are all capable of reading, so I am not going to read the thing out loud to you. There is a version online, too, that you can access. However, I made the mistake once of not printing these and a student said he never saw the syllabus and didn't know what was expected. Since then everyone gets a printed copy while I continue my murder spree of trees."

Nori leaned over and whispered, "At least the comments I have heard about him are true. I think I might survive this class."

Mr. Rodriguez went over the highlights of the syllabus and what was expected, the assignments, due dates, and required material. By the time all of that was done, he dismissed class and told them to enjoy a rare break and he would see them all on Wednesday.

Her English class was a Monday and Wednesday class. Once Eve packed everything up in her backpack, Nori was ready to go. They walked over to the dining hall and grabbed a snack and some coffee. Well, Nori grabbed some coffee. Eve refilled her water tumbler. Then they found a spot outside and settled down on one of the benches.

Nori turned sideways and criss-crossed her legs. "Alright, now that we have some time, what classes are you taking this term?"

Eve took a drink of water to buy some time and gain some composure. "Well, as you know I have English Comp 101. In addition to that, ASL 101, College Algebra with Trig, Astronomy, and World Geography."

"That is a heavy course load. What is your major?"

"I haven't narrowed it down really, but I am into Astronomy, so I might go into something with that, or chemistry. I am hoping after a couple of classes, I will be able to make a decision. What about you?"

"I am sort of like you, but I do know right now I am a math major. They have some really cool professors here in that department. Who do you have for Trig?" Nori took a long pull on her coffee cup.

Eve's face scrunched up as she thought about the question, but she couldn't remember. "Oh, hold please. Let me look at my printout." Eve opened her backpack and pulled out the crumpled piece of paper from earlier. "A Professor Edison."

Nori's eyes widened and she sat up straighter and squealed, "OMG! YOU ARE GOING TO LOVE PEYTON!"

Eve leaned back a little at the level of exuberance coming from the person across from her. It was a good thing that she had a leg on each side of the bench to balance herself or Eve might have fallen off the bench.

"I am getting the feeling you like this particular teacher."

"Ummm. Maybe. Yeah." The air shifted slightly and Eve watched as Nori's cheeks flushed a bit. "My best friend, Ian, teases me all the time that I have a crush on her, but it isn't anything like that. Trust me, you will see what I am talking about when you meet her in her class."

"Sounds like two of the five so far are solid. Do you know anything about a..." Eve looked down at her paper and read, "Let's see, a Dr. Trinidad, a Wallace, or a LeForge?"

"As in *Star Trek Next Generation*? That is so cool. I bet he or she gets teased all the time."

"I didn't even think of that at first. Hmm."

"To answer your question, I haven't heard anything regarding Wallace or LeForge, but I heard that Dr. Trinidad is a stickler and demanding in class. As long as you know your stuff you will be okay. Oh and don't sit in the first two rows of his class if you can help it. He will call on people randomly and I have heard that sometimes his breath is strong after certain meals."

"Wow. That is a bit specific."

Nori shrugged. "I don't like gossipping, but wanted to give you a fair warning based on what I have heard. Good luck on the other two. Most of the people I have met so far are in my classes and more majoring in the same thing as I am. How's your roommate?"

Eve bit her lip a little not wanting to share her concerns with someone she only just met. "So far, things have been okay. We will see as time goes on."

"Hopefully things work out. I have the same one as last semester and I think we learned to co-exist. She does her thing and I do mine. We definitely don't hang out in the same circles. I am here to study and work on setting myself up post college. I am not here to party and blow off half of my classes."

"Wow. That is crazy. Maybe things will get better." Eve looked down at her watch and realized a lot of time had passed and it was time for her next class which happened to be with Dr. Trinidad. "I need to go and thanks for the advice as World Geography is next. I will see you on Wednesday in class?"

"Good luck. Sorry, I am still hyper from winter break. Need help with directions?"

"It looks like it is in the McIntosh Building."

Nori pointed across the courtyard. "That is it over there."

"Thanks. It was nice meeting you, Nori. Have a wonderful day."

"It was a pleasure meeting you, too. Welcome again to Sterling U."

Eve got up and waved as she hurried down the sidewalk to see what fortunes awaited her in her next class.

Keeping Nori's comments in mind, Eve walked in and chose a seat about three rows back in the middle of the room. She still preferred to be in the middle so she could hear and focus on conversations around her. Thankfully that class went quickly and there weren't any instances of foul breath. She was done for the day early so she had time to get back to her dorm and start in on some of the reading she needed to have done before Wednesday. It was a bit of a hike back to her dorm, but she didn't mind it when the weather was pleasant like today. The sun was shining and it was fifty-eight degrees. One of the things she liked was the fact it rarely snowed here.

By the time she made it back to her room, her stomach was growling. She didn't think it was going to be silent until dinner so she opened a granola bar as she settled in on her bed with her English textbook, making sure to set her timer so she would have time to get dressed and drive to work. She was working the early evening shift today. It was her last weeknight at the restaurant

She got a job at the library on campus as part of a student-work program, but she also was keeping her job at Michelangelo's on the weekends. The tips she made there were good most nights and it would help her with cash during the week. However, they wanted to know if she would be able to cover this evening to help them out. She agreed since it was the first week of classes and her first one tomorrow didn't begin until 11am.

The timer went off on her phone and she was so engrossed in reading that she almost threw her textbook. Regaining her composure, she marked her spot and sat her book aside. After changing into her black slacks and button-down shirt, she grabbed her purse and headed out the door. Just as she was leaving, her roommate was coming into the room and they almost collided.

"Ugh, watch out!" Bentley called out as she scowled at Eve and gave her a disgusted look after taking in her appearance. "Where are you going? To a funeral?"

"To work." Eve didn't have any time nor inclination to explain herself to the other woman. Even after only a few days, Eve knew that if she could, she would switch roommates in a heartbeat. "I have to go." With that Eve went around Bentley and hustled down the stairs. When she arrived, she put on her red tie and double checked her appearance in the rearview mirror before heading inside.

Carlos, the executive chef, was issuing orders to everyone when she went back into the kitchen to put her purse in a locker. When he saw her, he sent a wink her way and kept on shouting out what needed to be done for the evening.

Oddly, she felt right at home there, unlike several of the other places she had worked before. Eve clocked in and went to let everyone know she was there and ready to go. Looked like the right time as a party of eight was heading inside. Adam logged them in to her section and she went to move two tables together. Then she walked to the front to lead them back to the table herself. She placed a menu in front of everyone and asked what they wanted to drink. For the rest of the evening she was steady, but it wasn't chaotic like during the weekend. She was glad it was her last weeknight because she wasn't sure how she could take classes during the day, work at night, and get studying done in between everything.

By the time she finished up, it was 10:30pm and she was driving back to the dorm. Carlos sent her home with some leftovers that she could warm up. That was the one good thing about the restaurant, you were able to eat a meal there on break. The man might have also snuck some dessert in there that she knew she would have to hide. No one came between her and her dessert.

Eve climbed the stairs and was looking forward to taking a shower and crawling into bed. She wanted to try and get in another

30-45 minutes of studying before sleep. However, as she approached her room, that thought popped like a balloon blown up too much. There was a loud ruckus coming from the other side of the door. More than one person's voice by the sound of it. Dread washed over her and she turned the door handle worried about what she would find on the other side.

Her roommate and three others were all sitting around drinking. Closing her eyes for a moment, Eve prayed that when she opened her eyes, they would be gone. Cracking one eye open, she let out a deep groan internally. Nope. They were still there.

"Don't just stand in the doorway, come inside before someone sees us!" her roommate shouted. Eve was sure the woman didn't realize that her loud voice would be what drew someone's attention, not the fact that Eve was standing in an open doorway. "Where have you been anyway? You look a mess."

"Work. I am going to shower. Do you know how long you all are going to be..." Eve tried to think of a polite word, "socializing? I need to get some studying done and sleep."

"Ugh. You are such a party pooper. It is day one. There isn't much homework yet. Come on and relax a little. Do you want a drink?" Bentley raised a glass up in the air and waved it.

"No, thank you." Eve slid her bag with food in it under her bed and behind some other stuff. She didn't need the drunk quartet to get the munchies. Then she dug out and grabbed her toiletry bag, along with a change of clothes, and went down the hall to the showers. Originally, she was going to take a short one to wash off the smell of food, but given the fact her room was taken over, she took a longer one in an effort to buy some time that the others would be absent upon her return.

Eve moved cautiously back down the hall to her room. It was quieter than when she left. She held her breath as she turned the knob and eased the door open. With a loud whoosh of air, a sense of relief washed over her as everyone, including her roommate, had vacated the room. Maybe this wouldn't be too bad this semester and she would be able to survive. She reached under her bed and pulled out the food she brought back. Slipping the box out that held beef wellington, grilled potatoes, and asparagus in it, she put it inside her mini fridge. It was one thing that she saved up and brought with her when she moved in the dorms.

Eve pulled back the covers, climbed onto the bed, and started reading the first chapter of her world geography textbook. When her eyelids kept closing and she wasn't retaining any of the material any longer, she gave up, sat the book on the desk beside her, turned the lamp off, and let sleep claim her attention for the next several hours.

CHAPTER 2

EVE

The next morning Eve woke up and put on a pair of jeans, a red t-shirt, and a gray pullover hoodie. After donning some shoes, she grabbed her backpack and double checked she had everything inside. Once she was set, she headed to the cafeteria for some breakfast. She noticed her roommate was still sleeping when she slipped out the door. She was excited about her classes today. Plus, tonight was the first night she would begin work at the library. There was a full day in front of her.

As she went through the line, her mind wasn't paying attention to her surroundings until a friendly and familiar voice brought her back.

"Hey, Eve. How are you doing?"

Eve turned and saw Nori standing beside her. She smiled, thankful for the happy person. "Hey, Nori. You getting some breakfast?"

"I just sat down with mine. I saw you and thought I would see if you wanted to join me and a couple of other people."

"Uhh. Sure. Let me check out and I will be right over. Where are you sitting?"

Nori pointed as she spoke, "I can wait on you if you want."

"That's okay. You go on ahead and I will be there in a moment."

Nodding, Nori took off. Eve hoped the people that Nori was going to introduce her to were more like her and not like Bentley's group. As Eve approached, she noticed they were all laughing and had an aura around them that radiated kindness. Relaxing her shoulders, she sat her breakfast on the table and then put her backpack on the floor in between her feet once she was seated. There were five people around the table, one guy and four girls.

Nori took charge, "Hey, everyone, this is Eve, she is new here this semester. Eve, this is everyone. Starting on my left you have Logan, Katherine, Abigail, and Melissa."

Katherine waved and spoke first, "Welcome to Sterling University. Everyone calls me Kat, so you may also if you would like."

The girl Nori said was Melissa spoke up to Eve's right. "Are you a freshman or a transfer student?"

"I'm a freshman. It is my first semester at the college."

"Eve and I have Comp 101 together. I think I am going to take her under my wing," Nori declared.

As everyone chatted, Eve's attention kept landing back on Abigail. She wasn't sure why, but the woman drew her in a different way than Nori's friendliness did.

"Logan, here, is outnumbered often and surrounded by too much estrogen," Melissa said.

He hugged Katherine to his side as he replied, "The things we sacrifice for those we care about."

Eve must have looked confused because Abigail explained, "Those two have been dating for a few years now. They came to college as high school sweethearts. A real Hallmark movie in the making."

Eve smiled and took a bite of her breakfast sandwich to hide the laughter that wanted to boil up.

"We will be sure to get the right person to cast as you in the production," Logan shot back. "However, I do have to bid you ladies good-bye because the director is calling me on set elsewhere." He gave Katherine a quick kiss and then rose up.

Everyone called out, "Bye, Logan." "Later, tiger." Eve just waved not knowing what to say exactly.

"Are any of the rest of you in relationships?" Eve asked as she wanted to keep them talking so no one thought to ask her any questions.

Katherine looked over at Nori and grinned. "What do you have to say to that, Nori?"

Eve watched as some pink flooded her new friend's face. The girl's expression transformed into this gooeyness. "Actually, over Christmas break while I was back home, I met someone. Her name is Jess."

Oh, Eve thought. She wasn't expecting that. Not sure why the announcement of her dating a girl surprised her, but it did. It obviously didn't change the way Eve thought of Nori, but it came as a bit of a shock.

Nori continued, "We went on several dates before I had to come back to school. We decided to commit to one another despite it being a long distance relationship. She is so sweet, talented, funny, and beautiful."

"Awww. The beginning stage where everything is cute and wonderful. I miss that stage." Katherine sighed.

"You and Logan are wonderful together and love each other to pieces," Melissa voiced.

"Yes, but we are well aware of one another's flaws and get into arguments like every growing couple does. The honeymoon stage is where you both think the other is perfect and can do no wrong. Wait until the other is comfortable and farting in front of you all the time, including when you are out on a date or around other people." Katherine scrunched her nose up like she suddenly smelled something putrid.

"What about you, Eve? Do you have a special someone you are dating?" Nori asked, innocently.

"Umm. No. I am not dating anyone at all." Eve wanted to escape before more questions could be asked.

Katherine joined in right as Eve was about to stand up to run away. "Are you interested in dating someone?"

Shrugging, Eve said, "Sure. When I meet the right person." She gathered up her trash and before she could make her excuses that she needed to get to class, Abigail, the quiet one so far leaned over to ask her the question she didn't want to be asked right then.

"Is the right person male or female?" After a brief moment, she added, "Or other?"

Eve's heart was racing and the food she ate was sticking to the walls of her stomach and making her feel claustrophobic. "Ummm."

However, she was spared any more discomfort when Nori piped up. "Leave Eve alone. Besides, I have an eleven o'clock class and need to hurry."

Glancing down at her watch she cringed. "Dang it. I do, too, and I need to find the class. Thanks for letting me sit with you and nice meeting you all." Without another word, she turned and bolted out of there fast.

Eve managed to find her classroom in plenty of time. She was looking forward to taking American Sign Language. She had already started learning a little of it from YouTube videos and was eager to absorb more. This classroom was tiny and only had about thirty spaces compared with the bigger auditorium-style classrooms. There were already several students in seats. There were rows of desks with three seats at a table on each side of an aisle going down the middle. She was hesitant to choose one right next to a stranger, so she picked one along the wall that left the middle seat free. Sometimes her introverted self sucked when it came to social situations.

The teacher stood up in front of everyone and began to speak as someone slipped into the space next to her. Eve didn't even look at the individual, it not being of importance at the moment. Her focus was on Mr. Wallace at the front of the room.

ABIGAIL

As Eve flew out of the cafeteria, Abigail felt horrible for asking her question so openly and directly. She and her friends didn't care what anyone's sexual orientation was as they were a mixed bag of preferences. She figured since Nori opened the gates so to speak, talking about Jess, it was the perfect time to gauge what Eve's interests were. Abigail could only blame her own attraction to the female across from her for opening her mouth and inserting her foot.

Nori's face fell into a frown and she whispered, "I hope we didn't scare her away. If I don't see her again before tomorrow, I will talk with her in English and ensure she is okay. I think she could use some friends. Plus, I will definitely get her number so I can reach out in between classes. Maybe I will invite her to hang out and watch a movie with all of us. What do you think?"

"How about you all come over to my apartment? That way we have more space. I am sure Logan won't mind. He can either have a girl's night with us, retreat to the bedroom, or go have a guy's night playing sports." Katherine offering up her place worked perfectly in Abigail's opinion.

"How about this weekend? I can check with Eve and see when she is available," Nori asked the group.

Abigail hated to dismiss the idea, but she knew she had a conflict. "Let me check my schedule. I am working at Farenheit this weekend. I might be free during the afternoon and on Sunday. I will text you. I have to rush to class, but I wanted to hang back for a few."

"Later."

Abigail snatched up her bag and sped walked outside. Once she hit the outdoors, she ran across the lawn to where her 11 o'clock class was. She opened the door and stepped inside looking for a seat. Mr. Wallace was about to begin class, so she barely made it. As she glanced around, her eyes settled on Eve. Looked like favor was with her today. Or at least she prayed it was favor as she wasn't sure what the reaction from Eve would be. She eased down into the seat and noticed that Eve didn't even stir or peer her way. Soon enough, the reveal would be had.

Mr. Wallace was a hearing teacher, but he informed them that starting next week, they would have to begin speaking only in sign language for most of the time. "Alright, you have the syllabus and can review it on your own time. As this is a language class, you will be graded on class participation, homework, written exams, and signed conversational exchanges. We are going to take advantage of the time we have today and start working on our alphabet and numbers." He pulled up a stool in the front of the class. He went over the proper hand placement for finger spelling. "How many of you already know your alphabet?"

About eight hands shot up around the room including hers and Eve. It was at that moment that Eve turned, probably to notate who raised their hands, and saw Abigail sitting next to her. The surprise was clearly expressed across Eve's face by the raise of her eyebrows, eyes growing larger, and mouth slightly opened.

Abigail waved a small half wave before turning back towards their teacher as he continued. "Great. Once we go over the alphabet, we will break off into groups of two or three and practice fingerspelling words. You that have experience or knowledge, spread out at that time so you are in different groups. Alright, let's start. This is the letter A." He held his hand up, palm forward and closed his fist. His thumb was on the outside of the fist, sticking up. "You will notice that this looks like a lowercase "A" that has been printed. Everyone try it." He waited as everyone did as instructed and then continued on with the next letter. He worked his way through the entire alphabet. Then he went back through it a little faster.

Once they went through it several more times, he passed out a list to everyone and broke everyone up into groups. Since both she and Eve had raised their hands earlier, Mr. Wallace had them separate. Then the groups practiced spelling and reading one another's words. They did that and worked on fingerspelling their names. Soon class was dismissed. Abigail gathered up her bag and followed Eve when she left.

"Hey, Eve, wait up."

Abigail slowed her steps to Eve's as they strolled down the hallway. Abigail was easily six inches taller than the other woman. "I wanted to apologize for what I asked at breakfast. I didn't intend to make you uncomfortable. Will you forgive me?"

"Yes."

"Where are you headed now? Do you have another class?"

"No. My trig class doesn't start until three. I thought I would go hang out in the library and study until it is time. I don't feel like going back to my dorm. What about yourself? Do you have class?"

"At two. Chemistry lecture. My lab for that class is this evening. Would you like some company on the way to the library?" Abigail asked even though she was still following beside the adorable woman.

After a few moments, Eve spoke, "Sure." Then with what seemed like a bit more hesitation continued. "If you have something to work on and want to join me in studying until your next class, you are welcome. I don't want to appear rude, but with my schedule, I have to take advantage of all the time I have free when I can."

"Yeah, I have plenty to do. I would love to join you." They walked in companionable silence for a minute or two before the urge to get to know Eve teased Abigail's senses. However, she didn't want to overwhelm or scare off the woman again, so she kept it to school conversations. "Who do you have for Trig?"

This seemed to get a smile from Eve. "Apparently, one of Nori's favorite teachers."

"Peyton, huh?" Abigail knew immediately of whom Eve referenced. "She isn't just her teacher, but she is Nori's advisor, too. Peyton is a good teacher, but I think it is her personality and likable character that endears her to students."

"Why does everyone call her Peyton instead of Professor Edison? In fact, I have found the titles for different people run the gambit here in the way the professors are addressed."

They had reached the steps of the library and Abigail placed a hand on Eve's arm for a moment. "In regards to Peyton, you will see when you meet her. She is very informal and welcoming of everyone. I think she is working on her PhD, so soon she will be Dr. Edison. I have had her for a few of my classes. As far as the others, we follow what each instructor wants us to call him or her. Most of the ones with doctorates, we call doctor so and so no matter what, out of respect for their position. Not sure that really answers your question. Ready to get our study on?"

"It does somewhat. Let's go." Eve and Abigail ascended the steps and opened the double doors into the library.

It didn't matter how many times Abigail came to the library, the smell that permeated the air was one of her favorite scents. She loved the smell of new and old books alike. It made a person think about all the work and dedication that went into the craft. Not only that, but it gave her a sense of connection to other times and places that she couldn't get outside the building's walls.

Abigail pointed in the direction of a winding staircase and then led the way upstairs. Once they were up there, she headed in the direction of a particularly quiet corner. She had a feeling that solitude and peace was at the top of Eve's required list. She gestured and spoke low, "Do you want to sit in the poofy chairs or at the desk? I am not sure what kind of work you need to do."

"I am reading for now. Are the chairs as comfortable as they look?" Eve eyed the green squishy armchairs.

"More so. Let's go. This is one of my favorite spots."

They both settled in. Abigail watched as Eve criss crossed her legs in the chair and was jealous, but she had a way of folding her legs underneath her that worked. She took her shoes off first so she didn't disturb the fabric.

At first Abigail kept sneaking glances over at Eve, not able to resist watching her deep concentration on what she was focused on. However, eventually, Abigail became absorbed in her own reading. She knew that her instructor this afternoon was the type that started off the semester with the subject matter and expected you to have looked at the syllabus ahead of time. At one-thirty, her alarm went off causing a small shriek to come from Eve. "Sorry about that. I knew if I didn't set an alarm, I would get absorbed and miss class. Thanks for letting me study with you. Maybe we can do this again."

Eve nodded and took a drink from her water bottle. "Yes, that would be lovely. Have a good class, Abigail."

"Please call me Abby, most everyone does."

"Very well. Have a great rest of your day, Abby. If I don't see you before, I will see you in class on Thursday."

The urge to lean down and kiss the top of Eve's head was strong, so she swiftly departed before she made any more blunders for the day. As she was leaving, she sent a text to Nori.

ABIGAIL: YOU WILL NEVER GUESS WHO WAS IN MY 11AM CLASS.

Useless, Not relevant, Monotone voice, Too hard, Pointless, Waste of Time." On and on for a few minutes the answers came.

"Exactly. Now I will disagree with you all on some of the points that it is too hard or pointless; but, that is why you are in my class. My goal for this semester is not to simply teach you how to perform and solve a problem based on particular rules and have you do the step a hundred times until your eyeballs want to fall out. Don't get me wrong, that will be part of it for sure. Give or take a bit. But, my goal as your professor is to teach you purpose, relevancy, the point. How certain aspects come into play with whatever your field of study is. Even if your major is English, I will find something to relate to it. By the end of the semester, I want you to leave having an appreciation, note I didn't say love, rather an *appreciation* for the subject. If you give me your hardest and you put in the effort, then I will meet you along the path wherever you are."

Eve could see now why Nori would choose this instructor to be her favorite. Eve was half in love with the woman herself and it had only been a short time.

"Now that you got my spiel about my personal goals for this class, I am going to pass out the syllabus and we can get started." A groan was heard all over the room. "Yes, my students, we are going to start our journey today."

Peyton passed out the syllabus and Eve pulled out her notebook and pencil ready to absorb whatever knowledge the woman in front of her was willing to impart. Eve was actually looking forward to what was to come.

After class, she gathered up her stuff and headed back to the library for her evening shift.

She went to the main desk and introduced herself and told the girl behind the desk that she was there to see Meredith. The girl disappeared and then a few minutes later returned with a woman in her early fifties next to her smiling. When they reached the desk, the woman held out her hand to Eve. "Hello, I am Meredith. Welcome, let me show you around and get you started. You can stash your backpack under the desk there so you don't have to carry it." Once Eve had safely tucked her backpack underneath so it was out of the way, she followed the kind lady. They walked around the library on a quick tour where Meredith pointed out different areas and some of the specialized rooms. Once they had toured both the first and second floor, they ended back at the desk. "Tonight I am going to have you shelve books as they come in. There is a cart full from the day also. This will help acclimate you to where everything is. Tomorrow we will focus on learning the computer software. Feel free to wander about or ask if anyone needs assistance. When you don't have anything to do, you are welcome to work on assignments.

"Thank you. I will get started now on filing the books." Meridith smiled and returned to the other part of the library and Eve grabbed the cart and loaded up the remaining books. As she put the books on the cart, she sorted the books into the different sections so they were easier to shelve. Once all the books had been shelved, Eve joined the other student at the circulation desk. The other girl was deep into her book so Eve pulled out her homework. When quitting time arrived, she had finished up the reading for both her English and World Geography classes the next day.

Eve's stomach was growling by the time she made it to her second floor room back in the dorms. It had been a long time since breakfast that morning and she had only had a couple of granola bars and an apple to snack on since then. She was looking forward to warming up her leftovers and eating while she worked on some of her math homework. When she entered the dorm room no one was in the room and a sense of relief washed over her. However, it instantly went away and was replaced by anger when she opened her fridge and found the food from the previous night was gone. She had every urge to find her roommate and demand an answer for why she stole her food. However, she knew that wouldn't solve anything and now wasn't the time to confront Bentley. Instead, she fixed herself a peanut butter sandwich and looked to see if her dessert was still hidden. It was. So, after the sandwich, she dived into the rich, chocolatey goodness, allowing it to melt her anger.

She was sitting at her desk with a pencil in her right hand and a fork in her left. She would work a problem or two and then take a bite of the cake. It was so moist and creamy with a layer of a chocolate mousse in between the layers of sponge. The outside was covered in a rich, dark-chocolate ganache that wasn't too thick. Her taste buds danced in pleasure. About halfway done with the dessert her eyes were starting to close, so she put away the cake and called it a night on her homework. She knew she could finish it up tomorrow in between classes or after her geography class. Not trusting her roommate even more than she previously hadn't, she hid the remainder of the cake again and changed into her pajamas.

A couple of hours later, she was awoken when her roommate stumbled into their room and knocked over a lamp. She ignored her and attempted to go back to sleep, but each time slumber almost claimed her attention, Bentley did something else to jar her awake. Frustrated, she turned over and sat up on the edge of the bed and spoke before thinking.

"What is your problem? Can you be any noisier? Do you not see that I am trying to get some sleep over here? Are you going to get drunk every night? Also, while I am thinking of it, why did you go into *my* refrigerator and eat *my* food? Do you know how rude that is?"

Eve sat in shock as all of that flew out of her normally peaceful mouth. Guess two days at college had already changed her. Not that she particularly liked these changes. However, her roommate wasn't going to take all the questions quietly and without firing back.

"It isn't any of your business what I do with my time. I can already tell you are going to be some boring stick in the mud who wouldn't know a good time if it was wrapped up and labeled for you. Half of this room is mine and I have a right to do what I want to. As far as your precious food, I was hungry and figured if you could afford to have those kinds of leftovers, then you could buy yourself some more food. Although, you might think about buying yourself a new wardrobe and personality instead. You are just some prude, uptight dyke. I heard about the group of people you were having breakfast with. A bunch of freaks. Well, except the one who has a boyfriend. She better watch it, though. A sexy man like that might get stolen from her."

The rage boiling in Eve's blood at that moment could have cooked a potato in three minutes.

She took a few deep breaths as she had been taught and regained her composure because she knew that there wasn't anything that yelling at each other was going to solve and she was probably disturbing the people in the rooms around them. "Look. I don't think calling each other names is going to solve our problem. There isn't any reason we can't come to some sort of agreement and some rules that we both can live with. Let's get some rest tonight, then have a conversation when we are both a bit more clear headed. What do you say to that?"

"Whatever. I am going to see about possibly switching rooms with someone else."

Good luck with that, Eve thought. *You would be doing both of us a favor if you managed to do that. My chances of getting someone better has to be higher.* What she said out loud was, "I hope you can find a roommate that is more compatible than I am."

Eve wanted to snatch up her backpack and a change of clothes and go sleep in the library for the night, but instead, she rolled over and did a meditation in her head to lull herself back to sleep.

The next morning, Eve woke up and threw her hair in a ponytail before sliding on a pair of leggings and a long shirt. It was going to be a long day so she was going to be as comfortable as she could be. She stuffed some granola bars and a few other snacks in her bag and grabbed her water bottle before leaving. She drove her car over to the library's parking lot and then walked to English class from there. Leaving work at 10pm tonight, she figured it would be safer to only have to walk to her car instead of walking all the way to the dorms.

She entered the classroom fifteen minutes before class started and was eating a banana when Nori walked in and plopped down next to her. "Morning, Eve! We missed you at breakfast today."

"Not sure I will be getting to the cafeteria before this class very often. I brought something with me. Have to start the day off right." She waved the banana in the air.

"Please tell me you have something other than a banana."

"Sure, I have a protein bar for now and some granola bars for later. I will go get some lunch after my geography class." Eve pulled out her computer. "Did you get the readings done?"

"Yeah. Hey, I wanted to ask you a question. The girls and I thought we could get together at some point during the weekend to watch a movie. Have kind of a girls' night out. Would you be interested in joining?"

"Depends on the time. I have to work most of the weekend. I generally work evenings on Friday and Saturday. Sometimes for special occasions, I work on Sundays."

"How about Sunday afternoon if you aren't working. Say around 2pm? Here is my phone number. Text me and let me know. I know Abigail works on the weekend, too. Guess we better pay attention now. Mr. R is looking serious with his vest and glasses on today."

The two girls laughed as Eve took the piece of paper from Nori. She programmed the phone number into her phone and then handed it back to Nori. She wasn't going to be responsible for it getting lost and ending up written in every bathroom stall over a five-state radius. Although, Texas is pretty much its own five-state radius.

Both of her classes went well and they had lively discussions on the subject matter. She had to write a persuasive essay for English class by the following Wednesday. By Monday, five essays were required to have been read along with a rebuttal composed on two of them. In Geography, they were studying South America first and had a quiz the following Monday on all the countries and capitals when given a blank map.

For lunch, she was craving a burger so Eve gave in and ate. She wanted a big order of onion rings, but she settled for a side salad to try and balance it out. She was halfway done eating when Abigail strolled through the area. She had to admit the woman was pretty. The whole group was. But, for some reason, there was something that made Abigail stand out to her. She was surprised she was single.

When the other woman caught her eye, Eve waved. A few moments later, Abigail had weaved her way over next to her.

ABIGAIL

"Hi, Eve. Do you mind if I join you?"

"No. Of course I don't. I still have some time before I have to report for my shift at the library." Eve took a bite of her burger.

"You are working there?" Eve nodded. "Did you know about it the other day when I was showing you the spot I liked?" Abigail asked.

"No. Last night was my first shift and I only worked a few hours. Mostly shelving books and some orientation. Where do you work? Nori mentioned something about getting together and you needing to check your schedule."

"Yeah. I am a hostess and sometimes waitress at Fahrenheit 212."

Eve grinned. "Oh cool, I waitress at Michelangelo's on the weekend."

Abigail had just picked up her club sandwich, as Eve said that, she sat it back down. "Wait, you work at the library during the week and waitress on the weekends plus take a full course load?"

"Yeah, seventeen credit hours. I want to make up for not attending last term."

"Wow. I am impressed, but it has to be hard on you."

"Yeah." Eve spoke the next part quieter, but Abigail still heard her. "Especially having a rude roommate like my own."

Abigail tucked that piece of information away for a different day to discuss. If there were already issues after a couple of nights, then that didn't bode well for the future.

"If you ever need to talk or need an escape. Let me know. I'm your girl." How she wished that meant on other levels, too.

"Thanks."

Abigail caught Eve staring at her onion rings. "Want one?"

"I'm not taking your food. I almost got me some, but then decided I better not."

Pushing the tray closer to Eve, she insisted, "Please, take a few. I won't eat all of them. However, they are some of the best ones I have ever had."

Before she even replied, Eve had reached out and snagged one. "If you are sure."

Then the woman moaned around the food and Abigail's mind went straight into the gutter. Plunged deep into that dark abyss. She was thinking about all the other ways she could get Eve to moan. She was so lost in her thoughts, that she didn't hear Eve talking to her. Finally the throat clearing and hand waving in front of her face caught her attention.

"Sorry about that."

Laughing, Eve looked over at her with a smirk, "Did you leave the planet for a moment or at least the college?"

"I went somewhere else for sure."

"Do I want to know?"

Whispering low and leaning in, Abigail didn't want to tell her the truth, so she said, "I was communicating with my home world. When I do, I phase out of this realm."

Watching Eve's face go from a smirk, to a worried look, to a 'what the hell,' and back to a smirk with a roll of the eyes was entertaining.

"Haha, Abigail. You almost had me fooled. Keep your secrets."

With a wink, Abigail simply replied, "I will for now," before taking a big bite of her sandwich.

"So, how often do you work?" asked Eve.

"This semester, mostly the weekends. Once I get settled in a couple of weeks, I might pick up an extra shift during the week if they need help. Then again, I might find myself too busy studying at the library to work." Abgail barely restrained herself from winking as she spoke.

"Do you have a heavy course load?"

The fact that Eve didn't pick up on the flirting and hint that she would be coming by the library to study just to see her, amused Abigail. She had a feeling this girl was going to be fun to tease while at the same time torturing herself. If only she knew which way Eve swung.

"I have a couple of science classes so those are more intensive due to the fact there is a lecture and lab part, but I try to balance it out with lighter classes. I am happy to see we have a class together. Maybe we can find some time to practice our signing with each other. I think learning the words is easier than seeing someone sign and catching everything said."

"I would appreciate having someone to practice with."

Abigail popped a piece of onion ring in her mouth and then revealed, "By the end of the semester, we will be able to talk with our mouths full. Plus, we can exchange words with the others around us and they won't even know it."

Eve laughed, "So, you are taking the class so you can have a secret code?"

"I mean, it isn't a bad thing. Before you, I hadn't even thought that. I found the language fascinating. That and I have had a few deaf customers at the restaurant and would like to be able to communicate with them."

"I never thought of it that way." Abigail watched Eve look at her phone and then jump up and start gathering her things. "I'm sorry. I lost track of time. I have to hurry."

"Go on, I will take care of your trash and everything."

"You sure?" Eve had pulled her bag on her back.

Abigail waved her off. "Go, go."

Eve was already headed away and called over her shoulder, "Thanks."

Abigail reclined back in her chair and observed the little kitten scramble away. Once Eve was out of sight, she gathered up their trash and tossed it. She now had a plan to execute for the night.

First, she called up work to see what nights she was on the schedule for the weekend. Thankfully, she had Sunday off. She sent Nori a text letting her know she confirmed Sunday was a go. Secondly, she was due to work that evening, but she knew that Samantha was wanting some extra hours. She pulled up her phone number and tapped the call button.

A familiar voice answered, "Hello, Abby."

"Hey, Sam. I know it is last minute, but are you still looking for some extra hours?"

"Sure. What time are you scheduled for?"

"Five to ten."

"No problem. Have you cleared it with bossman yet?"

"No, wanted to see if you wanted the time first. I can do it if needed, just something came up and killing two birds with one stone. I will call and clear it and then text you."

"Sounds good. Have fun doing whatever or whomever it is you are getting out of work for."

"Haha. Will do. Thanks."

After she hung up, she called back to the restaurant to speak with their boss. He didn't have a problem with Samantha coming in instead. Abigail shot off a quick text and then went to round up part two of her plan.

It wasn't anything romantic or embarrassing. In fact, it wouldn't even seem like anything out of the norm really. Eve might get suspicious when Abigail showed up at the library, but lots of students studied there. The fact that Abigail had a dinner packed for the two of them for whenever Eve got a break would be coincidental and lucky. Or she would say, when she was packing something for herself, she thought the other woman might enjoy something, too, and she wanted to do a kind deed for a new friend.

Reality was that Abigail was going to start wooing Eve and see if she could decipher what the woman's thoughts were romantically. Maybe in the end, Abigail would be lucky and discover that Eve's interest could possibly align with her own. She might have to get some assistance from Nori in that department, too. Pick her mind. It was now time for Abigail to become a hunter.

CHAPTER 4

EVE

Books that had been returned were stacked up on carts ready to be shelved. As soon as Eve stored her backpack under the desk, she got to work on completing that first. She loved the peace and quiet the libraries afforded, but knew that as the semester got going a bit more, there would be more noise in areas as study groups were formed and met. For tonight, though, it was the quiet swish of a book sliding in between two others or an occasional thunk as one fell to its side.

She worked for about thirty minutes shelving books before returning to the front desk. Meredith began giving her a tutorial on their computer system and how to operate it. Eve shadowed Meredith for the next forty-five minutes as they assisted some students needing to check out some books, look up some information, or reserve a couple of rooms. A few of the professors came in to request copies of DVDs and blu-rays be set aside for an assignment.

Eve was making her way around the library to see if anyone appeared to need assistance when she saw Abigail sitting in one of the chairs with a textbook open and her laptop perched on the arm of the chair. She almost left the woman alone to study, but something drew her closer. As she crossed the floor, Abigail lifted her gaze from the textbook and smiled up at her.

"Right on time," Abigail said.

Eve stopped and asked with a tilt of her head, "I am? For what?"

"For me to take a break. Also, what time do you go to dinner tonight?"

"Umm, I am not sure. I think 7:30 maybe. Why?"

"Because I am going to need a food break and brought some. Thought we could maybe share a meal."

"Oh, well. I was going to just eat a few of the snacks I had in my bag, but sure. We can eat together."

"I meant I brought enough dinner for both of us." Abigail continued to smile so genuinely up at Eve and she wasn't sure what to make of that.

"Okay. If you are sure. Thank you. Want me to come over here when I go to break?"

"That works for me."

"Alright. I will let you get back to studying and I will continue my rounds."

"See you soon, Eve."

Eve waved a little and continued strolling around, trying to figure out why Abigail would bring her dinner. Then she chastised herself for questioning someone being nice. After all, they all were aware that Eve was new to the university and didn't have friends.

It was a slow night as far as the number of people that were in, but it was busy because Eve was learning everything. She took notes on a few of the procedures, or particular ways to look up specific references.

When break time arrived, Eve went to find Abigail even though it felt a little awkward. She wasn't sure why she felt like that, but it might have to do with questioning intentions or reasons behind things.

When she made it where Abigail was, she found the girl had already set out two meals. It wasn't much. There were two sub sandwiches, two bags of chips, a couple of cookies, and two bottles of water.

"I take it you were definitely ready for some food tonight?" Eve laughed as she motioned around at everything.

"Yeah, and I know how breaks are. They go by faster than the work does. Wanted to be prepared and have everything ready to go. It isn't a gourmet dinner or even a warm one, but I thought it might be good."

"It is wonderful and thoughtful. Thank you again." Eve sat down in one of the chairs at the table. "I will have to do something to make up for you bringing me dinner."

"That isn't necessary. If you think about it, you are saving me from having to eat all alone tonight."

"Still, I will think of something." Eve took a bite of her food as a plan came into her mind. "Oh, I have an idea. Do you like chocolate?"

"Don't most people?"

Nodding, Eve covered her mouth as she chewed from a rather large bite. As soon as she was able to swallow most of it down, she continued. "The restaurant where I work serves this amazing chocolate cake. I will bring you a piece of that. It is one of the best cakes I have ever had. They have other really great desserts, but not all of them are so easily transportable or keep well. Now I am rambling. Sorry."

Eve looked down at her food and deliberately made sure she took a smaller bite. Why did she have to be so awkward around people all the time? She wished she could simply be normal and social.

Abigail touched Eve's arm. "I like your rambling. It is cute."

"Thanks." Eve couldn't look up at that moment because she knew her face was pink from embarrassment. She wasn't sure how to take that statement. Was Abigail flirting with her? Did she want Abigail to flirt with her? She needed to change the topic quickly. "Where did these sandwiches come from? Did you make them?"

"That would be a no. I mean, I can. I have to say I make a pretty great sandwich, but I got them from a Deli shop down the street from here."

"You would think a sandwich was a sandwich, but these are really good."

"Yes, they are. I think it has something to do with the bread and that they bake it fresh there. I discovered them before and have gone back lots of times. It is a quaint little 'mom and pop' place."

"Well, they are delicious. I will have to check them out." *Sandwiches? Seriously, Eve, we are talking about sandwiches?* Eve thought to herself. She wanted to groan and sink into the floor.

They made small talk for the next ten minutes or so and then Eve gathered up her trash. "I appreciate the dinner and I will bring you some dessert as soon as I can. Maybe this weekend. I need to get back." Eve stood up and made her escape without even giving the other woman a chance to say anything.

For the rest of the night, Eve avoided that one part of the library in case Abigail was still there. She wasn't sure what she was feeling and it was making her confused and questioning everything. Class tomorrow was soon enough to have to worry about talking again.

She didn't have much time for studying that night until about eight-thirty when Meredith went home. By that time, she was told she could shelve the few books that came back and then work on studying at the circulation desk unless someone needed to check out a book.

At the end of the night, Eve drove back to her dorm, stared up at the second floor, and dreaded going up there. She didn't want to have a confrontation once again with her roommate. She was determined to not make a big deal of anything and to just try and take care of herself.

She opened the car door and reached in for her bag. As she did, she heard someone whistle and yell out a snarky comment. Eve whipped around so fast, prepared for someone to be near, but there were only a few guys walking past her. She let out a deep sigh and slung her backpack over her shoulder. After checking that the door was locked like three times, she trudged up to the dorm and to the second floor. The anxiety beating up her mind right then was so high that it almost turned into a panic attack by the time she got to her room. She knew it was stupid and that anyone else would think this was silly, but she couldn't explain it. Eve sucked in a lungful of air and turned the knob.

When she pushed the door open, immediate and immense relief flooded her system to see that the other half of the room was silent and absent of any individuals. Eve grabbed her shower bag and went down the hall. She returned wearing her comfy, blue, soft, fuzzy pjs. They were a gift to herself this past Christmas and they made her feel like she could take care of herself and everything would be okay. Who knew clothes could affect your emotions so easily. Some people had power suits, but she had power pjs. Once everything was put away, Eve took thirty minutes to read a book for pleasure before turning off the lamp and snuggling down into the blankets.

ABIGAIL

When Eve left to return to work, Abigail wasn't sure if the dinner was a good thing, or if it pushed Eve away. She packed up and left for the night. After all, Eve might not be into women. However, she wasn't a quitter and she was going to let Eve see if nothing else, they could be good friends. Her entire circle was a great group and they all already liked Eve. Tomorrow in class was another day and hopefully Eve wasn't avoiding her after the cute comment.

She texted Nori when she got back to her dorm.

A: Hey. Do you have Eve's number?

N: Maybe. Why???????

A: Can you text to see if she wants to join us for breakfast?

N: Why?

A: Because I think it would be nice to see her hanging out with us.

N: WAIT A MINUTE! Are you interested in her?

A: Thought you picked up on that. Too busy in your own heart bubble? LOL

N: Hold on.

A moment later Abigail's phone pinged with a new message. When she looked to see who it was, she found it was the group chat with the four of them.

Group chat

N: Hey girls. Did you know Eve piqued Abby's interest?

K: I thought I caught a couple of glances.

A: Seriously Nori? All I was wondering is if you wanted to invite her to breakfast tomorrow morning with us since we know her first class is at 11 am.

M: I think you are jumping the gun Nori. Leave Abby alone.

M: Abby, you better have some patience.

A: *Groans* You all are crazy. Nevermind. I am skipping our breakfast meet up tomorrow morning.

A: In all honesty, yes, I am intrigued. Mostly, I wanted her to have more time with you all as a group to become friends. That is all. If it was only seeing her, I have other ways of doing that.

N: Do tell.

M: Yep.. Are you becoming a stalker????

K: Logan is wondering what is going on.

A: I AM GOING TO BED NOW, I AM TIRED. SEE YOU IN THE MORNING

M: THOUGHT YOU WEREN'T COMING TO BREAKFAST.

A: I LIED. YOU KNOW I WILL BE THERE.

N: WE WANT MORE DETAILS LATER.

A: WHATEVER

K: LOGAN SAID DON'T FORGET TO USE PROTECTION.

A: THAT DOESN'T DESERVE A RESPONSE.

N: YOU KNOW... NEVERMIND, NOT GETTING INTO THAT CONVERSATION TONIGHT. NIGHT. LOVE YAS.

M: LOVE YOU TOO NORI. I HAVE MORE STUDYING TO DO. THANKS FOR THE BREAK.

K: ♥

Abigail loved her friends, but sometimes they jumped into the deep end. She finished getting ready for bed and then set her alarm to get up early to go for a run.

The next morning, when her alarm went off at seven, she wanted to snooze it; but, she was disciplined enough to wake up. She put on a pair of jogging pants, a hoodie, and a pair of running shoes. Pulling her hair back up into a ponytail, she made sure she had her keys before leaving. Running helped to clear her mind and gave her some quiet space to think and let everything flow out and into the universe. Sometimes she listened to music on headphones and sometimes she didn't. Today was one of those 'music on' days. She put on a playlist and took off after stretching a few minutes. There was a nice path through the college that gave her a good three mile stretch to work off some of the fog in her head. She passed some people heading to breakfast or early classes and was glad she didn't have any of those this particular day.

Once she made it back to the dorm, she luxuriated in a long, hot shower before dressing for the day. She wrapped her hair up in a tight bun on top of her head and left it wet. A few of her light-brown locks were too short and hung around her temples and the nape of her neck. She took a little more care in dressing for the day in hopes that maybe a certain someone would notice her. Who knows? But, she was going to try and put some extra pep in her step.

Packing up the necessities for the day, Abigail wrapped the strap of her bag across her body and was out the door in time to meet the gang for breakfast at the usual time. When she arrived, the only person she saw at first was Melissa. Abigail swore that woman never slept and was early for everything. She would probably be a whole day early for her own wedding. Dressed, hair done, and everything twenty-four hours before she would need to be. She made everyone feel like they were late if they were on time for something. She didn't set out to intentionally make anyone feel that way, but how else are you supposed to feel when a person is the first to arrive at every single event. Maybe Melissa was really a time traveler and she set her watch to be at the location early when in reality she was actually late, but her trick saved her. That was an interesting concept.

By the time Abigail made it to the table, Nori had joined Melissa. Abigail sat down between Nori and Melissa leaving an open space on both sides of her. She opened her breakfast burrito and poured salsa all over it. She looked forward to diving into it. As soon as she took a bite, she moaned at the taste. The other two girls simply looked at her with their cereal and yogurt. "What?"

"Do we need to leave you alone there?" Melissa asked.

"No. It just tastes good and I was craving one this morning. It is like a veggie omelet wrapped up inside of a warm tortilla blanket and it is chilly outside this morning."

Nori said, "That is nothing. It is 21 degrees back home in Broken Arrow and snow is falling. My mom said they are supposed to get about 4-6 inches. I told Jess she better go make me a snowman and take a picture of it."

"Please tell me you will share the picture with us. I wouldn't mind if it snowed down here," Melissa commented.

"You haven't looked at the weather, have you?" Nori asked.

Immediately both Abigail and Melissa pulled up the weather app and their mouths dropped in surprise. That was the moment when Logan and Katherine joined them.

"Are you two trying to catch flies for your breakfast?" Logan asked while pointing at the two girls.

Nori shook her head. "Nope, they just say we have a small chance of snow on Sunday for our get-together."

"Oh really? Wow. Well, if it does, I won't be able to get the boys outside. We might be holed up in someone's room playing video games. At least you girls are having an indoor day. But, really what are the chances it will actually snow?"

"Hey, it could happen. Don't steal my hope," Melissa shot at him. She paused and looked around the room. "Did you text Eve last night?"

Nori replied back, "I did. But, she didn't respond, so I am not sure. She seemed up to hanging out on Sunday when I spoke with her yesterday."

They all looked at Abigail as if she held some magical explanation. "Why do you all keep looking at me?"

Then her eyes widened as she looked behind their group. Before she could cut them off, Nori said, "You are the one that asked me to text her last night."

"Wait, what?" Eve stood looking confused and a little in shock.

Nori turned around and transferred that beaming smile up at the short, dark-haired beauty.

"Good morning, Eve. Sit down next to me before you drop your food."

"I don't know if that would be a good idea. I thought you wanted me to come by this morning."

"Oh, girl, I do. I just wasn't thinking that you didn't know the time we met or that you were welcomed automatically to join us. Abigail, here, asked me to text you since no one else had your phone number."

Abigail was so thankful that Nori worded it that way. She watched the on-edge female step behind Nori to sit down between herself and Nori. She wasn't going to complain one bit having the adorable, shy girl sitting next to her.

"Okay. If you are sure that is all it is. I am not going to stay where I am not wanted or people are talking about me." Eve eased down and opened her juice.

Nori leaned over and gave Eve a hug from the side, "I promise that is all it is. I would have been sad if you weren't here this morning." Abigail wished it was her comforting Eve on what was going on.

Katherine joined in on the chat meaning her first cup of caffeine was demolished, "I would ask how classes are going, but I know it is only the fourth day of the first week. Have you met all your teachers yet?"

Abigail watched as Eve's face transformed from worried and apprehension to happiness and excitement. All the lines smoothed out and muscles relaxed, her posture straightened as if she was more confident. She liked the look of this Eve.

"No. I have my Intro to Astronomy class tonight. However, I think I am going to enjoy the others if first impressions hold up. I mean some are more personable than others, but they were all at least positive and happy. You all were right about Professor Edison, though. At first I thought she was a teacher's assistant until she started talking."

The whole group laughed. "She was the only reason I survived my math courses," Logan admitted.

"That reminds me I need to reach out to see when she is doing the volunteer work at the elementary school this term so I can see if it works with my schedule," Nori added.

"Volunteer work?" asked Eve

Abigail jumped in before Nori could explain. "Yes, she volunteers at a local elementary school and takes students from the college. They tutor and work with various teachers in the classrooms once a week. The students love it. I have had the opportunity to help out several times myself."

"Wow. I love that. I wish I could help out, but my schedule is really full." Eve looked sad for a moment and then smiled. "I hope you get to go, Nori. Then you can tell me all about it."

"I will be happy to do that. I am sure Abigail will be also. I imagine Peyton will announce it in all her classes as per her usual procedure."

Abigail grinned, "You know I will. I am willing to share whatever you would like to know."

Nori cleared her throat and took a drink before speaking. "So, are we all set for Cinema Sunday?"

"I'm in. I am bringing the popcorn," Melissa chimed in from Abigail's right.

Katherine added her contribution immediately, "And I will have drinks chilling and queso heating up."

"I will swing by and pick up sandwiches on my way," Nori offered.

"What do you all want me to bring?" Eve asked.

Nori shook her head. "Nothing. You are our guest this time, so you don't need to bring anything."

"That isn't right. I will bring a dessert from work. Might be a few different offerings that are leftover at the end of the night, but they are always delicious."

Abigail placed her hand on Eve's upper arm. "I think that sounds marvelous. I, for one, wouldn't mind a sampling of some of Michelangelo's desserts."

"Wow. You work there? I can't afford a place like that. Heck, yes. As long as you aren't having to pay for the food then I am in full support of this," said Melissa.

"It sounds like I should be jealous of all this food and pretend to be sick Sunday so I can stay at the apartment," joked Logan. An elbow to his side silenced him on the matter. "Or not."

Abigail straightened up. "As much as I enjoy all this talk about food, Eve and I need to get to our class." Looking at the woman, she asked, "You ready?"

"Yep." They both gathered up all their stuff and waved to the others. "Bye, you all. Thanks for inviting me to breakfast."

"Here is your formal invitation to join us any Tuesday and Thursday at the same time. We always get together," said Nori.

"Thanks. I will see you this Sunday," Eve called as she started maneuvering around the maze of chairs.

When they got outside, the wind was gusty and their clothing was flapping about. Abigail had to hold tight to her bag since it liked to slap against her backside. By the time they made it into the building, despite Abigail putting her hair up for the day, there were bits and pieces falling down around her face and head. "How does your hair not look a mess?" she asked Eve.

"Simple. I took a moment to put my hoodie up and over my head so it didn't get as disheveled.

"Smart woman. Well, I will have to redo my bun. I think I will put it back into a messy bun, so it looks like I did it on purpose. Let's get to class and then we can figure out the state of my hair."

They both walked down the hall and made it to class in plenty of time for Abigail to fix the messy bun. Then about that time, Mr. Wallace walked in and the lesson began.

That day in class they reviewed the alphabet and followed the teacher's instructions then they grouped up to practice saying hi, how are you doing, what's your name, answering, and saying nice to meet you.

Since they teamed up with those around them, Eve and Abigail ended up in the same group. They had a nice relaxing class and it was becoming one of Abigail's favorite classes. Afterwards, they both headed to the library to study.

EVE

Once their ASL class was dismissed, the two of them walked to the library to study. They didn't really need to eat again since it had only been a couple of hours. The wind hadn't died down any while they were in class. This was a rare occasion when Eve was thankful for heavy doors because they didn't catch the wind as much and slam open banging the wall behind them. Eve always hated when that happened and everyone turned and stared. But, with the thick wooden doors, they just had to fight against the weight. It was easier opening when the wind was going in the same direction as the opened door.

This time when they entered, Eve knew exactly where to head and took the lead. She figured since Abigail had studied in the same spot twice, then that was their area. Their area, now that sounded a bit more intimate in her head than it should. Did Eve want it to be an intimate thing? Did she even know to whom she was attracted? She never really thought about it much at all growing up and as a teenager because she was aware that she wasn't in a situation that was conducive to having relationships. Her only thought was surviving and getting through high school so she could try and get a start somewhere. She never thought about college or anything loftier than getting through the first eighteen years.

However, here she was attending a university and meeting new friends. Ones that she could possibly hold on to over the next several years. It was mind blowing.

Abigail cleared her throat lightly and brought Eve out of her musings. She must have walked on auto-pilot all the way to the second floor.

"Everything okay?" Abigail asked. Eve could see the concern in the way the other woman's hand reached out part-way then paused and her forehead was scrunched.

"Oh yes. I left the planet and got lost in my own thoughts. I'm sorry. Did you say something?"

"Nothing of importance. Anything you want to discuss?"

"Nah. I appreciate the offer, though. Shall we get started?"

Eve watched as Abigail settled in the big, cushioned chair. Since Eve was mostly reading right then, she mirrored Abigail's position in the other chair ninety degrees to the left of Abigail. The astronomy textbook balanced on the arm of the chair and there was a little table to the side of both of them that she could sit her water bottle on. Eve got lost in the words on the page and was grateful she set an alarm when her phone let out a bird sound. She hated the ringtones on her phone so she set up some that she didn't mind hearing when alarms and timers went off.

Eve stretched out her muscles from sitting in the same spot for so long. "I might need to set reminders to stand up and move every so often. She glanced to see that Abigail was sitting at the table instead of in the cushion chair. How did your work go?"

"It went well. I needed to work on some homework problems so that unfortunately required more of a table and wider area to work. At least for today. How was the world of astronomy?"

"You know how it goes. The first chapter is always more of an introduction type of thing, but I like it all. I am excited for more of the observation part of the class."

"You will have to share what you learn. I was going to ask if you wanted to trade numbers. That way if you ever wanted to practice sign language, not that you need it, or go test out a few of the local college dives you have my number and can message me. Or if I am needing the dirt on how stars are aligning you can clue me in."

Eve laughed, "Remember, astronomy, not astrology. But, sure. Nori has it and if you wanted it bad enough, I know that woman would give it to you without much of a struggle." Eve rattled off her number as she put her book away. "I am not sure I will have an opportunity to see you before, so have a good weekend at work. I will see you on Sunday." Eve left Abigail behind to keep problem solving as she headed off in search of the stars.

Later that night after she had completed showering and crawled into bed to relax, she pulled out her phone and noticed she had a couple of text messages. Wow. I'm getting popular with two in one day. She didn't really have a big need for a phone since there was no family or others that cared. Mostly, she had it for emergencies, work, and a few games.

Because of this, she didn't look at her messages very often during the day and it stayed on silent so she didn't forget to switch it off. She tapped the message icon and noticed that one was from Nori and the other was from an unknown number. She opened up Nori's first.

N: Hey Eve. Available for lunch tomorrow? Wasn't sure of your work schedule. LMK

Eve replied back to the message.

E: Has to be an early lunch. I go in at 2:30pm. Would 11am work?

Eve exited out of that message chain and clicked into the unknown one.

Abigail: This is Abby. You gave me your number, but didn't take mine. I know you are in class and will see this later tonight. Wanted you to have my number. Sleep well and see you soon.

E: Hi Abigail. Hope this doesn't wake you. Got your text. Yeah, I was in a hurry. You are now saved in my phone and aren't a creepy "unknown."

E: Not that all new numbers are creepy.

E: Actually yours is the only one in a long time.

E: I am closing my phone now. Have a good night yourself and sweet dreams.

A: LOL. You are funny. Glad I am not a creeper too.

E: Definitely not. Happy work this weekend.

A: Night Night.

Eve put on her headphones and started up an audiobook to listen to while she played a couple of games on the phone. After about thirty minutes, she fell asleep on her phone and woke later when her roommate stumbled in the door, knocking some things over in an effort to get to the bed. Eve kept her eyes closed tight and prayed that she would settle down and Eve could get back to sleep. She was thankful she didn't have an early class the next day. After several clumsy minutes, there was silence once more.

Cautiously, Eve rolled over and saw that Bentley had collapsed in the middle of the floor and didn't even make it to her bed. The bad thing was the door was left propped open by a foot and partial leg in the path the door swung. Eve groaned and threw back the blankets. She marched over and shoved Bentley's lower body out of the way far enough so the door closed. Then she made sure she was in a position where she wouldn't drown in her own vomit if she woke up sick during the night. She couldn't even imagine what the weekend was going to be like since those were the typical party days. Maybe her roommate needed some help and an intervention. Eve was surprised that someone hadn't gotten her help before this. Grabbing a pillow and blanket from the other bed, Eve lifted her roommate's head off the floor and then slid the pillow into place before covering her up. Knowing her good deed for the week was done, Eve crawled back into bed, put her headphones in, set the sleep timer, and listened to the book until she fell back to sleep.

The next morning, Eve woke up and found her roommate wasn't on the floor any longer. She must have woken up at some point during the night and gotten up in her bed. Good for her. That meant that Eve didn't have to try and sidestep her while getting dressed. Since she had no desire to be in the room when Cruella woke up, she dressed in a pair of warm running pants and a Sterling U t-shirt under her hoodie. She grabbed her second set of clothes for work that was on a hanger and her trusty backpack and crept outside in the hallway. She figured it was early enough that no one would be awake, but she was wrong. There were plenty of people coming in and out of doors. The room across from hers opened and a tall redhead stepped into the hall.

"Good morning." Eve smiled and tried to project happiness.

"Morning. Are you Bentley's roommate?

The smile on Eve's face deflated quicker than a balloon released of its air. "Yeah. Why?"

"Well, she started banging on my door late last night. When I opened it, she thought I was you."

"I am so sorry about that. She seemed to have, umm, been a bit... ummm, not one hundred percent."

"Drunk is the word I believe you are looking for. Wasted, trashed, sloshed, pissed... Shall I continue?"

"No. All I know to do is apologize. Trust me in that it has been one week and I am already over it."

The redhead's demeanor relaxed a fraction before continuing. "You might need to say something to the RA if it keeps up. Better from you out of concern, than the testy individuals that live on this floor."

"I will do my best. Again, I am sorry she woke you up. I need to go now."

Eve hurried down the flight of stairs and out to her car before any of the other students caught her attention. She made it to her vehicle without any more interruptions.

Eve drove away from the campus glad to have a small reprieve from everything. She wanted to go to college and get an education so she could do more in life and not become another sad statistic of foster kids. She was more than how she was raised. Growing up she had a few teachers that believed in her and encouraged her. It was because of them and Carlos that she was attending the college. At the rate this week was going, she was beginning to think maybe continuing as a waitress and finding a second job would be better than roommates that came in at odd hours drunk or having people over in her dorm.

The restaurant where Nori wanted to meet came into sight and Eve pulled into the parking lot. It was busy and by the looks of it, they might have to skip lunch. However, Eve got out and went inside. Instead of a crowded restaurant and groups of people waiting to be served, she found it mellow and a buzz of people chatting, but there wasn't anyone waiting on a table. Maybe the restaurant was owned by a relative of Mary Poppins and could serve more than it appeared to. At first she didn't see Nori, but then someone waved and Eve saw her friend.

When she arrived at the table, she half expected the whole gang to be there. Instead, it was only Nori. Eve felt simultaneously relieved and saddened by this; relieved that she could relax, but a little disappointed that she wasn't going to be able to see a certain someone. She genuinely enjoyed Nori's company. "Hey. I thought it would be more chaotic here, but it isn't bad." Picking up a menu, Eve looked it over. "Have you eaten here before? Do you have a favorite?"

A laugh came from the other side. "I like that you ask if I had a favorite and not if the food is good."

"I figured it was or you wouldn't have suggested it." Eve thought she would go with the chicken taco and cheese enchilada combo.

"I have and I love Tex-Mex food, so it is hard to pick out a favorite." The server arrived to take their drink order. "I will have a Coke please."

"May I have an iced water, please." When the server left, Eve eyed her lunch companion wondering what made Nori invite her out for lunch.

"I imagine you are wondering why I wanted to meet you." Dang, was Nori psychic? Her expression might have shown her shock as the other woman continued. "I figured you were wondering about that since you have to go to work and I still wanted to meet."

A bowl of chips and salsa was placed on the table along with their drinks and Eve dived in. Pointing one of the chips at Nori, she replied, "This is very true."

"Mostly I wanted to see how your first week went at the university."

"And the 'not mostly' part?"

Nori shrugged, "I wanted to ask you something, but wanted to make sure you felt comfortable."

Immediately, Eve sat down the chip she was holding. "Okay. That sounds suspicious. Let's start with that part."

"Aww. No, it isn't bad or anything. Please don't worry. I know on Tuesday we kind of caught you off guard when we were talking about who all we were dating. It was asked who you were attracted to or liked. I wanted to follow up on that conversation."

Eve cleared her throat and scooted back a few inches in her chair. "Umm. I don't think–"

Nori interrupted Eve, "Don't worry, Eve, I am not going to ask you the same thing. I only want to clarify and share a bit with you if I may."

"Go on." Eve sat with her hands in her lap, fingers laced together, twisting them back and forth. Her heart was beating quickly and she could feel little beads of sweat starting to form at the nape of her neck despite it being cool.

"It is hard for most people to say who they are attracted to if one isn't straight. Our small group knows this and we all have stories, good and bad. Kathleen and Logan are as straight as a ruler, but they don't judge or think any differently of us who aren't. As you know I am a lesbian and my best friend Ian is as gay as Logan is straight. One night, I will video conference with him and let you meet him. He is a riot and will have your stomach hurting from laughing. Melissa is bi and loves males and females. Then there is Abigail. I am not sure if you have picked up on it, but in the few days we have known you, she has grown interested in you."

Eve sat up straight and she could barely hear the rest of the words that Nori said after that from the pounding in her ears. Who knew you could hear your own blood pump. The pressure in her head was mounting and she knew that soon it would rupture something. She took a few slow breaths and finally was able to understand what Nori was saying again.

"That is why I wanted you to know."

Oh dang it. She missed out on something major while she was having her little internal freak out. "Okay."

"We want you to know you are able to be yourself around us and we aren't going to judge. Now, ready to dive into the food?"

Eve looked down and sure enough, it seems not only did she not hear part of Nori's speech, but she wasn't aware of the food arriving at their table. She was in trouble now. She wanted to know the missing information, but was afraid to let Nori know she'd freaked a bit. Better to play it off and hopefully she would discover it later.

For the remainder of lunch, they enjoyed the food and chatted about classes, teachers, and horrible roommates. Nori was of the opinion that if Eve's roommate continued to come back that way, then something needed to be done. Once lunch was over, Eve headed over to Michelangelo's to become the server for everyone there. A role reversal from lunch.

CHAPTER 5

ABIGAIL

Sunday morning, Abigail woke up with a horrible headache and groaned. She felt like someone slammed their fist into the side of her head. She hoped she wasn't getting sick. She rolled out of bed and was grateful her roommate wasn't there. She brushed her teeth and put on a pair of baggy pants before remembering it was movie day at Katherine's. So, she took two pain relievers, took a shower, and changed into a pair of leggings and a long sweater. The day wasn't going to be one where she was going to be all primped and stylish. Nope, she was going to be comfortable and pray the meds kicked in.

Tossing her hair up into a messy bun, she grabbed what she needed for the girls' afternoon and drove over. As she parked, she saw Eve walking up the sidewalk. She opened the car door and called out.

"Hello, Eve!"

Abigail watched as the bag in Eve's hand almost went soaring away. Abigail would have felt bad if that happened. She ran to catch up. "Sorry. I didn't mean to scare you."

"It's okay. I think I am extra jumpy today."

It was then that Abigail noticed the extra packages in Eve's other hand. "Do you need help carrying anything?"

"No. I am afraid if you took something that it would unbalance me more. Although, you could knock or ring the bell for me."

"Of course." They got to the door and Abigail knocked, even though she normally might have gone on inside. However, she didn't want to appear impolite to Eve. When she heard shouting from inside, Abigail opened the door called inside. "Guess who I found!"

The door swung open and three women came racing immediately over. They all grabbed an item from Eve and then gave her hugs. Abigail hadn't even thought to do that and missed her chance. The three others wrapped her up in hugs also.

"Come on in and welcome to my humble apartment, Eve. Please make yourself at home. I know it will be needed at some point, so let me show you where the bathroom is."

Katherine swept Eve away for a minute and Melissa whispered when they were out of sight. "Did you both arrive together?"

"No, she was walking in when I parked. I should have offered to bring her here, though."

Nori was unpacking bags and placing stuff on the counter. "I did offer, but she said she wanted to drive because there was a slight chance that she might have to go to work tonight."

"Dang."

The two women entered back into the kitchen-living room area.

"Alright, ladies. Does anyone have an opinion on what movie we watch first?" Katherine asked as she turned on the television.

Abigail settled on the couch hoping she might get lucky and have Eve sit next to her. "As long as it isn't a Nicholas Sparks movie, I am game for most things."

"I want a hot woman to ogle over," Nori shot out.

"We have to watch at least one movie that isn't a romance," Abigail demanded as she rested her head back against the cushion.

Eve suggested, "What about *Ocean's Eight*? There are lots of beautiful women in that movie and it isn't a romance. Or there is a movie with a name that has fives in it, I believe. It is a 'girl power' movie, too. I can look it up."

"Yes! Perfect. Eve, you are officially one of us, in case you didn't know that. You brought good desserts and have great taste in movies," Katherine said.

"Speaking of desserts, these look heavenly. I think you may get nominated for dessert duty. Abigail, why haven't you ever brought us desserts like this from your restaurant?" Melissa asked.

"Because I swear they keep them in a vault and don't like to give them away. Not really. I have brought desserts before," Abigail countered.

"Not as many or such a selection." Nori drooled from over a box.

Catching Eve's blush, she wondered what was truly in those take out containers.

Katherine walked back to the counter and opened the cabinet. "Alright, ladies. *Ocean's Eight* is locked and loaded. Fix your plates of food and let's get settled down for mayhem." Katherine handed out plates for everyone. "We are doing paper plates so cleaning up is a breeze. All the fixings for nachos are on the counter. Ice is in the door of the fridge and the water there is good, too. There are cans of soda in the fridge. I think we are set."

Each of the girls fixed their plates. Abigail rose up from the couch to grab some food. She didn't fix very much because she wasn't very hungry. They all settled down around the TV. Melissa claimed one recliner while Katherine took the other. Nori sat at one end of the couch and Eve sat on the floor.

"You don't have to sit on the floor, Eve. There is plenty of room on the couch. I will sit in the middle so you can have the end and have easier access to the table."

"I am fine."

"Trust me, Eve, that floor isn't comfortable. That is why we have all this furniture," Katherine rebutted.

"Okay. You win. Thank you." Eve stood up and took the space at the opposite end of the couch from Nori. Abigail sat cross legged with a bottle of water between her legs and her plate resting on top of her legs. Katherine started the movie and soon they were all engrossed in the action on the screen.

By the end of it, Abigail was still feeling kind of icky and her headache hadn't really gotten any better. However, she didn't want to break up the fun for everyone else, so she stayed quiet. They all got up to get refills of drinks and then decided it was time to dive into the desserts. One of the containers held several pieces of chocolate cake that looked like it was rich and moist and delicious. It called to her like a siren from the sea. Without trying to, Eve might have found her weakness. In another box were tall, thick pieces of cheesecake and on the side there was a choice of raspberry sauce, a caramel, or a chocolate sauce.

Eve started explaining what was in the last box, "When I explained that I was meeting you all this afternoon, Carlos made something especially for us, they are a part blondie and part chocolate brownie. This isn't sold at the restaurant very often. When it is, we serve the brownie warm with a vanilla bean ice cream and drizzle of caramel. He wanted us to have something fun."

"Who is Carlos?" Nori asked, as she pulled out one of the brownies from the pan. "Oh my goodness. These are delicious. Katherine, do you have any ice cream? I want to warm this up and eat it with some ice cream."

"I think there is some in the freezer," their hostess supplied.

Nori almost knocked Melissa over in her rush to get to the freezer. She opened the freezer and squealed, "YES!" Abigail watched as her friend pulled out a container and hugged it to her body as if she just found her long lost pair of jeans or something.

"You okay over there, Nori?" Abigail teased her.

Nori stuck her nose up in the air like she hadn't just been about to cry in happiness over ice cream. "Yes, I am. You have no idea the bliss I am about to be in. I swear Eve, if I wasn't already dating my dear Jess, I might woo you just for access to these desserts." Then that saucy minx sent a wink over at Abigail without anyone else seeing it. "Then again, if I explain the situation, she might forgive me."

Eve giggled, "I didn't do anything. Plus, I am not getting in the middle of you and your girl. Females fight ruthlessly. I like all my body parts attached as they are and not scarred."

Nori hugged Eve to her side. "You are quality stock. Now who is this Carlos?"

Abigail was wondering the same thing. She knew he was probably a cook or chef, but most of them wouldn't just release so much food to a waitress unless there was something else going on.

"Carlos is the Executive chef at the restaurant where I work. For some reason, he has—I guess you can say—looked after me sometimes. He and his wife are wonderful people and always giving back to the community and I think along the way, I became a project or someone they help out in small ways. I earn my keep and everything, but the past year or so has been a bit rough. Anyway, they are kind and you all get to partake in those rewards today. Eat up."

"While those brownies look good, I want a piece of that cake." Abigail pulled the box over to where she was leaning against the other side of the island. The pieces were huge and she didn't want to appear selfish, so she cut one of the pieces in half. Then careful to not break it, she lifted the piece of the cake out. Her mouth watered and even now a day later, she could smell the chocolate and sugar combination and it made her happy. She was careful to carry her piece back to the couch where she was sitting before.

Once everyone had their sugar high of choice, they all returned to their same spots and turned on the second movie. Lifting a forkful of cake to her mouth, she had to bite back a little moan that wanted to escape at the taste of the cake.

A whisper came from her right side, "It is good, isn't it? It is one of my favorite things."

Abigail turned her head slightly to see Eve watching her eat the cake. "It is." If someone asked later, she would say her hushed deep voice was due to trying to stay quiet and had nothing to do with the look on the other woman's face, or the twinkle in her eye that grabbed Abigail in the gut. It had been a long time since she felt this kind of pull from another person. Swallowing her own desires to thrust her hands into Eve's locks and tug until their mouths collided, Abigail took a long, slow drink of the water in front of her in an effort to compose herself. She would have sworn Eve almost had the same look in her eyes, but she might have been projecting her own feelings outward. Each bite of the cake Abigail took, she heard that whispered voice in her head asking, *it is good isn't it?* By the time the piece was done, Abigail was on fire and flushed. Despite taking several cold drinks, it didn't do anything for the flames that licked Abigail's body.

Later on, Abigail woke up covered in a blanket and stretched out on the sofa. She sat up and looked around trying to figure out what had happened. Melissa was snuggled up in one chair and Nori was passed out in the other chair. When Abigail went to find her phone to see what time it was, that same melodic voice spoke quietly from the other end of the sofa. “Hey. How are you feeling?”

“What time is it? Why is everyone asleep?”

“It is about 9pm. They all fell asleep early. You fell asleep during the movie. Nori went to tease you awake and found that you were burning up. We laid you down on the couch and covered you up. Somehow that friend of yours managed to get you to wake up long enough to down a couple of pain relievers. I don’t think you woke up as much as just doing what she demanded while sleeping on. Your eyes never even opened. Anyway, we all decided to stay until we knew you were going to be okay. Logan got home and charged into the place and not even that stirred you. I think you had some people worried.”

“You know, I think that is the most I have heard you speak at one time before.”

“I’m sorry.” Eve closed her mouth and Abigail regretted the teasing immediately.

“No. I like it. I enjoy listening to you talk. Plus, you can tell we are all chatty in this group. So, you didn’t fall asleep?”

“No. I worked on some studying I had with me.” Eve held up her textbook that Abigail hadn’t noticed until that moment. “It is nice and quiet here even with the low level of snoring or television from the other room.” Eve nodded in the direction of Katherine and Logan’s bedroom.

“Thank you for staying. I guess what I thought was a simple headache was something else. I probably should have stayed away today, but I wanted to spend time with you.” After a couple of seconds passed, Abigail added, “And them, but mostly wanted to be here for you. I knew it was the first time we were all going to hang out from school. Plus, I am attracted to you.”

A quiet, “I know,” came from the other end of the couch.

“You do?”

"Yeah, Friday, Nori took me out to lunch so she could explain a few things and one of the things she said was that you were interested in me."

"And?"

"And, I am not sure. I haven't ever been in this situation before."

"Where a girl likes you?"

"Anyone at all."

"Really? You are a beautiful and intelligent woman from what little I know about you so far. I am surprised." Abigail saw Eve shrug and curl up a little tighter on her end of the sofa. "Here, let me sit up so you can have more room." She scooted up on the sofa with her back along the arm and legs folded.

"You didn't need to do that." Abigail said.

"I'm awake and don't need the whole couch. May I ask you a question? If you don't want to answer it, then you don't have to."

"Okay."

"Does the idea of me being attracted to you freak you out? And if so, is it me in particular or the female aspect of it?"

"It isn't you, Abigail. I think I haven't ever explored that option in my mind at all. To be honest, I haven't ever thought about who I was attracted to."

"Thank you for answering. I know it isn't easy to talk about or even think about. Tell you what. How about we table this topic? You know where I stand. I am not going to pressure you or intentionally make any moves to make you uncomfortable." Abigail saw Eve let out a big sigh and quickly continued, "However, I would like to continue to spend time with you and develop the friendship that I feel is there. We could hang out together in both a crowd setting like today and alone like when we study together or have a quick meal between classes or work. How does that sound?"

"I am cool with that."

Abigail was thankful and at least she wasn't shot down completely. She could work with them being friends. Plus, maybe her feelings would weaken as they developed more of a friendship and solidified that. "Now, I think it is about time I wake everyone up and head back to the dorm. I probably will need some more meds and sleep soon. Classes wait for no one."

Abigail swung her legs over the couch and then went to the first chair and leaned over and spoke really quietly as she shook Nori. "You can quit pretending to be asleep now, but thanks for letting her think no one else was listening."

An arm came up and wrapped around Abigail's side. "You're welcome. How are you feeling?"

"Horrible. I hope it isn't contagious."

The two of them woke up Melissa and knocked softly on the bedroom door. Soon, everyone was packing and gathering everything up. Abigail walked out with Eve, Melissa, and Nori. At the parking lot they all split up to head to their places.

Abigail climbed the steps to her room and once inside, kicked off her shoes and collapsed onto the bed. She didn't even bother changing clothes but grabbed a blanket from the side and covered herself up. She did manage to swallow another couple of pain relievers to combat the fever. The last thing she thought before her eyes closed was that she should text and make sure Eve made it back safely.

Chapter 6

Eve

Tuesday morning arrived and Eve still hadn't heard anything from Abigail. She had texted her a couple of times to see how she was feeling, but nothing. She would have taken it personally, but Nori said she hadn't heard anything from her either and that Abigail must really be sick. So far, none of them had gotten sick from being in contact with her.

If Abigail didn't show up for their ASL class, then Eve was going to check on her. She wasn't sure when she would find the time, but one of them needed to go over. Maybe Eve could take some soup or something. Isn't that what they are always doing on television shows? Not that Eve had soup, but she could stop and pick some up from a restaurant. She skipped breakfast with the group because she had something she needed to finish up that morning.

Class started and there was no sign of Abigail. So, it was settled that Operation A was going into effect. When they had a break, Eve opened her phone and sent a text.

> Eve: Abby. You okay? We are getting worried about you.

E: NORI, ABBY DIDN'T SHOW. HAVE YOU HEARD ANYTHING FROM HER?

NORI: NOPE. I TOLD M AND K I WOULD GO BY THIS AFTERNOON.

E: LET ME KNOW HOW SHE IS AND IF SHE NEEDS ANYTHING. I'M ON BREAK FROM CLASS. WE ARE DUE BACK IN 5, SO IT MIGHT BE LATER BEFORE I REPLY.

N: NO PROBLEM. WILL LET YOU KNOW.

Eve shoved her phone back into her pants pocket and returned inside the classroom.

After class, Eve headed over to the library to get some homework done. It was hard to focus, but she did the best she could. The fact that Nori was going to check on Abigail helped to mollify the worry somewhat. She sat in her chair and had a pair of headphones on so she could block out all the noise. When her alarm sounded, it startled her so much that her book and papers fell off her lap. *Geez. Can't you be a little less skittish?* Once all the papers were gathered up, she lovingly placed them in the folder and backpack, keeping her frustration to herself. No reason to have wrinkled and ripped papers because she was upset with herself. She headed over to her Trig class. At least this class made her happy. All the classes did, but she was glad to be doing something that wasn't stress-inducing right now. Although with the way she was starting to explain and debate with her own mind, her mental status might be changing.

Eve found her spot and opened her notebook, ready to take notes. She'd submitted her homework online already. Peyton strolled in the door and stood in front of the class. Once the time hit the minute, she began.

"Before we begin today, I wanted to share something with you all. For those of you who don't know, I do a weekly volunteer at an elementary school. I take students over with me and we help out in classes, teach the kids, and really just bring some joy into their lives. I won't go into details here because the majority aren't interested.

However, if you want more information about it, I am holding a meeting in this room next Tuesday afternoon before class at two-fifteen. Coming to the information session doesn't mean you have to sign up, it is just for you all to ask questions and discover more about it. Now that we have that out of the way, let us begin." Peyton turned to the chalkboard and began writing and drawing on it.

Eve wanted to volunteer, but it would depend on the day and time. Between classes and work, she wasn't sure that the time would line up properly. However, she should be able to at the very least sign up for the information session.

The class went by quickly and Eve finally got to check her phone for messages. There were a couple.

NORI: WENT BY ABBY'S. SHE IS REALLY ILL. HAS BEEN SLEEPING AND NOT LOOKING AT HER PHONE. I'M DRAGGING HER TO THE HEALTH CENTER.

ABBY: I'M ALIVE. NORI IS PUNISHING ME FOR SKIPPING CLASSES BY MAKING ME GO SEE A DOCTOR. TELL HER TO STOP AND LET ME SUFFER IN PEACE. :(

Eve replied to both.

To Nori she sent off:

GLAD YOU ARE TAKING HER TO THE DOCTOR. LET ME KNOW WHAT HE/SHE SAYS.

To Abby she sent:

YOU NEED TO BE EXAMINED IF YOU ARE STILL THIS UNWELL AFTER 48 HOURS. NEED ANYTHING? I HAVE TO WORK, BUT CAN BRING YOU SOMETHING AFTERWARDS.

There was no reply coming immediately, so she put her phone away and headed to the library for her shift. Between working and studying, she felt like she could move in and no one would even notice. Now that it had been a full week working, she was better at the system. Plus, she was relaxing more into the role of helping students and pointing them in specific directions when they needed assistance with a topic. That part would take her awhile to get down as well as some of the others.

This was her short night since she had a later class. While she was reshelving books, her phone vibrated in her pocket. She pulled it out to find a text from Nori stating that Abigail had the flu. Poor girl. She shot back a quick reply thanking Nori and that she would check in on Abby later. If none of the girls got sick within the next day then they were probably in the clear. Eve might take over that soup after all and pick up some drinks for her to keep hydrated. She was going to need to flush that out of her system.

By nine-fifteen that night, Eve was ready to head back to her room. She debated going by the store that night, but decided to wait until the morning. Driving back to her dorm, she made a mental list of what she needed to get. For once her roommate was in their room, sober, and alone working on something. Eve didn't say anything and simply grabbed what she needed to take a shower. When she came back, she climbed into bed, and worked on reading her textbook until she started falling asleep. Giving up, she sat the book to the side and curled up on her side to sleep.

The next morning, Eve's alarm went off at 6:30am and there was some grumbling from the other side of the room. However, it quieted back down. Eve rolled out of bed and dressed for the day. She drove to the nearest grocery store and bought a few things for a care package for Abby. After her English class, she went by Abigail's dorm room. She knocked on the door and no one answered. She waited a few moments and knocked again. As she was getting ready to turn around thinking maybe Abigail felt a lot better and was in class, the door knob crept open a crack. There before Eve stood a version of Abigail she didn't think she would ever see. Her hair stood out in all directions and would definitely win in a bedhead competition. She was slouching and looked like she might crumple to the floor any moment. Oddly, Abigail's appearance sort of made her think of a piece of paper that had been wadded up tight and then attempted to be smoothed back out and nothing was quite right.

"Eve, what are you doing here?"

"I brought you a care package." Eve held up the bags of items.

"You didn't need to do that. You don't want to be around me right now."

"Come on. Let me in. Are you taking care of yourself?" Once Abigail opened the door, Eve took a quick look around and saw the place was a mess.

"Okay, guess the answer to that question is a no." There were tissues falling out of a trash can, wrappers of junk food littered the desk, and clothes were tossed haphazardly around. Although, the clothes it seemed might have been more of her roommate's than Abigail's. In fact, the person in front of her might still be in the same clothes she was in earlier this week. Eve pushed her way in. "Go sit down on the bed. Actually, no. Go take a shower and put on some clean clothes." Eve opened a bag and pulled out a mask. "Don't take offense, but I don't want the flu. Now shoo."

Abigail grumbled, but did as she was told. While she was taking a shower, Eve pulled on some gloves and got to work. She gathered up all the trash and tied off one of the bags before putting an empty one in the trash can. She found some clean sheets and changed out the bedding along with the pillow cases. Then she gathered up the dirty ones and shoved them inside of a bigger trash bag and tied it off. She sprayed disinfectant spray on every surface she could manage. So, by the time Abigail returned, the room had been sorted and cleansed. Sitting along the desk now sat a few bottles of water and gatorade along with a bag of vitamin C drops, Tylenol, ibuprofen, and a bowl of soup.

Abigail dragged herself back through the door and stood there like a statue. Eve grabbed her dirty clothes and shoved them in the laundry bag. "Do you have another blanket?" When Abigail pointed at a tote under the bed, Eve pulled it out and put it on the bed and then crammed the blanket in with the rest of the dirty clothes.

"Who are you and what did you do with Eve?"

At those words, Eve blushed and stammered, "Umm, well, sorry. I have had to help take care of several sick kids growing up. I guess I kind of take charge now and then. Trust me, I will be back to my normal shy, uncertain self soon enough. In the meantime, I am going to take your bedding to wash, but I have to go to work. Be sure to eat that soup and drink plenty of fluid. There are other things in the bag to eat later. There are two types of pain reliever on the desk. If you don't have any adverse effects, then you can alternate the two types every two hours if you have a fever. Any questions?"

"No."

Eve nodded and gathered up the trash and the dirty clothes bag and moved to the door. "I will check on you later. Call or message someone if you need something. Your friends care about you, Abby. Let everyone help because we all know you would do the same." She had opened the door when a weak voice called out behind her.

"Eve?"

She turned around and saw Abigail sitting on the edge of the bed with what looked like tears in her eyes. But Eve was sure it was just the girl not feeling well. "Yes?"

"Thank you for everything."

Eve smiled in a gentle way as if she was trying to reassure a young child and quieted her voice. "You are welcome, Abby. Don't forget, fluid and soup." Abigail nodded and laid down on the bed. "Rest well."

Then Eve hauled the stuff she brought along with the two bags and quietly shut the door behind her. She had to hurry so she would make it to the library in time for her shift. Even though she knew what she was doing, the whole time Eve was waiting for Abigail to kick her out or tell her to leave her alone. Surprise, surprise, that wasn't the case at all.

CHAPTER 7

Abigail

Thursday morning Abigail felt a little better and had to admit that it was probably partially to do with the fact that Eve came over the previous day. Not that seeing her beat the germs away by her beauty, but rather the fact that she cleaned and forced Abigail to shower and wash the germs down the drain. The change in clothes and bed linen along with knowing she was clean seemed to have charged her cells. Plus the soup, water, and vitamin C aided, she had no doubt. However seeing Eve did settle her spirit and allowed her to rest, so maybe there were some medicinal qualities in attraction after all.

She found that while she wasn't up to leaving her corner of creation to venture out into the wild of the student jungle, sitting up and reading a bit to catch up was sustainable for bursts of time in between resting. And by the end of the night, she had managed to tackle the work from Monday's classes and finished an assignment that was due by the end of Friday.

Despite being in some rather larger classes, Abigail emailed her professors that she was down with the flu, but would do her best to complete the work on time. They all sent her well wishes and told her to let them know if she needed some office time to understand any concepts she missed in lecture.

By Friday, Abigail was itching to get out of her room and she hadn't had a fever in twenty-four hours. She did go ahead and call out Friday night not wanting to risk anyone by accident. However, she had to admit she was surprised she hadn't heard anything from Eve though, especially to update her on their sign language class. She tried calling her, but after five rings, the phone went to voicemail. Typing out a quick message to Eve, she asked if she was doing okay.

While she was waiting on a reply, she pulled out her tablet and logged into Disney+. Today she was going to dive into a little Marvel mania.

Abigail reached out to Nori when by Friday evening, there was still radio silence from Eve.

Abigail: Hey girl. You okay? I haven't heard from any of you in a bit.

Nori: It isn't like it has been days. It was yesterday morning. 🙄 Anyway… Knew you were sick. Been busy with classes, Ian, and Jess. How are you feeling?

A: Better. Wanting to get out of the room. Tried to call Eve earlier, but haven't heard anything back. Have you by chance talked to her?

N: Did you try texting? You know how some don't talk on the phone. Ex. This convo.

A: Do you want me to call? The dial feature is on all phones nowadays.

N: Actually the majority of telephones don't have a dial feature as much as a push numbers and call feature. It would be rather cool if you could enable the old time rotary phone on cell phones.

N: CAN YOU IMAGINE HAVING A LITTLE 3D THING POP OUT OF THE SCREEN?

A: N? YOU ARE BEING A LITTLE PEDANTIC. PLUS YOU ARE OFF TOPIC. HAVE YOU TALKED TO EVE?

N: I AM NOT. YOU ARE SIMPLY JEALOUS THAT MY MIND WORKS DIFFERENTLY AND YOU DON'T THINK UP SOME OF THE CREATIVE IDEAS THAT I HAVE. THINK WE COULD GET LOGAN TO ENGINEER SOMETHING LIKE THIS?

A: NORI!!

N: GEEZ. NO NEED TO YELL. I AM RIGHT HERE. WELL, I GUESS YOU MIGHT NEED TO YELL SINCE I CAN'T ACTUALLY HEAR YOU FROM YOUR DORM ROOM. STILL, IT ISN'T NECESSARY MY FRIEND.

Abigail wanted to both laugh and scream at her friend's antics. She hit the call button on Nori's contact and listened to it ring. After four rings, she was about to give up and drag herself down to Nori's room, when a voice on the other side picked up.

"Abby. It is so nice of you to call. My fingers were starting to get tired."

"Okay, what is going on with you? I swear I am beginning to think either aliens have inhabited your body or I am on some weird hallucination trip from medicine."

"Let's go with option two."

Abigail rubbed her head. "Forget it, I am hanging up and going to try calling Eve again. All I wanted to know was if you had heard from her. I know she is working right now so most likely won't listen to my message until tomorrow. Let me know when the aliens have replaced you with your normal self."

Abigail pulled the phone away from her ear to hang up when Nori spoke one word. "Wait."

With a deep breath and more patience than she had in her state of recovery, she settled back down to listen.

"I'm here."

A noise on the other end of the phone that resembled a sigh of resignation was heard before Nori continued. "I was trying to keep a promise to Eve."

"What promise is that? And what could she possibly want to keep from me anyways?"

"She didn't want you jumping to conclusions, but she caught the flu."

"From me."

"This is why she didn't want you to know. She was worried you would blame yourself."

"It is my fault."

"We were all exposed to you. Who is to say she also wasn't exposed to someone else. Maybe that is the person she got sick from."

"She was in my room on Wednesday cleaning. Plus, she hauled off all my yuckiness that day. I should have stopped her, but I wasn't thinking right and was only happy to see her for a few minutes. How long has she been sick?"

"Since yesterday morning. She asked me where the health center was. And before you go and do something rash, just keep your butt in your room. I have got this handled. I didn't know it was possible, but she is more stubborn than you are."

"What do you mean?"

"I tried to swing by her dorm room, but she wouldn't open the door. She said she knew what to do and would tend to herself. Although later, she texted me and mentioned that it meant a lot for me to come by. Then she messaged that she might just stay sick if it meant her roommate stayed away and she had some peace. I don't think she meant that last part, though."

Abigail laughed, "Well, maybe tomorrow I will venture over and take her some soup. Let's see if she keeps me shut out after barging into my own room."

"Good luck. Jess is waiting for me to video chat with her. You promise you are good?"

"Yeah."

"Glad to hear that. Let me know if you need anything and let me know how it goes with Eve."

"Will do. Night and tell Jess I can't wait to meet her."

"I will. Bye."

Abigail hung up and immediately pulled up Eve's name and sent a text.

A: Heard you took the flu bug with you when you left the other night. Sorry about that. How are you doing? Please message when you can.

Within about three minutes, Abigail had a response.

E: Nori warned me she caved. *sighs* I'm alive. I am taking my meds and drinking lots of fluid. I will get better quickly. How are you?

A: Lots better. Will you let me bring you soup?

E: Nope. Stay far far away. You don't want this again.

A: What if I just show up?

E: Is that you knocking on the door now?

A: No, I'm in my room. Who is there?

Several minutes passed and Abigail texted again.

A: Eve?? Who was at the door?

When fifteen minutes passed by and still no response, Abigail stood up to put on her shoes and go over to physically check on Eve. She had one shoe on when her phone beeped.

E: Sorry. It was a delivery guy. My boss sent me food over from the restaurant.

A: I was getting ready to charge over and see if

YOU HAD BEEN KIDNAPPED OR WERE BEING ASSAULTED. I MANAGED ONLY ONE SHOE WHEN YOU MESSAGED BACK.

E: AREN'T YOU THE LITTLE HEROINE.

A: HAHA.

E: REMINDS ME OF A LITTLE NURSERY RHYME. DIDDLE DIDDLE DUMPLING.

A: WHAT DOES?

E: YOU HAVING ONE SHOE ON AND ONE SHOE OFF.

A: I DON'T KNOW THIS ONE.

E: GOOGLE IT. GO ON, I WILL WAIT.

Abigail took a few minutes and did that and laughed at the song and why it made Eve think of it. She realized it was even funnier because she was in fact leaning back in the bed with the one shoe still on.

A: I GET IT NOW.

E: 🙂

E: SPEAKING OF NURSERY RHYMES, I AM GETTING SLEEPY NOW.

A: SWEET DREAMS. MESSAGE ME LATER WHEN YOU WAKE OR IF YOU GET BORED.

E:

Abigail kicked off the remaining shoe, opened a bag of popcorn, and settled back to watch another movie for the evening, thinking that Eve's boss must really like her to send food all the way over from the restaurant. Good for her. She deserved people that cared about her.

EVE

The sun streamed in from the windows and straight into Eve's eyes. It felt like someone took ice picks and plunged them into her eye sockets. She rolled over and hid her face against the wall, but then the dust and lack of oxygen had her coughing so she had to move again. This time she simply put a pillow over her eyes, but left her nose and mouth free so she could still breathe. The sharp pain of a headache eased back a little bit. She swore she felt worse today than yesterday and she wasn't sure how that was possible.

She forced herself out of the bed and changed into a different pair of pajamas. She really hoped she went on the mend soon because she was going to run out of clean clothes and have to venture to the laundromat soon. Plus, Abigail's stuff was in her car and she needed to return that to her. But, all of that was going to have to wait. Right now, it was more pain reliever, some cough medicine, and a glass of water. Then she sat up in the bed trying to read her astronomy textbook, but after eighteen minutes and reading the same page five times, she gave up. She wasn't retaining any of the information and it wasn't aiding in her pain level. She sat the book aside, turned an audiobook on her phone, and set the sleep timer for fifteen minutes. Then she turned the volume down low enough where it didn't kill her head, but loud enough she could hear it. At least it gave her brain something to occupy itself while she rested and until she fell back asleep.

The next time Eve woke, it was because her bladder was demanding attention. She was even dreaming about trying to find a bathroom to use, but nothing was working. Finally, her brain aroused the rest of her body to wake up and function. She hurried and was happy to have made it before an accident occurred. Returning, Eve grabbed her phone and noticed several missed calls and text messages. She called Carlos back and reassured him that the food last night was great and she still had plenty. After promising to let them know if she needed anything at all and that she would be in the following weekend only if she felt better, she was able to hang up the phone.

After that, she almost didn't call Nori back, but knew she couldn't do that to her new friend. She dialed up the phone and smiled when shortly after Nori said hello, a male's voice in the background shouted, "Tell her hello from Cali and that she could be here with me in the warmth."

"Let me guess, that is the infamous Ian. Tell him hi from me as well."

"Oh, doll, she put you on speaker, so I can hear you loud and clear. How are you feeling? Do I need to hire someone to come nurse you back to health? I am sure I can find just the right nursemaid to come give you a sponge bath!" Ian exclaimed.

"I appreciate your kind offer, but I'm okay. I think I should be getting better here very soon."

"Well, you just let Ian know and I will make some medical magic happen," Ian said.

Nori interjected, "How are you feeling, Eve?"

"Today is bad, but hoping..." Eve had to stop talking to cough for a minute. She held the phone away to try and cover part of the sound from Nori and Ian. When she returned it was quiet. "I'm sorry. As I was saying, I hope this is as bad as it gets and I recover soon. I won't interrupt you all any longer. Ian, it has been a pleasure meeting you verbally at least. Nori, I will talk to you soon." Eve hung up before they could tell her she wasn't bothering them.

Eve drank more water and curled up to watch a TV show on her tablet. It was propped up against the wall so she didn't have to hold it. She fell back asleep before the first episode was even over.

The next day was spent the same way. She had kept in touch with her friends via text messages and they all tried to come and check on her, but she kept them away. By Monday morning, she was tired of being inside her dorm room. However, her fever had been broken for less than twenty four hours, so she stayed inside one more day.

That night, she wanted fresh air. She took a shower and then dressed in some leggings and a long shirt. She wandered outside and found a spot that was void of people for the most part. Eve wasn't crazy or stupid, so she ensured she had some pepper spray and her phone in case she needed either one. Her phone buzzed and it was Abigail.

A: HEY EVE! WHAT ARE YOU DOING TONIGHT? WANT COMPANY?
E: I AM OUTSIDE LOOKING UP AT THE SKY. NEEDED OUT OF THE DORM.

A: ON CAMPUS?

E: SORT OF. NEAR THE PARK ON THE SIDE WHERE MY DORM IS. IT IS DARKER AND NOT AS MANY STREET LIGHTS.

A: FEEL LIKE SOMEONE TO SIT WITH YOU?

Eve debated on whether or not to have Abigail come join her. When she was honest with herself, she missed seeing and hanging out with the other woman.

A: YOU CAN SAY NO. IT WON'T HURT MY FEELINGS...MUCH.

E: HAHA. NO, I WOULD LOVE YOUR COMPANY.

A: BE THERE SOON.

Eve snuggled into her shirt starting to get a little chilly since it was in the forties outside. She probably should have brought a hoodie along, but she wasn't thinking and didn't think she would be out long enough. She almost messaged Abigail to see if she could bring one that Eve might borrow, but quickly dismissed that idea as silly. Plus, it might come across as something more and Eve wasn't ready for that yet if ever. For now, she could keep herself warm or tolerate the cool air. She knew she could be quite stubborn.

Fifteen minutes later, Abigail was strolling up to where Eve was sitting on the bench listening and looking. "Hi, Eve, glad to see you are better." Abigail settled down next to Eve.

"You seem to be back to your normal self." Eve turned her head to look at her friend.

"I am mostly there, still get tired easily. I worked last night for a shorter shift and that went well, but I was happy to get back and call it an early night. It felt good getting out, though. I take it you have the 'tired of looking at the same four walls' syndrome.

"Yep. I needed to feel the wide-open space around me and thought what better way than star gazing."

"Speaking of star gazing, what made you interested in Astronomy, Eve?" Abigail asked as they were looking up at the night sky.

"I don't know. I think growing up in homes where you weren't sure how long you would be staying and feeling like you didn't fit in made me look to outside things. I would look up at the sky from the bedroom window when I should have been sleeping and it made me think about how much of the world the stars saw and observed. They looked down on all the happiness and sadness and watched it all play out. It made me feel like maybe there was hope one day for something better. I know that sounds crazy."

"No, it doesn't. It sounds like it was a way to escape where you were and it allowed you to not become a bitter person about your situation. I admire that."

"Thanks. Plus, I used to visit a couple of my classmates' homes and we would watch some sci-fi shows or movies and the thought of visiting other planets or traveling around on a big spaceship fascinated me." Eve leaned her head back and rested it against the top of the bench to take in even more of the beauty above. "What made you interested in chemistry and what is your specific degree or what do you want to do post college?"

Abigail sighed, "I am not totally sure. I thought about going to pharmacy college and then into research maybe. Or becoming a pharmacist. Then I thought about changing my path a bit and becoming a chemical engineer. It is all up in the air. However, my passion in a way came from my childhood, too, but not in the same manner. As a child, I liked to bake and was amazed at how you put together a bunch of stuff and based on how much of specific ingredients were included, you wound up with cookies, cakes, pies, breads, and whatnot. They all had similar ingredients, but reacted differently depending on proportions. Plus, I liked stirring granules in liquid and observing how fast or slow it dissolved depending on the temperature and how fast you stirred it. Of course, I didn't know any of that was part of a chemical process until later. In high school, I had a chemistry class that changed my view of the world and my passion. Sorry about the long soliloquy."

"No. I like listening to you talk and getting to know you. Sometimes I question my choices on what to study and wonder how any of us are supposed to know what we truly want to study at this young age. I know we feel old, but really we aren't. Thanks for sitting out here with me tonight, Abigail."

"It is my absolute pleasure, Eve."

The two of them sat in relative silence and Eve knew it wasn't awkward. She didn't feel the need to force some sort of conservation. The fact that there was that comfortability warmed her heart and caused the rest of her body to shiver.

"Are you cold?" Abigail asked from beside her.

"A little. I wasn't thinking of the weather when I left my room." Eve wasn't going to tell her that she shivered due to an effect from the woman herself.

"Here. Take this." Abigail took off her zipped up hoodie and handed it over to Eve to put on.

Eve opened her mouth to argue, but Abigail shook her head and Eve simply closed her mouth and slid her arms through the holes. She wrapped it around her and let the warmth absorb into her skin. Movies always showed the man sacrificing his coat or something to save the woman he was with from being cold, wet, or naked, but Eve never thought people did that in reality nor would she have ever thought something like that would have happened to her. It made her a little happy and sad at the same time and that confused her.

Eve's voice caught a little as she whispered, "Thank you."

"You are welcome, Eve."

"Abby?"

"Yes?"

The next words were weird to say, but Eve plunged ahead while staring straight up at the twinkling darkness. "Can I cuddle against you?"

Instead of hearing a reply, Eve felt an arm wrap around her shoulder as the side of Abigail's body pressed up against her. Then a hand pressed the side of her head down to rest against a shoulder and she felt warm to her bones by this gesture as another whispered question came from above, "Better?"

"Mmmhmm."

"Good." Abigail said before Eve felt a kiss being placed on the top of her head.

"I hope I don't make you sick again."

"Don't worry about that. I am made of sterner stuff."

Eve wasn't sure how long they stayed like that, but the next thing she was aware of, she was being nudged.

"Wake up, Eve. Let's get you back to your room so you can recover more."

"Don't wanna. I am comfy here." Her pillow laughed and vibrated under her causing Eve to shoot straight up, looking around. "Oh no. I went to sleep."

"It's okay. I let you be for a few, but the temperature is dropping and I didn't want your recovery to be set back. Let me walk you back to your dorm."

"You don't need to do that."

"Yes, I do. I will worry if I don't. Let's go." Abigail stood up and held out a hand.

Eve took it and was glad she had because she wobbled a bit when she got vertical.

They walked next to each other on the way to Eve's dorm room. When they arrived, Eve wasn't sure whether to invite Abigail in or not. However, Abigail solved the problem by giving her a hug as she spoke quietly, "Get some rest and maybe we will see you at breakfast in the morning if you are feeling up to it."

"I will be there. I have missed too much class as it is." Eve had just closed the door when she realized she still wore Abigail's hoodie. She opened the door back up, but Abigail was already gone from the hallway. "Guess I will have to return it to her when I give back the rest of her stuff." Eve muttered as she changed back into some pajamas. She couldn't quite bring herself to put it into the dirty clothes hamper, though. She laid it on the top of her bed thinking maybe she should keep it close in case Abigail needed it sooner. Or at least that is what she told herself.

Her little catnap charged her up a bit and she was able to read some of the material she'd missed while sick.

ABIGAIL

The whole way back to her dorm room, Abigail had a smile on her face. Even though the temperature had dropped into the thirties, she didn't feel any of it. The happiness and joy she felt kept her warm.

When she woke the next morning, she showered and dressed and went to put her favorite hoodie on. Then she remembered she let a beautiful girl borrow it the night before and the silly grin returned recalling the feel of having Eve up close to her. Abigail knew she was making a bigger deal out of the whole scene than was warranted, but she saw it as a little bit of hope.

She hastened her steps and this morning was the first one to arrive for breakfast at their table. Nori was right behind her by only a few minutes, though.

"Morning, Abby," Nori said before yawning.

"Restless night?"

"Spoke with Ian too late last night because he forgets sometimes I am two hours ahead of him. Then Jess called and while we didn't talk all night, it was for a good hour. Then I was working on homework until 2am." Nori yawned again. "I almost skipped breakfast this morning so I could sleep a little longer, but I wanted to see everyone."

"Well, if you don't stop that yawning, I am going to send you away," Melissa said as she sat down next to Nori. "Here, drink your coffee, you loon. Be glad I love you because the line at the coffee shop was long this morning."

"COFFEE!!" Nori wrapped her hands around it and held it close to her as if it was a long lost loved one.

Abigail took a long swig of her drink before piping in, "Melissa, you are definitely right about her being a loon."

"She isn't the only one. I wasn't sure if Eve was joining us or what she drank. I should have messaged her," Melissa said. "Now I feel bad."

"Don't. She said she is coming this morning, but that she was looking forward to having a big mug of hot chocolate," said Nori after she swallowed a big gulp of her drink. "I feel a bit more human now."

"Thanks. How is she feeling?" Melissa asked.

"I texted her this morning and she said she was up to attending classes and having breakfast with us. She said she might take a nap in between classes, but would play it by ear."

Abigail set down her fork and added, "I saw her last night and she was looking better."

Nori leaned in close, "I didn't hear about this. Why didn't you share the deets with me?"

"Because you don't have to know everything, Ms. Nosey, and here she comes, so zip it," Abigail hissed before pushing a chair back for Eve. "Here. Sit down before you collapse."

"Thanks." Eve sighed as she eased down into the chair. "I underestimated how much energy was required to go through the line and get food. I feel like I need to rest even after that."

"Sounds like the flu hit you harder than it did Abigail," said Melissa.

Eve shrugged. "Maybe. I don't get sick often, but when I do, it knocks me out."

Nori jumped in immediately and offered, "We are here to help. I know that Abby has class with you this morning and can take your books to class for you and then maybe can make sure you get to Trig this—"

Eve interjected, "She doesn't need to do that. I will be fine."

"I was actually going to offer anyway before Nori volunteered me."

"You are still recovering yourself, Abby. Oh before I forget, I forgot to return your hoodie to you last night before you left. I thought I would wash it with the rest and then give it back to you later. Unless you need it today."

"No, there is no hurry." While Eve had been talking, Abigail noticed the looks exchanged between the other two girls and Nori's interest.

"Okay, good. Sorry about that. I was so warm and wasn't thinking when you left. I opened the door to catch you, but it was too late." Eve began picking at her food and eating her toast.

"Sooo... you two hung out last night, did you?" Nori asked and Abigail wanted to reach across the table and slap her friend. Instead, she leaned back and glared at Nori out of sight of Eve.

Eve didn't notice anything unusual in how Nori looked because she answered as nonchalantly and normal as if nothing was being inferred. "Yeah. I was feeling caged in and went to sit outside. Abby texted me while I was still outside and then came and kept me company for a bit."

"That was nice of her," Katherine said as she sat down. She and Logan caught the tail end of the conversation.

"How did you end up with the hoodie?" Nori continued the inquisition.

Abigail kicked her friend under the table, except she missed and kicked Melissa. "Ouch."

Mouthing sorry, she nodded at Nori.

Eve answered, "I wasn't thinking when I went outside and didn't take a jacket or anything. So, when I was getting cold, Abby offered up her hoodie to save my pride."

"She can be sweet like that when she wants to be."

"Yeah." Eve blushed just a fraction, but you had to be watching to catch it. Hopefully she was remembering their night together, too, and the parts she wasn't sharing.

In an attempt to get Eve off the hot seat, Abigail threw the hot potato at someone else. "So, how is Ian doing? When is he going to come out and visit with us again?"

Nori laughed, "Not until it gets warmer." Then Nori shared a story or two about what Ian had been up to in California.

While everyone's attention was diverted, Abigail risked reaching under the table and squeezing Eve's hand for a moment. The other girl squeezed it back and held on for a few extra seconds before releasing it. Those few moments put hope into Abigail's heart even more.

She tuned back into the conversation and finished eating breakfast while they all discussed what was going on in each of their lives. Once everyone was done eating, Abigail grabbed Eve's backpack despite the protest from the other woman. She easily wore Eve's on her back and her own cross body one so it hung along her side. "See, I am good to go."

Melissa popped up, "Actually, you look a bit lopsided. We could fix the problem and have you put a backpack on your front and then another like yours to lay the opposite direction. Then you would be even. I can volunteer mine to help." Melissa raised her own backpack from the floor to emphasize her point.

"That will be fine, Mel. Keep your own bricks to yourself. I don't know what you have in there, but it always weighs more than the rest of ours."

"That is my secret." She winked and easily swung it up on her back as if it held feathers instead of half of a house.

Abigail laughed and shook her head at her friend before turning back to Eve. "Ready to go?"

"Sure. I still think I can take care of my own backpack."

"Either I wear it or you put it on your back and I carry you on my back. I am open to either option."

Abigail had to refrain from laughing as Eve's face contorted and relaxed as a look of shock, fear, and resolution crossed her face. However, the little firecracker did narrow her eyes as she spoke, "I am giving in only because I am worried you are insane enough to try and pick me up if I don't allow you to do this and I don't want to be late for class."

Eve was right. Abigail would probably do exactly that. Since she wasn't fully recovered, it might result in both of them on the floor and as much as Abigail would enjoy having Eve sprawled on top of her, in the middle of the cafeteria wasn't the place for that to happen.

"Our quiet class awaits. Better to save your strength for signing." Abigail pushed in their chairs, "Bye, everyone. Talk soon."

Then the two girls left to head toward class before they were, indeed, tardy. Thankfully class wasn't bad and there wasn't a lot of conversation practicing because that is when more energy was used up. However, by the end of class, Abigail knew that Eve needed a break and perhaps a nap, especially when there was no resistance to assistance.

"I am not even going to fight or argue with you carrying my stuff. Thank you. I was going to go to the library to study, but I am not sure if I can stay awake. I worry if I go to the dorm to take a nap, I will oversleep and I don't want to miss Trig class again."

Slowing her steps down a bit, Abigail offered, "What if I come over and study while you take a nap. Then I can wake you up before I go to Chem and that will allow you time to fully wake and get to Trig."

"Oh, I can't ask you to do that. Plus, I am always complaining about my roommate's friends coming over. I don't want to give her any ammunition by having you there. I don't have the mental fortitude to battle with her right now."

"Then you come over to my place. My roommate is out all day with classes and doesn't return until later."

"Abby, that is sweet of you to offer–"

"Good. Let's go." She knew there was a but coming and Abigail refused to allow Eve to voice it.

Letting out a long sigh, Eve relented, "Alright. You win. Again."

"Hey, you won when you came over to my dorm room while I was sick, but it isn't a contest. I care and want to help out."

"I appreciate that, but I have a hard time letting anyone help because I am so used to taking care of myself and being my own support. When you are it, there isn't really an opportunity to lean on anyone. You get sick, you take care of yourself. You have financial problems, you get more than one job or figure things out. Car breaks down, you call a tow then walk or call for a paid ride. Sorry, that makes it sound like I don't have friends or anything. I don't mean it like that."

"I understand what you mean. Don't worry. Well, in our group, we will force you to submit under our ruling thumb and take the help whether or not you want to." Giggling, Abigail nudged Eve's shoulder as they walked.

"I have noticed. From day one, Nori has pretty much pulled me along."

"I believe she has adopted you as her sister and thus, you are now part of the collective."

Eve stopped and turned to face Abigail and asked quietly while backing up. "Are you all part of the Borg? I will not assimilate."

Abigail couldn't help it, she busted out laughing so hard she had to stop and lean against a tree.

"You are laughing, so I am thinking I might be safe. Never saw any of them laugh. Then again, maybe you have more of a processor function that allows you to tap into the humor of humans. I am wondering if maybe I need to run away while I can. You know, change my identity and location." Eve bit her lower lip in worry.

Abigail held up her hand. "Please stop... I can't... breathe..." She bent over and of course that shifted the balance of books causing her to collapse to the ground and laugh even more.

"I think maybe your processors are now not functioning properly. Maybe I need to take you to see a doctor or perhaps you need to regenerate and that will help?"

Eve stood there so serious and without cracking a bit of a smile and that is what really aided in the uncontrollable laughter. Abigail would never have been able to have delivered so many lines without breaking character. She held one finger up in the air to signal Eve to give her a minute.

"I believe that most people hold up the middle finger, not the pointer finger, do they not? Is the Borg different? Does the significance of the first finger indicate something?"

"Stop."

"Drop and Roll? I don't think rolling around on the cold ground would be good for my health at this point. Actually, it probably isn't good for you to be sitting on it as well, especially now that you are coughing. I will behave now. Let's get you up before you relapse and the rest of your collective comes after me chanting 'Resistance is Futile.'"

Eve held out her hand to Abigail and once she calmed down and resumed breathing without coughing, Abigail grabbed it and hoisted herself up off the ground. Then she grabbed their bags again and they resumed walking. "You were amazing. How could you keep going with a straight face?"

"Drama class. But, thinking of you as the Borg helped a lot, too."

"You definitely have skills, dear."

"Thank you."

They chatted for a few as they finished walking to Abigail's dorm. By the time they had climbed up to her room, Eve was really pale and slow. "You definitely need to lie down and take a nap." Opening the door, Abigail let their bags slide to the floor next to the desk before helping Eve to sit down on the bed.

"Come on now. Lay back and rest. Here, I will get you a fresh blanket." Abigail rummaged in her tote and pulled out a soft one and covered up Eve. "Go to sleep and I will wake you up in time for your next class."

"Thank you, Abby." In less than three minutes, Eve was asleep. Not wanting to be a weird creeper and watch her sleep, Abigail pulled out her own homework to work on. She set the alarm so she didn't lose track of time and then began working.

When the alarm sounded, Abigail quickly turned it off and stretched. Then she turned to look at the sleeping woman in her bed and admitted to herself that she liked seeing Eve amongst her things. She sat down on the edge of the mattress and spoke softly. "Eve, time to wake up for class." The woman didn't stir. Maybe she was a sound sleeper. Abigail reached out and shook Eve gently on the arm. "Eve, dear, time to wake up." That got a little movement and mumbling out of the woman. "Come on now, you will get mad at both of us if you don't wake up." Abigail moved part of Eve's hair and ended up touching her forehead. The girl was warm. She hurried up and dug until she found a thermometer and was glad it was one you could use on the forehead. She looked down and it read 101.1. "You will have to hate me later, but you aren't going to class."

Debating on whether or not to make Eve wake up to take some pain reliever and water or to let her sleep, Abigail finally settled for giving her 30-45 minutes and then check her fever again and see where she was at.

One thing was certain, she needed to call the library and let them know that Eve wouldn't be going to work that night, either. She went on the campus website and located the phone number for the library and called them. When someone answered, she asked to speak to someone in charge and then quickly explained the situation. The woman was very nice and understanding and told Abigail to make sure that Eve rested and to reach out tomorrow and update them.

After that call was done, she knew she wouldn't be able to concentrate and ended up pacing the floor a bit and doing some quiet cleaning. After almost forty minutes passed, she took Eve's temperature again and it showed 102.4. Well, that settled it. She grabbed a lukewarm bottle of water and two ibuprofen from the bottle Eve left for her when she was here and set them on the table. Then she sat back down on the bed and peeled the blanket back from Eve and ran her hand up and down the woman's arm to try and help wake her.

"Eve, hun, I need you to wake up enough to take some meds." The other woman didn't stir. She tried again. Shaking Eve lightly this time to try and stir her, Abigail spoke a little louder, "Come on, Eve, please wake up so I don't have to call someone for help. You are worrying me."

With that Eve mumbled and cracked open her eyes just a fraction. "Let me sleep, the monkeys were playing peek-a-boo."

"I need you to sit up so you can take some meds." Abigail sat down and helped Eve to raise up and prop up against Abigail's side. Reaching over to the table, she grabbed the two pills and ordered, "Open up your mouth so you can take these ibuprofen and take this bottle of water." Eve did as requested, but she started to drop the bottle, so Abigail grabbed ahold of it to help. Once she managed to get the pills down Eve, she helped the other woman to settle back down onto the bed. She really was getting concerned about her. She decided she better text the group. She hated to leave Eve, but she did need to get to her next class if one of the others could come sit with Eve. She already missed her Chem lecture for the day.

Abigail: Hey guys. Eve is in my room asleep and has a fever. I am worried. I finally got her to take meds. Anyone free this afternoon to sit while I attend class?

Nori: Poor girl. Why is she in your room?

Melissa: Not the point Nori. I am free Abby. Be there in 15.

A: Thanks Mel.

N: I'm sorry. I was just curious why she wasn't in her own was all.

N: Need anything from the cafeteria or the store?

A: Actually, some water and maybe Pedialyte or Gatorade? Fluids. I need to see what I can do for her.

N: How high was her temp?

A: 102.4 when I gave her some meds.

N: Keep a sheet on her rather than a blanket and maybe a cool cloth along her neck. If it goes up any more, we can take her to the health clinic. I will get some stuff and meet Mel back at your room.

A: Thanks. I wouldn't leave, but I have already missed so much class.

M: Almost there. She probably is having a setback from the flu. I have a mask and a book

TO READ.

K: HEY. WAS IN CLASS. JUST SAW THE MESSAGES. LET ME KNOW IF YOU NEED SOMETHING AND LOGAN AND I CAN COME OVER.

A: THANKS GUYS.

Abigail put her books into her bag and switched out the fuzzy blanket that was over Eve for a sheet. She wasn't sure if it would help, but it would probably make Eve more comfortable, so Abigail removed the woman's shoes and socks. She leaned down and kissed the top of Eve's head and heard a gentle knocking on the door.

Opening the door, Abby found Melissa on the other side. "Hey, Mel! Come on in. Thanks for coming by. I am sure she would kick both of our butts if she knew I requested a watcher, but I didn't want to leave her alone. I need to rush. Make yourself at home as usual. I will be back as soon as my class is done."

"No problem. I am going to take advantage of your roomie's bean bag chair and read something that isn't a textbook."

Abigail smirked and picked up her book bag and hurried out the door.

CHAPTER 8

ABIGAIL

Class was over and Abigail had never been so happy. She had a hard time focusing on what the professor was lecturing on, but she did her best to take notes so she could review everything later. It was a good thing she did show up, though, because there was a pop quiz in class that could not be made up. Luckily, it was on previous material and she was up to date on everything so she felt like she fared well.

Once the students were dismissed, she rushed back to her room. If she had been thinking, she would have checked in and seen if anyone needed anything or if she could bring back some food. But, her concern over a certain dark-haired astronomy student overrode all of her niceties.

The door to her dorm room was cracked and Abigail eased it open to find two of her friends sitting there whispering. Two heads turned towards her and each one held a finger up to their lips in the universal sign to be quiet. Like she was going to come barging in with a full drum line behind her.

"How is she doing?"

Nori frowned. “She hasn’t woken up at all. We tried once to get her to wake long enough to drink something, but she didn’t respond, so we left her asleep.”

“Yeah, she wasn’t easy for me to wake up, either. I am not sure if it’s due to the fever and recovering or if she is a deep sleeper.”

“Do you want us to stay with you?” Melissa asked from her perch in the bean bag chair.

“Nah. I should be good now. I will message Alex and see if she can camp out elsewhere tonight. That way I can sleep in her bed.”

Nori stood up and hugged Abigail, “Keep us updated and I can easily come back over since I am just on another floor.”

“Will do.”

Melissa stood up. “I guess my break time is over and it’s time for me to go grab some dinner and do homework.”

“Homework is such a taskmaster.” Abigail grinned and gave her other friend a hug. “I appreciate you all and I know Eve will, too, once she wakes up.”

Once both of her friends were out the door, she took Eve’s temperature and noticed it was about the same as before. “At least it hasn’t gone up. However, Sleeping Beauty, you need some fluids and I am the beast that is going to make you get them or else you will end up in the clinic hooked to an IV.”

Abigail found a cup with a straw and poured some water into it. Then she eased onto the bed next to Eve and shook her awake. “Wakey, wakey, Eve, I might not be a firefighter, but I am going to do my best to help you cool the heat in your body.” Eve’s response was a bunch of mumbling that Abigail couldn’t understand. “Alrighty. Maybe I should have done this before the girls left.” Once again she tried rubbing Eve’s back and urged her to sit up as Abigail tried to help support her. “Drink some water, babe. It will help.” Abigail held the straw up to Eve’s lips and was happy to see her suck and swallow some of the liquid. After a few minutes and about half a glass gone, she helped to roll Eve over onto her side and then rubbed her back and hummed until Eve settled down and was resting once more.

“I think I need a nap after that myself.” However, she got up and found a snack to eat and worked on a project outline for a class.

After a couple of hours of working on homework, Abigail was tapped out. She checked on Eve again and her temp seemed to be staying around the same degree. The woman barely moved at all. Hating to wake her up again, she decided to lay down on her roommate's bed and take a nap. However, she did set her alarm for a couple of hours so she could get up and check on Eve again.

Abigail bolted up in bed having heard a scream. What was going on? She looked around the room and realized the scream came from her bed where Eve was sleeping. She scrambled over to the other side of the room and turned on a small lamp. Eve was curled up in a ball on the mattress with a blanket over her completely.

Abigail went to pull it back and heard a small whimper come from underneath the blanket. *What the hell is going on?* Abigail thought to herself. She immediately went into comfort mode and with ease rubbed Eve's back and spoke quietly. "Shhh. You are safe, Eve. This is Abigail. You are in my room, remember? You have been running a fever and sleeping in my bed. I need to take the blanket off of your head." She went to pull the blanket back over Eve's head and body once more and heard the small noise, but this time there wasn't any resistance. Moving to kneel on the floor, Abigail got in the line of sight of Eve. "Hey there, beautiful. You okay?"

Abigail watched as Eve's eyes grew large and her pupils were so big that there were only the thinnest lines of irises around the edge. She hadn't ever seen a person act like this. She tried to think of what she should do. Eve clutched the blanket in her hands and kept an eye on every movement Abigail made like she was worried something bad was going to happen. It was then that she realized that Eve must be in the middle of a fever-induced night terror type of thing.

Abigail held up her hands to show she wasn't going to do anything then sat back and ensured that she maintained a calm and soft tone and voice level. "Hey, Eve. It's Abigail. You have been asleep for a while. Do you want a drink or to go to the bathroom?" She knew the woman's bladder was probably bursting. She was glad she had a bathroom they shared with the room next door this year so she didn't have to try and get Eve down the hall.

Eve nodded her head a little, really slow and uncertain.

"Okay. Let me help you get up and in there so you don't fall. Is that alright?"

Again Eve nodded a bit even as those dark eyes darted around the room searching her surroundings. Easing up from the floor, Abigail stood up and held out a hand to Eve. She waited until Eve took it and then supported her as she stood and they crossed over to where the bathroom was. Abigail made sure the other side of the door was locked and then left Eve to take care of her business. Once she heard the sink running, Abigail debated on whether to open the door in case she was too weak to stand on her own or give her a minute. Before she could decide the door opened and Eve stood there.

They went back to the bed and Abigail handed her two more ibuprofen and some water to wash it down with. "Hey, go ahead and drink more out of this bottle of water. It is safe. See, brand new." Abigail cracked it open and handed it over as she opened one for herself and took a nice long drink. Eve followed and then once she had done that, she huddled up close into the corner of the bed and covered herself up with the same blanket as before. She began to rock and soon she had fallen back asleep.

Abigail's heart broke at what must be playing through her friend's mind right now. She waited about five minutes to make sure that she was good and asleep and then with as careful movements as possible, eased Eve back down horizontally. Then she took her temperature again. 104.3.

"Crap. This isn't good." Grabbing her laptop, she googled ways to bring down a fever. She went digging through her stuff to try and find some rubbing alcohol she had. Her phone beeped and she grabbed it to see who messaged. It was from Nori.

NORI: HOW IS OUR GIRL DOING?

ABIGAIL: NOT GOOD. I THINK WE MIGHT NEED TO TAKE HER IN. HER FEVER IS OVER 104. JUST GAVE MORE MEDS. WAITING 30 MINS.

N: I AM COMING OVER TO YOUR ROOM.

A: Okay. Do you have any Vicks?

N: I will check.

A: Thanks.

Seven minutes later, Abigail knew because she kept staring at the clock, Nori knocked on the door. Opening it, she let her friend inside.

“I didn’t have any Vick’s, but someone else did. What are you going to do with it?”

“One of the suggestions online was to apply it to someone’s feet and then put socks on, so it will help to pull the heat out of the body. Also, I need to put some rubbing alcohol under her armpits. I am going to try anything at this point. Thanks for coming by.”

“Has she woken up,” Nori asked.

“Yes, but it was weird. She was screaming and whimpering and not acting like herself. She has only been back to sleep for about fifteen minutes. If the medicine and this doesn’t help, then we are taking her to get help. I am worried, Nori.”

“Breathe. Let’s be glad she has us looking out for her.”

“True.” Abigail gathered the stuff and sat down on the bed looking down at Eve. “I think the feet will be the easiest to do first.”

“Agreed.”

They each took a foot and began rubbing it with Vick’s. However, when they started Eve began to flail about. Abigail relinquished her post and resume sitting next to Eve and rubbing her back and humming softly. Immediately, Eve calmed down, allowing Nori to finish up both feet. Abigail shot her an ‘I don’t know’ expression and shrugged her shoulders. Once that was done, they looked to see what the easiest way to do the next part was. Eve was wearing a long sleeve shirt. Hating to do it, they decided maybe they should change her into a baggier t-shirt of Abigail’s.

“How is this one?” Abigail held up a shirt and showed it to Nori.

“That will work. She is smaller than you so it will be nice and loose.”

"Should I take off the one first or just put this one over it and then try and take the other off underneath it." Abigail bit her lip worrying that Eve would think bad about them changing her.

"If this was Mel, Katherine, or myself what would you do?" Nori asked. But before Abigail could answer Nori answered herself. "You would take our clothes off and do what was necessary. This isn't any different."

"Yes it is."

"We don't have time, Abby. You have obviously never had to redress a sleeping baby or child. She is lying on her side. Remove one arm and then the other. Then lift it up and over her head. You can leave it on the front to shield her more if you want. Then you do the opposite in putting the shirt on. Put it over her head first, then one arm and the second. Once that is down, pull it down in the front and ease out the other one."

"You make it sound so..."

"Easy is the word you are looking for."

Both of the girls laughed for a moment and then Abigail did exactly as Nori instructed. It didn't end up being very easy to do because Eve fought her even while sleeping. They got it done, though. The sleeves were baggy enough that accessing her armpits was easy. Nori and Abigail tagged teamed again while one did the actual work and the other hummed and rubbed her back.

Once that was all done both Abigail and Nori were tired. "I am not going to leave you alone after that. Mind if I stretch out on Alex's bed? Think she will mind?"

"Nah, I messaged her earlier and I have already rested on it for a short bit."

Each of the women sat lost in their own thoughts and Abigail reset her alarm from when it went off earlier. She set a time for thirty minutes to check Eve's fever. Laying her head down on the table, she wasn't aware of falling asleep until the beep beep beep of the timer went off.

Nori stirred on the bed and sat up. "Geez that wasn't a very long nap."

"Sorry." Abigail found the thermometer and took Eve's temp again. "Dang it."

"No good?"

"It hasn't gone down any and in fact has gone up by a few tenths. Do we wait to see if things take effect soon or go ahead and take her in?"

Nori got up and grabbed her phone. "We are taking her to get help. I am going to go get my purse and keys and call Katherine and Logan. By the time they make it all the way over here, we will check to make sure it hasn't reduced by a good amount. If so, then we can apologize and go from there. You get dressed and find Eve's wallet for her identification."

They each split up to do their assigned duties. When Nori returned, she had Logan with her.

"Hey, Abs. Where is our fevered girl at?" Logan went over and picked up Eve and cradled her against him. "Katherine is in the car as close to the front door as she could get. Let's go."

Locking the door behind her, Abigail followed them both down the stairs and out to the car.

Nori headed off to her car. "I will be right behind you both. Abby, go with them to be with Eve."

Both cars loaded up and took off toward the emergency room. Once they were there, Katherine pulled up to the front door and let everyone out before she went to park. Logan raced in with Eve in his arms as Abigail rushed ahead of them. Someone at the reception desk saw them and inquired. "What is going on?"

Abigail rushed out stumbling over her words. "My friend has a high fever and hasn't really been lucid since she laid down to take a nap this afternoon. I have tried everything I know of to get her fever down, but it keeps getting worse. Can you please help? I wasn't sure if we should have come or not." All the emotions that Abigail had been feeling all day and night welled up and she found herself crying by the end of it. She sucked up everything and said, "I'm sorry. I'm okay now."

"I will get a nurse and we will get her right back, if you can sit down for just a moment. Why didn't you call an ambulance?"

"I didn't think to do that," confessed Abigail.

"What's her name?"

"Eve. I'm Abby."

"Okay, Abby. I will be right back."

The lady disappeared and Abigail turned to see that Logan was sitting on one of the couches with Eve cuddled against him. How Eve hadn't woken up she wasn't sure. He was rocking her a little, so she must have started to do that whimpering again. Either that or Logan naturally did that.

Two minutes later, the doors were opened and they were calling her name. Logan and Abigail followed the staff back. Once he had laid Eve down where the nurse indicated, he left telling Abigail he would be in the waiting room with the others when they needed her. She nodded.

The nurse began taking her temperature, blood pressure, and all the normal stuff while asking questions.

"Hi, I am Kathy. Can you tell me what happened?"

"Eve was getting over the flu and returned to class today. She was tired in between so I told her she could lay down in my room and I would make sure she woke for her next class. Except when I went to wake her, she wouldn't wake up and felt hot. I took her temp and then roused her enough to get some ibuprofen in her and made her drink some water. Then as the night went on she got worse. One point she woke up but wasn't like herself. She seemed to be in some sort of trance or dreamlike state like a child. Then she went back to sleep. Before she did, I was able to get her to take more meds and fluid. Her temp went up more and my friend and I tried a few techniques to get her temp to come down, but they weren't working. When she hit 104 I got worried and brought her in."

"You did good. We will hook up an IV and get some fluid going into her system to help along with some medicine. When did you last give her the pain reliever?"

"Umm." Looking up at the clock Abigail thought back, "Maybe an hour and half or so ago."

"The doctor will be in here shortly and I will be back with some stuff. I am sure the admissions desk will stop in to get all her details."

"Okay, I will do my best."

The nurse disappeared and soon the lady that was at the front desk stepped into the room. "Hi. Your friends out front filled out part of the information, but could you look over and see if you could fill in any of the missing information?"

"Yeah, but not sure how much help I will be. I have her wallet so I will see what I can find out."

"I will be back for the paperwork in a bit." The lady turned and walked out and Abigail was left to sit and stare at all the equipment on the white walls while holding a clipboard full of papers. *It's a rather large room as far as emergency rooms go,* she thought.

A vibration in her pocket alerted her to the fact there were some people that might want to know what was going on. She pulled it out and saw in a group chat where Nori had messaged everyone. Melissa woke and asked why no one called to fill her in. She said she would be there shortly to wait with the rest. Abigail locked the phone and took a deep breath as she opened the small wallet that held all the mysteries that was Eve in it.

Abigail found an insurance card, a driver's license, and a slip of paper listing allergies in it. She had never known of anyone that carried something like that around with them. It was folded up in the same slot as the insurance card. Opening it up, she saw a couple of medicines listed, but wasn't sure what they were exactly. However, she listed them on the form and filled out a bit more of the empty slots. The section on the patient and family history was left blank. Other than being in foster care, Abigail had no idea what kind of family knowledge Eve had and she definitely had no idea about past medical incidents with Eve herself. She sat the clipboard to the side and soon the nurse returned along with a doctor. "Hello, I am Dr. Fitzgerald. Glad you brought our patient in tonight. We will get some fluids and medicine into her and hopefully get this fever knocked off. I imagine once it reduces she will wake up if not before. However, we are going to run some blood tests and do a couple of throat cultures to check for a few things."

While the doctor was talking, the nurse was inserting the needle into Eve's arm. As soon as the needle punctured her arm, Eve screamed out loud. Abigail jumped up to head to the side of the bed, but Dr. Fitzgerald waved her back. She could hear the doctor speaking gently to Eve.

"Eve, you are in the hospital. I'm a doctor. You can call me Simone. Look at me, honey. I need you to relax and calm your breathing for me. Nice even breaths now. There you go. Good girl." The doctor spoke to Nurse Kathy, but Abigail didn't understand what was said fully. The nurse left, though. Then the doctor waved Abigail over. "Hey, your friend Abigail is here with you."

A small voice croaked out, "I want my mommy."

Dr. Fitzgerald looked over at where Abigail had walked up. "Do you know how to reach her mother?"

Not wanting to stress out Eve and confused about what was going on, Abigail shook her head and whispered, "Foster system."

Nodding, the doctor returned to focus on Eve. "Eve, we need to put an IV into your arm so we can give you medicine to make you feel better. Do you think you can be brave and let Nurse Kathy do that? She will be quick and then it will be over. I can hold your hand if you would like."

"Okay."

While the doctor was speaking, the nurse had returned with a few things including a pitcher of water and some ice chips.

Doctor Fitzgerald gave some directions and then she took a hold of Eve's hand. "Now, while Nurse Kathy is working on that side, I want you to tell me about something you like. You might feel a small pinch, but it won't last long." Abigail watched as the doctor kept Eve distracted and the nurse worked quickly and efficiently. "Now, what do you enjoy?"

"Stars," Eve said.

"What do you like about the stars?"

"They are pretty and magical. You make wishes on them."

"Yes, they are pretty. What else?" The doctor nodded at something the nurse said without ever taking her focus off of Eve.

Abigail stood away from the bed, mesmerized by what she was witnessing. Not all doctors were like Dr. Fitzgerald and damned if she might not have developed a small crush. Next thing she knew, Eve's eyes were shut and the nurse was throwing stuff and her gloves into the trash can.

"Okay, I gave her something to help her sleep easier until her fever breaks. I am not sure what is causing these episodes. The mind is a strange and fascinating thing. I was able to get the cultures I needed. Someone will come back in about fifteen minutes to take some blood. Best thing to do now is monitor her. Are you staying or do you need to leave? You mentioned she was in foster care growing up? Do you know if she has anyone we need to contact?"

"No. Other than her work and the friends she met at the college this semester, there isn't anyone from what she has told me. And yes I am staying. I want to stay in the room for as long as I can. Or if not, I will go to the waiting room."

Dr. Fitzgerald smiled. "You can stay. Things might change, but for now, you are good."

"Thank you."

The doctor reached out and patted her arm. "Go on. You need some rest yourself. You look exhausted."

Abigail walked to stand by Eve's bed and stroked her head a little then she kissed the hand that wasn't plugged up to something. "I will be right back. I am going to update the rest of our friends."

The moment Abigail crossed the emergency doors, all four of the others stood up. Nori opened her arms and Abigail walked into them and let the tears she had sucked back flow. She cried silently and held on for a few minutes before pulling back. When she did, she found that the others were a little waterlogged, too.

"How is Eve doing?" Melissa asked.

"She is sleeping peacefully again."

"Did she wake up?" inquired Katherine.

"Yeah for a bit, but she wasn't her normal self. It wasn't as bad as last time. The doctor gave her some medicine to help her sleep and fight the fever. They are going to run some tests to see if there is anything else going on. You all need to go and get back to school. Everyone has class tomorrow."

Nori spoke up for the whole group. "So do you. But, I am guessing you aren't going back are you?"

"No. But, if one of you could bring me my computer if you get some free time, that would be great. I am not sure how long we will be here. Text first."

"Are you sure you don't want one of us to stay with you?" Nori asked even while she yawned.

"Yes. I am going to curl up and try to sleep myself. I just want to be here when she wakes. She doesn't need to be alone any longer."

"Here, keep my car in case you need it." Nori handed over her keys. "I can catch a ride back to campus with Melissa."

Melissa wrapped an arm around Abigail's back. "Yep. Definitely on my way. Give me a hug before we leave you."

They all exchanged hugs and the four of them left as Abigail headed back to the room.

CHAPTER 9

ABIGAIL

Abigail woke again when she felt a hand move to touch her face. She sat straight up and stared into clear, caramel-colored orbs.

"Abby?" Eve coughed and then spoke again. "What happened?"

Never had Abigail been so happy and relieved to hear her name before. "Oh my goodness, Eve, so much." Tears of relief caught Abigail off guard. "You wouldn't wake up and I was scared and you were running a fever and other stuff. I am so glad you know who I am. Maybe I should tell the nurse you are awake."

"I am here. Hello, Eve. Let me check your temperature and then we will get you all caught up. But, you are in the hospital if you hadn't already figured that out. Very good, you have come down quite a bit. This is great news. Hopefully you will get to feeling better now."

"I don't remember coming here, though." Eve's voice was a little gravelly and Abigail went and poured some water into a cup and held the straw up to Eve's mouth. After taking a drink, she continued. "Thank you. Last thing I remember is laying down for a nap."

"I will leave the two of you alone for a few minutes and have the doctor update you when she comes around."

The nurse left and Eve turned toward Abigail. "I take it naptime didn't go according to plan?"

"No. I tried to wake you up when it was time for class, but you wouldn't fully wake up and told me to leave you alone." Abigail went on to fill in Eve on everything else that transpired. "And now you are awake."

"Wow. I am glad I didn't go back to my dorm room alone. Who knows what might have happened. Thank you for taking care of me. Will you update the others?"

"Of course."

The door opened again and Dr. Fitzgerald strolled into the room. "Hello again, Eve. I don't imagine you remember meeting me before. Glad to see your fever has come down." The doctor wheeled over a chair and sat down more eye level with Eve. "The tests I ran didn't show anything other than a severe strain of flu. That is the good news. However, with your fever, I want you to stay here until tomorrow in case you worsen again. I am practicing caution and don't believe we have anything to be concerned about. I want you to be able to rest and get lots of fluids and boosters your body is going to need. Let's see how you are doing between now and tomorrow morning and we can go from there."

"Okay. Thank you. Do you think I might be able to eat?"

"Yeah. First I want you to try some soft foods and then a couple of hours after that you can eat whatever you feel up to eating. You might even be able to talk your friend into bringing you some ice cream back. My friend swears that ice cream is a requirement after a hospital visit or surgery. I think it is from being around all you college-age students." They all laughed which caused Eve to cough. "Okay. You still need sleep. I know you don't think you do, but you do."

"I need to get some studying done," Eve sighed. "This means even more classes I am missing. I am not going to get caught up at this rate."

"Email your professors. I can sign a form stating you have to be absent in person for a bit of time if you think it will help. But, try not to stress or it will delay your healing. I will come back around later to check on you again."

"Thank you doctor." Eve said as she shifted on the bed.

"It is what I am here for. See you both soon." With those words, Dr. Fitzgerald stood up and left the room and the two alone again.

"Do you think it would be too much if we put something on the TV? This way when I feel like I am about to fall back asleep I can more easily. And you need to go back to the campus. No use in both of us missing classes. I will be alright. I promise. It isn't like I am going anywhere right?"

"I don't want to leave you alone."

"Abby, I appreciate all you have done for me, but you have your own schedule to attend to as well. I will feel emotionally horrible if you get behind in your classwork."

"It is just one day, Eve."

"Yes, but you were already out with the flu yourself weren't you?"

Abigail groaned inwardly knowing that Eve was right. With a huff, she tried one more tactic. "How about we compromise? I will attend my classes, but one of the others can come keep you company when they aren't in class."

"I will agree as long as no one misses class. As you said it is only one more day and I will be resting. It isn't a vacation and there are more than enough people here to take care of me."

"Thank you." Abigail grinned triumphantly.

"Don't be smug or I will rescind. Now, I want something to drink and rest."

After Abigail filled up the cup of water, she sat down and pulled up the group text. After updating everyone on Eve's condition, they all consulted their schedules and found some time they could come over and visit. She didn't care what Eve thought or believed, Abigail didn't want Eve to feel like she had to be alone in this situation.

EVE

She knew Abigail cared and wanted to be there for her, but it was hard to lean on anyone after all of this time. There were very few people in her life that had her back when she needed them. It was her first reaction to keep to herself and push everyone else away. Eve wasn't an idiot, though. She was aware that had she been alone with a temperature that kept going up that she might not have made it or she might have done other damage to herself. But, she hated to see anyone else sacrifice something for her.

In the end, she hoped that by accepting the compromise that everyone would get what they wanted as Eve didn't have the mental or emotional fortitude to debate any longer. She was both shocked and not surprised at the same time when she woke to find the darling girl asleep with her head on the edge of the bed. Out of everyone she knew it would have either been Abigail or Nori that was there caring over her. The fool was barely over her own bout of sickness and here she was bent over, sleeping sitting up in an uncomfortable chair. She almost felt a little like the Grinch and her heart grew a bit more in size.

It felt odd to have been passed out for so long and yet still tired. Before Abigail left, Eve had her turn the TV on quietly to the game show network as she had always enjoyed watching that. Abigail got her all sorted before reluctantly leaving for her first class. It wasn't fifteen minutes after she left and Eve had passed out once more.

The next time she woke, Nori was sitting in the chair with a textbook opened and a pencil in her hand. She was so focused on what she was reading that her eyes were squinted a little and there were little wrinkles on her forehead. This is probably where wrinkles really started. Studying. Eve couldn't resist simply watching Nori write something out and then erase it and then try again. It was very entertaining. Kind of like a silent movie without any sort of background music playing except the hushed noise outside of the room. Finally Eve thought maybe she should save the paper from having a hole in the middle of it from the amount of erasing.

"Having issues with your homework?"

Nori jumped a little in startlement, but thankfully nothing fell from her lap.

"Geez, Eve! You scared the numbers right out of me."

"So, you are only full of letters now? Does that make you a little like alphabet soup?"

"Ha ha. How are you doing?"

"You know, just lying about catching up on some relaxation without a care in the world."

"You are full of jokes right now. But seriously, how are you feeling?"

"Oddly thirsty. The stuff they have flowing through this tube doesn't do a dang thing for my thirst or appetite."

"They came in and filled up your water pitcher, so hopefully that will help."

"How's composition class going?"

"Straight to business, I see." Nori closed her book and set it to the side. "I did talk to Mr. Rodriguez after class and let him know what was going on. He said to email him when you were up to it and he would work with you on getting caught up. We were assigned another essay to write because it is a composition class, duh."

"I never got to turn in the last one yet. What is this one?"

"It is a compare and contrast essay. You have to pick two things that have something in common, but different and compare and contrast them. I am still debating on what I want to write about."

"What if I wrote an essay comparing the movie and book version of a story?"

"I think the contrasting would be easy."

"There are a lot of similar things between the two, but I could also introduce how both media are a viable way of getting stories across to different demographics."

"So, maybe instead of picking one particular story, you talk about the overall concept of both." Eve nodded and Nori got all excited. "I love it. Now to come up with something for myself. Hmm. After that idea, I need to bring my game."

They both laughed and Eve reassured Nori, "You will come up with something I am sure. Thanks for talking with our professor. As soon as I have access, I will email everyone and see what I can do or what I have missed. Hopefully there hasn't been any test or anything that I can't make up or submit late. I think my main worry is my Astronomy class and my College Trig class."

"I am sure Professor Edison will help you with that and you can schedule a tutor session with her."

"Did someone mention Professor Edison?" Dr. Fitzgerald walked into the room and Eve looked up.

Nori spoke up from her station in the chair. "Yeah, that is one of the teachers at the college we attend."

Dr. Fitzgerald came in looking at a computer screen. "Yeah, Sterling University. Peyton Edison is my bestie, but don't let anyone know that." She grinned and winked as if she was sharing a big secret.

Eve watched as Nori began to bounce up and down in her chair a little. She appeared like she was going to erupt at any minute and take flight. Eve was close to guessing correctly, but the eruption was Nori's mouth, "No WAY. I love her. Well, not love, love her, but love her as a professor. She must be so amazing to hang out with in person. Squeeee. Wow. And she is friends with a doctor, that is double cool. Eve, now you have proof that you were in the hospital. You can tell her that her bestie was your doctor."

Eve looked from Nori to the doctor and then whispered, "I am beginning to think she might need an oxygen mask and something to make her calm soon."

"Shut it. I heard that," Nori shot back.

"Your love of the professor is well known and the others will back me up on this. How does Jess feel about this?" Eve teased.

"She is well aware of my slight obsession." Suddenly Nori's face went red-hot and she covered her mouth.

Eve thought it fun to see the other woman squirm a bit. She had mercy on her friend a bit. "I am sure that the good doctor here will not mention your name when retelling this story."

"I swear I will not. I can't mention Eve's name due to HIPPA so you are safe. Besides, she probably wouldn't believe me anyways." Dr. Fitzpatrick said. "Okay, Eve. So far, so good. Keep up the progress and let the nurse know what you want to eat or if you prefer outside hospital food, I will allow it." Eve watched the doctor head to the door before turning around. "One last thing though, listen to your friend. Peyton will help you out and get you caught up. She is one of the most caring professors I know." With that, the doctor left.

"I can't believe I just gushed so much. I'm an idiot." Nori groaned.

"You are not. Relax. When do you need to get back to the college?"

"Not until tomorrow." Upon Eve's squinty look, Nori continued. "My afternoon class was canceled today. I swear. If you want to see the email, I will show it to you."

"I believe you. It just seems very coincidental is all."

"Trust me. I know. Abigail said the same thing and knew you would have doubts. How about I go pick us both up something to eat and bring it back."

"Okay. Only if you let me pay." When Nori went to open her mouth in what Eve had no doubt was an argument, she added, "I insist or no dice."

"Fine, but Abigail might still have your wallet."

"No worries. I need to make a phone call anyway. May I borrow yours?" Nori handed over her phone and Eve dialed up the restaurant's number. When Maribel, who was the business half of the restaurant, answered, she explained the situation and asked for a favor. "Can I send my friend over to pick things up and then as soon as I can get over there in a few days, I will pay for it?"

"Nonsense. What do you all want?" Maribel asked.

"Hold on." Eve turned to Nori. "What do you want to eat?"

"Something easy and that doesn't cost an arm and a leg. Do you think we might be able to get some cake? I still remember the last one you brought over."

Eve heard the chuckle from the other end of the phone. "Yes, I will add a couple of slices of the cake."

"Thanks. How about whatever your soup of the day is plus a couple of sandwiches quartered so we can both enjoy each."

"It will be ready. What is your friend's name?"

"Her name is Nori."

"You get to feeling better, Eve, and call me when you are and I will get you back on the schedule."

"I appreciate it, Maribel, and tell Carlos thank you, too."

Eve hung up the phone and told Nori, "Go over to Michelangelo's. It will be ready when you get there. Sandwiches and soup should be light enough for me to eat today. I am going to rest while you are gone."

"Need anything else while I am out?"

"Not unless you are going to bring me my phone and computer so I can get some work done."

"I don't have that. Be back soon."

Nori left and Eve tried not to stress over the fact that she wasn't only missing class, but she was missing work also and the income from not working. Plus, the cost of this hospital stay. She was going to have to tighten up her budget a lot for the next several months.

When Nori returned with the food, Eve's mouth started salivating from the simple smell of bread and seasonings. "Did they say what was in there?"

"No. It was all sealed up when I arrived and in two bags. They said one had dessert and the other had lunch in it. Shall we dig in?"

"Yes. I hope they remembered to put some spoons in there for the soup."

Nori dug into the bag and pulled out a couple sets of plasticware. "Yep, we are all good to go." Next she pulled out two containers that had a club in one and a French Dip in the other one. "Looks like we have a potato soup and a tomato one maybe."

"Oh good. I like both."

"Although, I think these are definitely more than a serving size," Nori said as she set two quart-size containers on the tray."

"Can you pour me some of each. I think I am going to wait on the sandwiches, but please pick one or both of them. Eat whatever you would like. The rest can be leftovers."

"They even provided two bowls. Are you sure you just work at this place?" Nori's face showed all the emotion that her words evoked.

"Haha." Eve took the bowl of potato soup and ate a nice spoonful and moaned as the flavor hit her tongue. "This is heaven."

Nori dug into part of the club sandwich and tomato soup. Once they were full, Eve watched Nori pack everything back up and throw their trash away.

Eve reclined the bed back more. "You can have dessert whenever you are ready, but you better save me some or else I will come out of this bed and hunt you down. I warn people that no one better come between me and my dessert."

Nori laughed and held up her hands in the universal 'I mean no harm' signal. "I swear I will save you some. I think there is more than enough for each of us to have a couple of pieces." After that they chatted until Eve's eyes started closing on their own accord.

Eve slept off and on for the remainder of the day and night. However, the later it got, the longer she stayed awake at a time. Overnight, she tried to keep quiet so she didn't disturb Abigail who was sleeping in the chair. The woman didn't listen to reason when Eve attempted to convince her to go back to the college and sleep in her own bed. The next morning when Dr. Fitzgerald came by before leaving for the day, she informed Eve that she could go home provided she rested and recuperated the remainder of the week.

"No returning to class, no working, no partying. Relaxing only. Take care of yourself or you might end up back here."

"Yes, doctor."

Abigail stood up and stretched, "I will make sure she behaves as I have no intention of living through that scary experience again."

"Very well. Good luck with all your classes and I hope to not see you again in the ER." Dr. Fitzgerald left and Eve almost whooped for joy.

"Who would have thought, I would ever be so elated to get back to my dorm room, cranky roommate and all?" Eve asked. "I wonder when I'll be able to spring this place?"

"Soon hopefully. That way I can take you back and get you settled in before class."

"At least you let me have my phone back last night." Eve held up the electronic device. "Not that I really need it that much, but it is still nice to have nearby.

Two hours later, Eve was climbing the stairs to her dorm room. When Abigail tried to stay back, she put her foot down. "I am going to take a shower, put on some clean pajamas, and curl up in my bed to study until I fall asleep. You need to go shower and get ready for sign language class before you are late for it. Someone is going to have to catch me up on everything I have missed in that class since it isn't in a book."

"Fine, but I will be back later."

Eve didn't reply, simply hugged Abigail at the door and told her thank you for everything. Then she closed the door and went to stretch out on her own bed. It wasn't much, but it was her stuff and it made her feel better just being surrounded by it.

She had to rest before she could gather up enough strength to scoot down to the showers. However, once she had washed her hair and her body, she felt tons better. There was something about a fresh shower to wake up your skin and make you feel alive.

Next, she gathered up her computer and started on makeup work. Two hours later, her eyes were droopy, she had a headache, and the words on the screen were crossing. Eve gave up and shut down her computer. She had just curled up on her side when a knock at the door made her glare.

"Who is it?"

"It's Abby."

"Come on in, the door should be unlocked."

Abigail opened the door and strolled inside. "Why is your door unlocked?"

"Because I didn't want to have to get up to let anyone in."

"Fair. I'm beat."

"Why didn't you go back to your room?"

"I wanted to check on you." Abigail let her bag thunk on the floor and then collapsed into the desk chair. "Would it be alright if I just took a nap right here?"

"I was about to take one myself. I don't think that chair is comfortable."

Abigail shrugged, "No worse than at the hospital. Heck, toss me a pillow and I will pass out on the floor."

Eve hated for Abigail to have to sleep on the floor. She really hoped her friend didn't read anything into the suggestion she was about to make. "How about you grab a blanket and curl up on the bed with me. It might not be a huge improvement over the floor, but I think it will be a little bit. I would kick you out, but I have learned. You won't go."

"Nope. You are stuck with me. Plus, I don't know if I am capable of leaving right now before I have a power nap." Abigail stood and then looked over at Eve. "Are you sure about this?"

"Just lay down before I think too much or change my mind. If my roommate wasn't such a butthead, you could have crashed over there." Eve waited and after a few moments, Abigail laid down next to her and it was a very snug fit.

Eve turned to face the wall in an attempt to give them more room. She called back over her shoulder, "You okay? Comfy?"

"It isn't a king size bed at a five star hotel, but it isn't bad," yawned Abigail.

Eve hoped she was able to go to sleep because ever since her mouth made the offer to have Abigail share the bed, her heart and nerves were wired. Would her friend think something extra was meant behind it? Did Eve actually intend for something more to be implied? After only a couple of minutes she heard a light, steady breathing of Abigail sleeping. Guess her bedmate really was exhausted. After all, the woman had been by Eve's side for a couple of days looking over her without much sleep. Taking solace in that, Eve released the anxiety and wrapped herself up in the comfort of knowing she was actually cared for by her new group of friends. Within moments she felt herself succumbing to the land of dreams.

ABIGAIL

Waking up next to Eve was one of the highlights of Abigail's week. She was thankful she woke up first and magically before her alarm so she could slip off the bed and not disturb Eve. She didn't want it to seem she was doing a runner of sorts, but she needed to get to Chem class and she didn't want to wake Eve. She took a piece of paper from her notebook and wrote out a quick note.

> Eve,
>
> I didn't want to wake you as you were sleeping peacefully. I had to go to class. I will check on you afterwards. Rest well.

Abby

She folded the note so it was laying where Eve would see it when she woke up. Then Abigail eased her bag off of the floor and crept outside of the room and closed the door without making much noise. Once in the hallway, she rushed outside and all the way back across campus slipping into a seat on the back row three minutes after the lecture already began. Hopefully Professor Upstein would forgive her.

After class was over, she went over to the cafeteria to get a late lunch. Abigail realized she hadn't had anything to eat since the night before when Eve shared part of the sandwiches and dessert with her. She was really hungry. She bought a chef's salad and an order of curly fries. She sat down at a small table along one of the walls with windows and dug into her fries. They tasted like heaven at that moment. Not remembering who she copied this technique from, Abigail dumped several packets of pepper onto the ketchup and then dipped a fry into it. Once all the hot salty and peppery fries were demolished, she turned towards the less enthusiastic salad. However, even that tasted good. While she was eating, she pulled up her phone and texted Eve.

ABIGAIL: HEY SLEEPYHEAD. HAVE YOU WOKEN UP YET?

EVE: YEAH. GOT YOUR NOTE. HOW WAS CHEM?

A: GOOD. WAS A FEW MINUTES LATE FOR CLASS.

E: YOU REBEL. I HAVE REALIZED YOU LIKE TO RISK GETTING THERE ON TIME.

A: OH?

E: AT LEAST WITH SOME OF THEM.

A: I THINK YOU JUST HAVEN'T SEEN ME AT MY BEST THIS SEMESTER.

E: OH, SO IT IS A NEW SEMESTER THING HUH? YOU

saying there is a reason for your tardiness?

A: Of course.

E: What is that reason?

A: A new student and the flu.

E: Haha. You can't blame me for you being tardy to class. I manage to get to our shared class on time, so I call BS on that excuse.

A: Call it all you want. I hold to my statement.

E: Nori said you are full of it too.

A: Is she there?

E: Yep. She said this argument should be held in the group forum.

Next thing Abigail knew she was getting a separate text message.

Nori: Okay gang, we need to have a vote on something. Do we think that it is Eve's fault that our dear Abby is late to her classes frequently this term?

Melissa: I think maybe like 60/40, no.

Katherine: I was going to say indirectly maybe, but nothing that Eve could do about it.

Logan: As the lone male wolf in this pack, I have to side with Abby on this one as I was rubbish when I first started dating Kat.

ABIGAIL: I AM GLAD EVE ISN'T IN THIS CHAT AT THIS MOMENT TO LISTEN TO YOU ALL.

EVE: BUT I AM. NORI ADDED ME.

A: OH HELL.

M: LOOK WHO IS IN TROUBLE NOW. LOL.

E: SHE SAID I AM OFFICIALLY A PART OF THE GROUP AND CHAOS AND THERE IS NO BACKING OUT NOW. SHOULD I BE WORRIED?

K: NAH

M: VERY

L: RUN FOR YOUR LIFE.

A: YOU ARE GOOD. SPEAKING OF WHICH, HOW LONG IS NORI GOING TO STAY?

N: I AM HERE ALL NIGHT WOMAN. YOU CAN HAVE EVE LATER. GO STUDY AND GET SOME SLEEP.

A: GEEZ. BOSSY MUCH.

N: YOU KNOW IT. SERIOUSLY, EVE AND I ARE WORKING ON OUR ENGLISH ASSIGNMENTS. SHE IS IN GOOD HANDS .

M: AWW. LOOK AT THAT, EVE, THEY ARE FIGHTING OVER YOU.

E: NAH. WE ARE TRYING TO STRONGARM ABBY INTO GETTING SOME SLEEP BEFORE SHE FACEPLANTS IN THE MIDDLE OF THE COURTYARD.

K: SO SWEET. YOU BETTER LISTEN TO THEM, ABBS.

A: GEEZ. I AM ALMOST DONE WITH MY SALAD AND THEN I WILL HEAD TO THE DORMS. NORI, SWING BY ON YOUR WAY BACK TO YOUR ROOM.

N: WILL DO.

They ended the conversation and Abigail finished her salad before swinging back and grabbing a sandwich to go for later that evening along with a cold Coke. She didn't want to go to sleep too early, so hopefully the caffeine would help keep the worst of the sleepies away.

Chapter 10

EVE

Eve knocked on the door of Professor Edison's office. A voice called out from the other side beckoning her to come in. As she opened the door, she found Peyton pouring water into a plant and talking to it.

Peyton turned her head around, "Hello. You must be Eve, come on in and have a seat at the table. I will be right there."

Following instructions, Eve sat down in one of the chairs at the small table that was situated in front of the chalkboard. A moment later, her professor plopped down next to her.

"Alright, now that Lily and Sherlock are taken care of, I am free to assist you."

"Lily and Sherlock?"

"My two plants. Yes, the rumors that I name and talk to my plants are true."

"I haven't heard any rumors about you other than students love you," Eve confessed. Although, she took a mental note to ask Nori about these rumors.

"That is sweet. I love my students, too. First off, how are you feeling?"

Eve smiled while pulling out her notebook. "Much better, thank you. I hated to miss all my classes so early in my first semester here."

"I am sure your professors understood. I hope they are being reasonable with you. Now, have you had a chance to look at any of the assignments or notes from the sections we covered while you were out?"

"Yeah. I reviewed everything and most of it I think I understand, but I have a few questions."

"Okay. Let's start with the first one you have."

The two of them worked for the next forty-five minutes on the various problems and questions that Eve had on the assignments. By the time they got to the end of the session, Eve's head was filled with so much information she thought it was going to start leaking out. Peyton must have noticed because she called a halt to the tutoring session.

"You need a mental break, Eve. We can schedule another session if you think you need it. But, let that permeate and soak into your brain first and then look at the problems again."

"Thank you, Professor."

"Anytime."

Peyton went to stand up and Eve stopped her. "Can I ask you a personal question?" She couldn't believe she was about to ask what she wanted to, but she wasn't sure who else to talk to. Eve watched a different sort of expression and guard come up around the woman.

"Sure. But, depending on the question, I might not answer."

"I understand. I would ask someone else if I knew who to talk to. On the first day of class you said that students could come to you about other things than school if they needed to talk."

"Yes. And I meant it."

Heat flooded Eve's body and she could feel her skin getting clammy along the back of her neck and forehead. She blurted out, "How did you know you were into women?" Eve looked down and avoided eye contact with Peyton.

"Oh. Well, I guess for me that happened when I was a young teenager. Some people know earlier and some later. I think it was when I noticed I was always checking out the other girls in my classes in high school and not the guys. Even then I really wasn't sure because I thought maybe I was trying to be like the girls or something. I tried to be interested in a couple of guys, but it didn't work so I knew the truth. Are you questioning your own sexuality?"

"Maybe. Yes."

"You know no matter what you feel, it is okay. Have you dated different types of people?"

"No. I haven't really ever dated." Eve felt like a loser admitting that.

"Nothing to be ashamed of. Lots of people don't date until they get to college or afterwards. Plus, if you find you aren't attracted to people at all, then that isn't something to feel bad about either."

"I am definitely not attracted to animals."

Peyton laughed, "That isn't what I meant. You have a sense of humor like mine. I like that."

"Oh?"

"Very literal and precise. It is why you absorbed what I told you today so quickly. But, that is beside the point. Why are you questioning yourself now?"

"There is a girl that has expressed interest in me. She said she is okay if we stay friends, but let me know that she would like more."

"And?"

Eve rubbed the back of her neck, "And... over the past couple of weeks, I have been thinking about it, about her. I think I might be developing feelings for her, but I am not sure."

"Do you think it would be helpful to talk to other people your own age about this?"

Eve immediately jumped up, "No! I couldn't do that. It is bad enough with my new friends asking and trying to be helpful. It is why I came to you. I thought you would be able to maybe give me some life advice. Forget I asked."

"Eve."

"I better leave. Thanks for the help."

"Eve, please sit down. I didn't say I wouldn't help or listen. I simply asked a question to see if it would help. Look, I will let you in on a little secret. Come on and stay."

Dropping her bag back to the floor, Eve slumped back down into the chair.

"Thank you. Now, I am sure if you know I am a lesbian then you probably also know I have a partner." Eve nodded, but kept silent. "When Nikola and I first started dating, it was chaos and a huge mess. I have no idea why she kept wanting to go out with me. First, I thought she wanted my brother, then I tripped and fell into things on our first date. I was constantly putting my foot in my mouth, and don't get me started with trying to accept flirting from her."

"Really?"

"Yes. I tell you that so maybe it will help you understand that dating is dating no matter the gender or sexual orientation of the people involved. You will fumble, make a mess of things, fight, misunderstand things, but if you are with the right person, none of that will matter. You will work things out. Let me ask you a question. You can answer me or simply think on it and answer yourself. What about this girl being interested in you worries you; and more importantly what about you possibly being attracted to her makes you scared?"

Eve thought about everything and realized that maybe Peyton had it right. Maybe it wasn't that she didn't know if she was attracted to Abigail, but rather she was scared that she was. "Thank you, Professor. I appreciate you taking the time to listen. May I come back if I need to?"

"Of course. I think you are going to be just fine though, Eve. You strike me as someone who is used to facing issues and not running from them. Good luck and I will see you in our next class."

Standing up, Eve grabbed her backpack and walked out of Professor Edison's office to go do some thinking while she worked at the library that evening.

Unfortunately, she was slammed at the library that night and to make matters worse her roommate, Bentley, was there along with her band of misfits. Eve was making her rounds filing books and discovered them in one of the study areas. She was surprised her roommate actually ever studied. As far as she knew, it was only partying Bentley was into at college.

When Eve walked by, Bentley called her over. “Hey, you. I need assistance.”

Groaning inwardly, Eve retraced a few of her steps and stopped in front of the group. “How can I help you all?”

Snickering, Bentley leaned over and squinted at Eve, “You could tell me where I could look up ‘How to Get Rid of an Unwanted Dyke Roommate.’” Leaning back, Bentley laughed and her friends joined in with her.

It took everything in Eve to not attack the sorry excuse of a human being. However, she needed her job at the library so she bit her tongue and didn’t say anything nasty. She did reply with a smile on her face. “You are welcome to submit for a room change. In the meantime, I will work on locating that information for you.” Eve turned and continued to file the books. When she returned to the desk, she looked up a few topics and printed out two short articles. Something inside of her mind told her to leave it alone, but she didn’t listen to it. Instead, she returned to where Bentley was still sitting and placed the articles in front of her. “Here you go, the information you need.” Eve didn’t stick around for the aftermath, but she still heard the loud gasp and growl and knew that Bentley had read the titles. They, of course, were “*How to Tell if You are Homophobic?*” and “*Living Your Best Authentic Lesbian life.*”

She had no reason for doing what she did, but after everything Eve had been through since the beginning of the semester, she was at her breaking point. If Bentley requested that one of them had to change rooms, she wouldn’t be sad at all. Heck, at this point, she would rather have a room just big enough for a cot to sleep on than to continue to endure Queen Snooty McPartyton. Thankfully, the remainder of the night there were no more sightings or encounters.

The drive to the dorm didn’t take but a few minutes and some nights she wondered if it was worth driving to the library, but as exhausted as Eve was at the end of that night, she was ecstatic to have a few less feet to walk. However, the moment she stepped onto her floor and saw the mess in the hallway, she knew it wasn’t even close to being done. There in the hallway tossed everywhere were her clothes, her books, and her snacks. It didn’t look like Bentley threw everything out into the hall. Eve marched down the hall and unlocked the door. When she turned the knob, the door wouldn't budge open. She banged on the door and heard snickering coming from behind it. "Bentley, open this door! You are being childish right now."

"No. You and your stuff can find somewhere else to stay tonight. Come back for the rest later. You are finished!" yelled Bentley

Not wanting to cause an even bigger scene than they already had, Eve slid down the wall and pulled out her phone. She hated to impose any more than she already had on her friends, but she didn't have anyone else. It was either message them or carry everything to her car and sleep in there for the night. She pulled up the group text message box and sent out a text to everyone.

EVE: ANYONE AWAKE? I NEED A HUGE FAVOR.

Instantly her phone began chiming back.

ABIGAIL: WHAT DO YOU NEED?

NORI: OF COURSE.

MELISSA: JUST STUDYING HERE.

KATHERINE: LOGAN AND I ARE STILL AWAKE. WHAT HAPPENED?

E: HAD A FIGHT WITH THE ROOMMATE AT THE LIBRARY. CAME TO ROOM AND SHE HAS TOSSED PART OF MY STUFF INTO THE HALL AND WON'T LET ME IN. THE DOOR IS BARRED. ANYONE HAVE A PLACE I CAN STAY?

N: YES. I CAN ROLL OUT A SLEEPING BAG FOR YOU.

A: THAT WITCH. I SWEAR I AM GOING TO COME KICK HER ASS.

K: LOGAN SAID OUR COUCH IS YOURS AS LONG AS YOU NEED IT.

N: ABBY. NO FIGHTING OR THIS WILL ESCALATE.

M: I WAS GOING TO SAY YOU CAN SLEEP HERE, BUT THEY ARE WEIRD ABOUT WHO SLEEPS IN THE SORORITY HOUSE.

K: OH AND SHE BETTER BE GLAD SHE ISN'T A GUY OR LOGAN WOULD HAVE A FEW THINGS TO SAY OR DO.

A: I AM ON MY WAY TO HELP.

E: YOU GUYS ARE GOING TO MAKE ME CRY.

N: I WILL COME WITH ABBY.

E: KAT, ARE YOU SURE YOU DON'T MIND? YOUR COUCH SOUNDS PERFECT TO ME.

K: WE WILL GET SOME EXTRA BEDDING FOR IT. NEED US TO COME HELP YOU GATHER YOUR STUFF?

E: NAH. I GOT IT.

N: EVE, TAKE PICTURES OF HOW EVERYTHING IS. WE NEED TO GET YOU A NEW ROOMMATE OR HELP YOU FIND SOMETHING BETTER. ABBY IS FURIOUS. WE ARE BRINGING SOME BAGS.

N: SEE YOU IN A FEW MINUTES

E: THANK YOU EVERYONE.

Eve stood up and took pictures of the mess and the hallway before she started folding things up. A few of the girls stepped into the hall as she was texting and asked if she needed help. They came back out and began to help her with stuff. It was nice to know that all the people weren't as horrible as her roommate was.

They were almost done with most of the things by the time Abigail and Nori arrived. The two friends were carrying a tote, an overnight bag, and a couple of bags. Abigail dropped down and hugged Eve tight before glaring at the door. She spoke quietly so as only Eve could hear. "Nori talked me off the ledge so I didn't come in guns blazing, but seriously that girl needs to get bent."

Nori started putting clothes into a tote. "Eve, pick out what you want to wear for the next couple of days. We will put those items and a few other things into this overnight bag. This way you only have to carry up one extra bag tonight. You will have to tell us the whole story of what happened once we leave."

"I don't want to keep you all up any longer."

"Nonsense. We are all going over to Kat and Logan's. Mel is on her way there now."

Eve was about to object when Abigail reached out and touched her arm and shook her head. Sighing, Eve gave in, "I can't stop you all and I am grateful for all the help. This is partly my fault anyways."

They had everything packed up in a few minutes and were heading back down the stairs to load up Eve's car. Abigail reluctantly agreed to ride over with Nori so Eve could have some space to relax and compose herself before they got over to Kat's apartment.

Once she pulled up, Eve grabbed her backpack and Abigail was beside her taking the overnight bag to carry to the apartment. As they approached, the apartment door was thrown open and all three of the girls were rushed inside.

"Come in, Eve, we made some hot chocolate and have some cookies to go with it. If you need something more, I can make you a sandwich," Katherine offered.

"This is perfect. Thank you."

Everyone grabbed some cookies and a mug of cocoa before settling down around the living room. "So, what happened?" Abby asked as soon as everyone was seated.

Eve explained the details of the night leaving nothing out. When she got to the part about handing over the magazine articles, everyone laughed. She finished her story with "and now we are sitting here. I know it has only been a few weeks into the semester, but I swear it has been an intense few weeks between dealing with her, getting sick, and trying to keep up with my class schedule." What Eve didn't say was her growing and confusing feelings about Abigail.

"I still think I should be allowed to go kick her butt," Abigail exclaimed.

"That isn't going to help anything. What we need to do is figure out a solution and work from there. I agree that you can't continue to stay in your dorm room not knowing what is going to set off your roommate. Plus, if she does have some ill views toward you or what you support, then she isn't going to simply change her mind overnight no matter what you say or do."

"She can't ignore this, Nori," protested Mel.

"Oh, neither she nor we are going to. We just need to be strategic on what we do so it doesn't cause any more backlash than it already has," reassured Nori.

Eve finished her hot chocolate and she was worn out. All she wanted to do was curl up on the couch and go to sleep and forget about things for a few hours. But, she didn't want to be mean to the people who once again stopped everything they were doing to help her out tonight. Apparently, others noticed her fatigue, though.

Abigail spoke up, "Hey, guys, I think now that Eve has told us the story of what happened, we take tonight to think about things and can regroup in the morning. I imagine she is ready for some peace after school and work today."

Eve glanced over at Abigail and mouthed the words 'thank you' to her. With a simple smile and slight nod, Eve knew that Abigail received her meaning. "I appreciate again all of you jumping in tonight. Abigail is right about one thing, I might pass out on you all soon with as tired as I am. I don't think I am even going to be able to get any studying done. I might try to wake up early instead."

Melissa hopped up from the recliner where she was perched and walked over to give Eve and then everyone a hug. "Have a good night, everyone. I will see you in the morning." With that, she disappeared out the door.

Katherine brought over four pillows, a couple of sheets, and a couple of blankets. “Here you go, make yourself at home. If you get hungry, please help yourself to whatever is in the refrigerator or cabinets. You already know where the bathroom is. We are going to say good night.”

Eve stared at the stack of linen and wondered why Katherine would think she would need so much. The answer was quick in coming.

“We decided that you might feel more comfortable tonight with more people around you in a new place, so we are going to have a sleepover of sorts.” Nori grabbed one of the pillows and a blanket and leaned back in the recliner.

“Ummm. You all didn’t need to do that. I will be fine and I am not alone. Kat and Logan are in their bedroom,” Eve reasoned.

“Don’t argue with Nori. Mother hen and all. I swear she has gotten worse since coming back from Christmas and dating Jess.” Abigail laughed.

“I can hear you, Abigail. I am not asleep that quickly. Now hush up,” Nori chastised from her chair.

“Yes, ma’am.” Abigail turned back to Eve, “Let’s get your sheets on the couch and then you can go change clothes and shower if you want.”

“A shower would be nice. But, I don’t want to—”

“The next words out of your mouth better not be ‘impose’ or some variation on the word. Trust me in that if you can handle staying awake longer tonight and want a shower, it is best to take it now. Come the morning, you will be fighting everyone.”

“Okay.” Eve picked up her overnight bag and disappeared into the bathroom.

ABIGAIL

The minute Eve disappeared into the bathroom, Abigail let out a deep breath. Apparently, Nori was waiting for such a moment, too, as she spoke up quietly from the chair.

"You know we are going to have to go with her to get the rest of her stuff at some point tomorrow. I think it will be easier and better if Eve moves instead of trying to force her roommate into giving up and relocating. Are there any empty rooms in our building?"

"I don't know, Nori, but we can inquire. Too bad, we didn't go ahead and get an apartment this semester like we talked about instead of waiting until the Fall."

"True. Then she could have easily roomed with us. We will work it out. Make sure she gets to bed soon. You do the same. I am going to try and get some beauty sleep. Need to keep up my appearance for Jess."

Laughing, Abigail called out, "Night, Nori." She stood up and spread one of the blankets out over the couch and then took one of the pillows and blankets and set them beside the other recliner. Then Abigail cleaned up the kitchen and put the mugs into the dishwasher. By the time all of that was accomplished, the door to the bathroom was being opened and Eve strolled out in a pair of pink pajamas with white bunnies on them and a towel wrapped up on top of her head. She looked so cute and adorable.

"Feel better, Eve?" Abigail asked.

"Much. It almost gave me some additional energy. I would be tempted to do a little studying, but I know how I feel is false and as soon as I stop moving, I would be falling asleep over my textbook."

"I know that feeling quite well."

"Do you need the shower next? I tried to leave some hot water if you did."

"I already took my shower earlier this evening, but thanks for the kind gesture."

"Of course." Eve placed her bag at the end of the couch and then sat down in the middle of the cushions and began brushing out her hair. When she started to braid it, Abigail rushed to interrupt.

"Would you like for me to do that for you? I imagine it is easier for someone else to braid your hair rather than doing it yourself."

"Sure if you would like to."

"Come sit on the floor in front of me and it will be faster." Abigail knew she partly asked just so she had a reason to touch Eve again, even if it was just her hair. There was something intimate about the act of brushing and braiding Eve's hair. The entire time they were quiet and didn't speak much. There was a slight tension in the air. Not bad, but an awareness.

When Abigail was done, Eve stood up and then bent and gave her a hug. "Thanks, Abby. I keep saying that, but I mean it. Let's get some rest. Morning will be here early."

"Good night, Eve." Abigail picked up the pillow and blanket from the floor as Eve turned off all the lights except a small lamp that left the room with a slight glow to it. She hoped that they both were able to sleep well that night.

The next morning, Abigail woke to the smell of bacon and coffee. When she concentrated, she heard Eve and Logan laughing behind her. She smiled and stayed as she was. Guess maybe they weren't going to the cafeteria for breakfast that morning. A knock on the door interrupted her musings. "I'll get it." She hopped up and almost tripped over the blanket. Before she righted herself, Nori was helping to stabilize her as Katherine called out, "It's open, Melissa."

The door opened and Melissa walked in carrying a box of doughnuts. "Hey, guys. I stopped for pastries. I figured we all could use some. Oh, the smell of caffeine. I need a big mug of that." She crossed the small room and set the box down before taking the cup that had been poured.

"The food will be ready here in a few minutes. Eve got started before Kat and I were even awake," Logan said as he pulled out six plates from the cabinet.

"I studied for a few and then when my stomach started growling, I thought I would treat you all to some omelets and breakfast potatoes." Eve flipped the egg mixture in the pan and then continued. "Logan came out and demanded bacon, so I told him he could make that. It wasn't ever my thing really."

"So, you cook, huh?" Abigail asked.

"Not a lot, but I can make a few things. While these aren't my groceries, I wanted to show my appreciation."

"No appreciation needed, but I will enjoy the fruits of your labor." Logan leaned in and hugged Eve. "Now, who is ready for a nice breakfast before we all split up and tackle classes."

There were a few hollow hoorays, but the action of everyone diving into the food left no doubt that the less than cheery celebration was due to the idea of lectures in front of them. In the end, there weren't any scraps left to toss in the trash and cleanup took only a few minutes with everyone pitching in to clean up and wash dishes.

"Don't forget you need to allow a little extra time to get to class today since we aren't in the cafeteria. No one can say they are late because of me," reminded Katherine as she tossed the washcloth over the sink. "I am going to get dressed as I have a bit longer than the rest of you. Eve, if you want to come back here tonight, you are welcome to stay as long as you need."

"Especially if you keep cooking like that," joked Logan.

"Thanks. I will let you know. But, now I need to hurry. Abigail, do you need a ride since we have the same class?"

Abigail jumped up out of her seat. "Yes, please." Looking down at herself, she figured she might need to change clothes. "Can you give me five minutes? I need something other than this to go to school in."

"Sure."

"Kat?"

"Go ahead and dig in my closet. I thought maybe you left your bag in the car."

"No, I didn't think of it in my hurry last night."

Nori laughed and Abigail threw a pillow at her.

"Four minutes and thirty-four seconds, Abby, and then I am leaving." Eve lifted up her phone where she had started a timer and Abigail saw the timer ticking down.

"Geez, woman." Abigail rushed into Katherine's room and went through her closet and found a big purple-and-black-striped shirt. Then she found a black belt to wear on top of that. Her black leggings she had on would work for the day. She rushed back into the living room where Eve was standing and wearing her backpack with her overnight bag in her hand.

"Look at that, with seventeen seconds to spare."

Abigail caught the wink that Eve sent to Nori and groaned. "You are a minx when you want to be, woman."

Nori picked up her own bag and joined them. "Someone needs to keep you on your toes. Later, everyone."

The three of them left to good-byes being called out behind them as they closed the door. It wasn't until they got to the car that it dawned on Abigail. She didn't have her book bag. "Curses."

"What now?" Eve asked.

"It's a good thing our class is a sign language one. I didn't even grab stuff I will need for class."

Nori's laughter was loud and could still be heard even after she shut the car door. Eve looked at her with a bit more sympathy in her eyes.

"Come on, we can swing by on the way if traffic is nice to us. If not, I will share."

"Thanks." Abigail shut the door and even though she knew why she forgot everything, she was still frustrated with herself. The time to the dorm didn't take very long and soon Eve was pulling up in front of the building. Abigail ran into the building and up the stairs. She didn't think Eve would leave her there, but she didn't want to find out. Alex was coming out of their room so Abigail didn't even have to take the time to unlock the door.

"You look like you are in a hurry, Abby."

"Yeah. I forgot my bag last night when I left. I wasn't thinking."

"Everything okay? Did your girl have a relapse?"

"Nah. She is healthy, but her roommate is being a witch and tossed her stuff out. We need to find her a new place to stay." Abigail crammed her textbooks and computer into her bag before looping it over her neck.

"Well, if she needs to crash here, you know I am cool with that."

"Thanks. It might come to that for a few nights. Got to go as I am almost late for class. See you later?"

"Yeah. Let me know if we need to rough someone up."

"I swear you could be a man sometimes." Abigail ran back down the hall to the sound of chuckling. She made it back down and into the car in one piece. "Okay, I'm good. Let's go."

"You sure? You sound a little winded."

"I didn't want you to flee in the getaway car without me."

In response, all Eve did was put the car into drive and laugh. Seemed everyone was finding Abigail humorous today.

CHAPTER 11

EVE

Once class was over, Eve and Abigail made their way over to the library where they were going to study for their afternoon session. Eve hoped that maybe if she gave Bentley some time to cool off she would be more reasonable. If not, Eve wasn't sure what she was going to do. She couldn't live off of the goodwill of her friends for the remainder of the semester. Besides she was paying to live there and she had a right to her half of the room.

"Earth to Eve."

"Huh?" Eve jerked her head up to where Abigail was talking to her.

"You didn't hear anything I said, did you?"

"Umm, no."

"What's going on in that mind of yours? I know you aren't studying because you have literally not moved for five minutes."

"It's nothing."

"It's something, Eve. Is it the room situation?"

Eve's shoulders dropped and she looked back down at her book. "Yeah."

"I think we need to—"

"Eve, I know you aren't working right now, but could you come with me for a minute?" One of the head librarians, Patricia, came up and interrupted what Abigail was about to say.

Sending a small smile over at Abigail she nodded. "I will be right back." Eve followed behind Patricia knowing that what was about to happen had to do with the altercation from the previous night. She didn't know whether to start off by apologizing or wait and see what was said.

Once they were in the office, Patricia waved at the empty chairs. "Please have a seat, Eve."

Eve sat down and clasped her hands together on her lap.

"Look, I hate to pull you out of your study session, but I thought it best to go ahead and deal with this now. We have had a complaint about you. Several in fact, but they are all around one incident."

"I'm so deeply sorry."

"So, you already know what was said?"

"No, but considering there is only one instance since I have worked here that I can think of, then I am guessing it was about last night."

"It is. I want to hear your side of the story."

"Okay, I am not sure what all to say since I don't know what the complaint was." Eve bit her bottom lip out of both a nervous gesture and fear.

Patricia smiled at her, "Just start at the beginning, Eve."

That one simple smile gave her the courage to speak, "It actually begins back at the beginning of the semester. Bentley is my roommate and she is not a fan of me at all. I am here to study and focus and she isn't. We have had several disagreements over the weeks. She has verbally harassed me about my friends and implied certain things about myself. Last night, when Bentley and her friends were here studying, I was walking by to shelve books and she called me over. I politely went to see what I could assist her with." Eve relayed the rest of the story leaving out nothing including her frustrated and misbehaved actions of printing off the articles.

"Is that everything?"

"Everything that happened at the library, yes."

"Go on, might as well tell me the rest, Eve."

"Okay, there isn't much more. When I got back to the residence hall, some of my stuff had been tossed outside into the hall and she wouldn't let me inside. I messaged a few friends and they came and helped me. I stayed at someone's apartment last night."

"Have you been back today?"

"No, ma'am. I was trying to give her some time to cool down. Usually after one of her outbursts, she is back to being tolerable for a few days."

"Very well. I can't ignore what you did. It wasn't professional of an employee at this library, student or otherwise." Eve's heart dropped into her stomach. "However, knowing this lady is a roommate who has been making you miserable, and wasn't a random person that mouthed off, makes me inclined to allow you to stay on."

"Thank you, ma'am."

"But, if you do something like that again with or without provocation, I will have to suspend or fire you."

"Understood."

"If I may give you a piece of advice." When Eve nodded, Patricia continued. "Go talk to your Resident Advisor and tell her what is going on. Maybe they can give you a different room. I suggest you go now and take your friend with you out there. Tell whomever it is that if they need to speak to me about last night to reach out."

"Will do." Eve stood up and left the office so grateful that she still had a job. She knew she could have gone back to working additional hours at the restaurant, but here she was closer and could study when she didn't have something immediate to do to assist someone.

When Eve arrived back at their study area, she was surprised to find Nori was there also. "What are you doing here, Nori?"

"I had a few minutes after class let out and Abby messaged that you were taken away in handcuffs."

"I did not. Don't exaggerate. All I said was that one of the ladies came and got Eve and I thought she might be in trouble." Abigail looked up at Eve. "Were you? In trouble that is."

Eve claimed her chair and nodded. "Yeah. You know who struck again. She filed a complaint against me and I am assuming had the others with her do the same."

"So, what happened?"

"Patricia asked to hear my side of everything and I was honest and told her everything. Basically, she said it was unprofessional, she understood, don't do it again, and for us to go talk to my RA right now."

Nori hopped right up. "Let's go do that now before your next class. That way you have backup and additional hands if we need to move more of your stuff out of your room."

"I am with Nori on this. What do you think, Eve?" Abigail began gathering up everything.

"I had already decided to go ahead and talk to her now. You sure you both want to go with me?"

"Yes," they answered at the same time.

"Then, let's go do this." Eve packed up her backpack and the three of them headed off before Eve changed her mind and lost her nerve.

When they arrived back at the dorm, Eve knocked on her advisor's door. Eve hadn't thought about what they would do if she wasn't there. But, Eve should have because why would someone be in one's room in the middle of the afternoon when the majority of classes were in session. However, the door opened and Eve braced herself for the upcoming conversation.

Before she could say anything the door opened wider and Alyssa beckoned them inside, "Come on in. I had a feeling I would be seeing you today. Have a seat."

"You were expecting me?"

Alyssa sat in one of the chairs around the table and crossed one leg over the other. "Yeah. More than one person has texted, emailed, or came by to tell me what happened last night. Plus, Bentley has been by telling stories and demanding that the two of you need to be separated. But, then again, she has been reciting the same thing since the beginning of the semester. She wasn't very happy about having to stay in this hall for this semester, so I didn't really pay it much attention. I probably shouldn't be telling you all of that. Go ahead and tell me what you would like to say."

Finding the strength and courage to speak her mind, Eve said in a very even and factual tone, "I think after last night and based on the last several weeks, it would be best if we were reassigned to other rooms. Honestly, I will be more than happy to move either in with someone else, or in a closet with electrical outlets at this point. If I need to find a place off campus, I will make that work somehow if I must, although I know that I have already paid for the term. I have tried to make compromises with her so we can both stay in the same room, but she neither likes nor respects me. I won't go into everything because that will sound like it is all her fault, but suffice it to say that last night was the last straw on more than one account."

Nori jumped in, "She even complained and almost cost Eve her job at the library."

"Nori, hush," Eve reprimanded, "That was something else. Patricia did say if you needed to talk to her about anything to contact her. I think more in case Bentley ran her mouth. I also want to apologize for all this drama. I swear I feel like I am in the middle of some theatrical production. Is there anything we can do?" Eve noticed that Abigail stayed quiet, but unobtrusively touched her back and that gave Eve more strength.

Alyssa paused a moment before speaking and Eve was worried that she would have to start trying to find a small box apartment to live in. "I appreciate you sharing that with me. Unfortunately, I believe some of the details will have to be shared and written out so we have a record of what happened. Good news is that someone left in the residence hall that Bentley was originally wanting to live in and she is going to be able to move in over there with a friend of hers. Therefore you will now have the room to yourself for the time being. Something could happen where we will need to room you with another person again."

"So, I don't need to leave?" asked Eve.

"No."

"Am I in any trouble?"

"None of that either. As I said, there were a number of people ready to share about Bentley tossing your belongings out and then others witnessing you coming back to find the stuff in the hall and not being allowed back in your room. Bentley will be out of the room today and we will change the locks on the door in case she thought to make a key to the door. If you can do me a favor and not come back until after 7pm, I would appreciate it. I gave her that long to vacate. Plus, let me know if anything is missing once you return to the room. How does that sound?"

"That is way more than I hoped for. Thank you so much."

"Of course. I am happy you stopped by so I didn't have to message you. News like this is always better delivered in person."

All of them stood up and Alyssa opened the door again. "Hopefully the remainder of your semester goes better and let me know if you have any other issues."

"Will do!" Eve refrained from hugging Alyssa, but once they were outside in the fresh cool air, she laughed and hugged both of her friends.

Nori celebrated right along with Eve and suggested, "I think this calls for ice cream sundaes tonight with everyone. What do you all think?"

"I'm game," Abigail agreed. "Eve, I am proud of you and thrilled that you won't have to stress about your living situation anymore. You might even need to burn some sage to get rid of the bad vibes tonight."

"That is so true!" Nori exclaimed.

The three girls walked back to the courtyard together then separated, each going to their next class for the day.

CHAPTER 12

EVE

The next week went so smooth for Eve, she was worried that something bad was lurking around the corner. After everything that had happened since the beginning of the semester, having days where she went to class, worked, and came back to a peaceful room to study was heaven. While she and the girls didn't burn any sage in the room, they did spray down and disinfect the whole room. Plus, they added a few touches like a fake plant, a few pictures, and a beanbag chair to the other side of the room so it didn't look like Eve lived in a half-sterile room. They also made up the bed. If someone moved in, then they could easily remove things. As Nori told her, "Now that you have your own place, we can come over here for a study or movie night, too, and we need space for everyone to sit." The bean bag was Melissa's idea since she loved Alex's in Abigail's room so much.

Eve had done a lot of thinking in the last week, too. She had time to ponder and analyze what Professor Edison told her. It was hard to deny certain things and feelings that were starting to bubble up. Eve wanted to make sure that it was, indeed, romantic emotions she felt and not simply gratitude or friendship. She worried that if she took a step with Abigail it could possibly ruin things. However, the saying 'nothing risked, nothing gained' popped into her mind.

Taking a deep breath, Eve grabbed her phone and pulled up Abigail's text message conversation. She wasn't sure why she was so nervous as they talked and texted all the time. Actually that was a lie. Eve knew precisely the reason the jitters had her hands trembling. She was about to take a huge step, no make that leap, out of her comfort area. Before she lost the nerve again, she held her breath and typed out a quick message.

EVE: HEY ABBY. WOULD YOU BE UP FOR KEEPING ME COMPANY TONIGHT WHILE I SEARCH THE STARS FOR MY ASTRONOMY CLASS.

Letting out a whoosh of air, she was happy she accomplished the first step. Now to move on the next one should Abigail agree. A ping alerted her to a reply on her phone.

ABIGAIL: OF COURSE. WHAT TIME AND WHERE?

E: HOW ABOUT 9:30PM IN THE SAME LOCATION AS LAST TIME?

A: I WILL BE THERE. SHALL I BRING SNACKS OR DRINKS?

E: NAH.

A: OKAY. SEE YOU THEN.

Eve tossed her phone down and went to shower and get dressed. After all, she didn't want to show up in her pajamas. Although, that wasn't too bad of an idea. But, meandering around campus with pajamas on would definitely lead to talk, especially when those pajamas had Christmas dinosaurs on them.

At eight-thirty that evening, Eve grabbed a blanket and shoved a couple of bottles of water into her backpack along with a few bags of chips, popcorn, and chocolate. Then she swung it onto her back and set out for the rendezvous location. She knew she would be early, but she did actually have some studying to do and maybe, just maybe, that would keep her distracted until Abigail arrived. Then the nerves would start their drumline again in her body.

She spread a blanket out on the grass and laid down on top so she could look up straight at the stars. It wasn't really easy to see the stars where they were now, but that was part of the assignment. They had to see how many of the stars they could identify here at the college and then go out farther away from the city where there weren't as many lights and observe. She was hoping to be able to do that Sunday night since she was off. There were a couple of places the professor shared that would be good, so Eve planned on utilizing one of those.

The sound of footsteps coming towards her had Eve rising up in a panic, but she saw it was Abigail and relaxed a fraction.

Abigail waved as she approached, "Hey, Eve. Sorry if I startled you."

"Nah, my fault. I was thinking too hard and zoned out."

"Already leaving the planet without me huh?"

"Ha ha." Eve waved at the blanket floor, "Care to join me?"

"I would love to." Abigail sat down next to Eve. "So, what are we doing tonight?"

"I have to see how many stars I can observe from around campus."

"Hate to break it to you, but I don't think you are going to be able to count all the stars in the sky. Plus, don't they come in and out of focus even if you just stare in one spot?"

Eve pushed Abigail's arm a little as she chuckled. "Lame, Abby, so lame. You know I didn't mean the whole sky. I have a list of stars. Plus, I have to simply scrutinize them and record my reactions and observations."

"Very well, I shall not share my own examination so as to not sway your own bias and deductions," Abigail responded. "I do like the ground pallet."

"It is a hard surface, but it makes taking in everything above easier." Eve laid back and waved her hand in a huge arc above her.

"I see. Maybe I should have brought us pillows."

"Next time. For now, here." Eve reached inside her backpack, pulled out Abigail's hoodie that Eve kept forgetting to return, and handed it over.

"That will work and are you saying there is going to be a next time?"

"I thought there might be. My next outing is a traveling one and thought I would see if the whole gang wanted to go and do some stargazing."

"Where are you traveling to?"

"Probably about forty-five minutes from here. Have to get away from the city lights."

"Wow. I imagine you could see so many more stars. Just ask them in the chat and see who is available."

"It is this Sunday night, though."

"That isn't a lot of notice, but I am sure it will be fine," reassured Abigail.

"Thanks."

They laid there in companionable silence for several minutes until Eve decided she needed to ask the next question in her plan before her brain freaked out with all the different scenarios running around on a rampage.

Eve turned her head and in a wobbly voice, whispered, "Abby?"

"Yeah?"

"Would you like to date me?"

ABIGAIL

Her ears and mind had to be playing tricks on her because she couldn't have just heard Eve say the words. Had she? It didn't matter because Abigail was going to act first and then apologize later for any misunderstanding.

Apparently, she contemplated too long because Eve sat up and Abigail could tell she was about to bolt. Needing to stop her immediately, Abigail shot up to her knees. She reached over and slid both hands along the sides of Eve's cheeks and lowered her mouth to place a long, lingering, soft kiss on the bewitching woman who had tied up her heart. When she pulled back, she saw heat had flooded all of Eve's face, from desire or embarrassment she wasn't sure.

"I guess that was a yes?" Eve grinned.

Abigail's smile lit up the entire night sky. "That was a hell yes, my darling girl!"

"Just checking."

"You better lay back down and finish your assignment before I do something to cause us to forget all about it. But, once you are done, we are definitely talking."

"Is that what you call what you just did? Because if so, then I might be up to another talk or two tonight."

Abigail's soul was full and it was going to take a lot to kill the smile on her face. She was trying to keep her heart and head in check, but as she continued to lay there underneath the dark sky full of hopes and dreams, she cast out a little wish and prayer and let her own mind continue the story she had started to weave that first day she saw Eve at breakfast.

Who knew how much time passed by while she was letting the young, fantastical love story play out in her head of the two of them together in college and then going on to make a life for themselves. Just because Abigail was a scientist didn't mean she only lived in reality. However, she did know better than to share any of those daydreams and musings with the one laying beside her and shaking her. Oh wait...

"Abby, did you fall asleep? Come back to Earth! Don't let the aliens take you away now."

Turning her head, she grinned over at the slightly annoyed woman beside her. "Sorry about that. You had your time visiting another planet, so I only thought it fair that I did. And don't worry, the aliens aren't going to take me away from you anytime soon. I would demand that they grab you, too, so we would still be together. After all, I can't date you from space."

"You are nuts."

"About you I am." Abigail watched as Eve's face flushed.

"Is this how it is going to be from now on?"

"Maybe. Does it bother you?" Abigail couldn't resist and propped herself up on her side and arm and tugged Eve towards her a little so their lips could meet in the middle.

"Mmm. That is nice."

"There are so many more where those came from. Did you finish finding your constellations?"

"I completed the observing part of my assignment, yes. Now I have to write everything up."

"Does this mean I get to keep you company in your room while you do that?" Abigail had other things on her mind to do inside Eve's room, but she would do her best to behave. She didn't want to scare Eve off.

"If you want, sure. You might be bored, though. I would wait to write everything up, but I want to do it while it is fresh in my mind."

Abigail stood up and held out a hand to help Eve up. "Come on, let's get going. I promise I won't be bored." She wrapped her hoodie around her waist since she was already wearing a different one. Then the two women folded up the blanket and were on their way back to Eve's in a few minutes. The urge to reach out and grab Eve's hand was like a sneeze that was tickling your nose, but you knew you had to fight it off. Slow and easy was the approach that Abigail was taking. Although the fact she kept kissing Eve might contradict that statement.

Once Eve opened the door and had it shut behind them and locked, the little minx commanded, "You can toss everything in the corner."

Everything? Like my clothes? Huh? Abigail knew she had missed something somewhere and was tempted to retrace their steps to see if the elusive item was along the path.

"Abby? The blanket and bag? You can put it in the corner and I will take care of it later."

Oh right. She'd carried items back for Eve. Looking down in her hands she saw everything was indeed in her arms. "Not a problem."

"You alright? You sure you don't need to get back to your own homework."

"Yeah. I am sure. I have nothing due tomorrow." Abigail went to sit down in the other desk chair, but then changed her mind and sat down on Eve's bed so she was closer to the bespelling woman. She hoped that whatever magic wrapped around her when Eve asked if she wanted to date dissipated soon because she felt a little hung over and all she did was agree and share a couple of kisses.

"I am going to type up my notes. Hopefully, it won't take too long. Don't feel like you have to stay, promise."

"I promise I want to be here even if we both sit and stare at the wall. I want to spend some time with you. I will leave soon enough as I have to get some sleep. Until then, I am all yours."

Watching Eve's eyes widened at those words pleased Abigail. Eve turned towards her computer and began typing and Abigail picked up one of the books beside the bed and started looking through it. She got caught up in reading and didn't notice how much time had flown by.

"You can borrow that if you want. I finished it," Eve spoke from beside her.

"What? Oh thanks. It kind of sucked me in. Sometimes it is nice to read something that isn't a textbook. What time is it?"

"It is one in the morning. I am surprised you are still here."

In response, Abigail waved the book. "I better get going. Did you finish?"

"Yes. All done on that assignment until Sunday night."

"Don't forget to message the group in the morning. Speaking of which, I have a question or two. I know you asked me if I wanted to date you, but I wasn't sure what that meant. Are we going to tell the others?"

"I think we better. But, can we wait until we are in person and not in the cafeteria?" Eve asked.

"How about Sunday night? That is only in a couple of nights and we will both be working between now and then." Abigail swung her legs over the edge of the bed and rolled Eve closer so her legs were stretched along the outside of Eve's. "Speaking of working and dating, when do we get to go on our first date?'

Eve cleared her throat and Abigail could see her swallow a couple of times before speaking. "Sunday night works great for filling in the others on our dating status. Maybe we can arrange a little day trip so it is more than simply driving to look at the stars. As far as the other, I assume Sunday doesn't count?"

Abigail leaned in closer and whispered only about four inches from Eve's mouth. "Sunday counts, trust me. But, I was thinking more of a one on one date."

"Ummm. Do you have a day and time in mind?"

"Now, but that isn't fair to you. How about next Friday morning we have a day date before we go to work."

"Next Friday?"

"Mmmhmm. You are a busy woman and I don't think you will be free before then. However, between now and then, we will have plenty of time to study and hang out like we have been. There just might be a few more perks."

"Perks?" croaked out Eve.

"Yes, ma'am. Like this." Abigail moved to tuck a piece of hair behind Eve's ear and then kissed the spot along her jaw at the bottom of her ear before placing another soft one on her forehead and along those lips that had parted and were panting a little. She couldn't wait until she was able to enjoy Eve a bit more. "Plus, now I get to charm you even more. But, for now, I think it best I leave so you can get some rest, darling girl."

Abigail stood up and walked to the door. "Keep my hoodie as a sign of who you are now dating and think of me when you wear it." Winking, Abigail opened the door and left, being sure to let the door click shut quietly before making her way out of the building. Once she was outside, she ran across the ground to her dorm room in an effort to work off some of the tension she'd caused in her own body. She had a feeling there was going to be even more running in the very near future.

Chapter 13

EVE

The next morning, Eve woke feeling both amazing and a little like what the hell had she done. She wasn't sure if she was going to survive the learning curve to dating Abigail if last night was any indication of how things were going to go. She had never kissed or been kissed by another woman romantically before and she still remembered the way Abigail's lips felt against hers last night. The shock of the first kiss kind of registered but didn't fully imprint into her memory as there were so many conflicting hormones and emotions bombarding her nervous system. Then the other ones definitely left behind evidence, especially when Abigail kissed her jaw and then spoke quietly to her. She didn't know that a person could feel like they were being caressed without a single touch. Maybe when they were laying on the ground last night, Abigail really did get replaced by a different species of organism; one that had a sort of magical quality that allowed for this sort of touchless sensual caressing. Eve had read it in plenty of books so it was possible. Myth and fantasy had to come from somewhere and sometimes it is from parts of true events.

Eve knew her mind was running away and falling down a rabbit hole, but she allowed for the momentary distraction and, of course, her brain was following. Eventually, she pulled her thoughts together and considered while she was thinking of the sky and foreign entities that she should text the group about Sunday night. She searched for her phone and at last found it had fallen behind the head of her bed. She fished it out and wiped off a little of the dust that had settled on the screen. She pulled up her text messages and found the group thread and typed out.

Eve: Morning. Would anyone be interested in a little trip on Sunday afternoon/night? I have homework and need to go check out the starry sky away from the city. Thought we could make a trip out of it.

She set down her phone and grabbed a banana and the peanut butter. She smeared some peanut butter over the banana before biting into the fruit. She was taking her second bite when the phone chimed.

Nori: Jess is arriving today. Would it be okay if she joined us?

E: Sounds good to me. I would like to meet the person you talk about all the time.

N: I don't talk about her that much.

N: But, I will see if she would like to do that.

Melissa: What are you all thinking about doing?

E: Awesome.

E: I am open. Definitely get some dinner, but we could do some shopping or go do an outdoors activity.

Logan: Where are you heading? I might have an idea for you.

E: There are a few options. Pretty much, I just need to be somewhere where it is dark

AND THERE AREN'T CITY LIGHTS. WHAT IS YOUR IDEA?

ABIGAIL: I ALREADY TOLD YOU I WOULDN'T MISS IT.

L: KAT HAS SOME FRIENDS THAT HAVE A RANCH ABOUT 45 MINS OUTSIDE THE CITY. SHE SAID SHE COULD ASK ABOUT GOING HORSEBACK RIDING AND THEN SHE WAS SURE THEY WOULD LET US STARGAZE THERE.

KATHERINE: YEAH. IF YOU ALL MIGHT BE INTERESTED I WILL REACH OUT.

M: I AM IN FOR HORSEBACK RIDING.

N: I HAVEN'T RIDDEN ON ONE SINCE I WAS LIKE 7.

E: NEVER BEEN ON ONE.

A: I'M GAME.

E: I AM WILLING.

K: LET ME ASK SINCE IT IS KIND OF LAST MINUTE AND SEE WHAT THEY HAVE PLANNED.

E: THANKS KAT.

By the time the chat died down, the banana was gone and she had a couple of dirty napkins from constantly wiping her fingers off from the stickiness. Now that the business was over, she pulled out her geography homework and worked on it for about an hour or so. When she was almost done, she had a ping on her phone.

A: THINKING OF YOU.

E: I HAVE BEEN THINKING OF EUROPEAN CULTURE.

A: OUCH WOMAN, THAT IS HARSH. IMAGINE ME

CLUTCHING MY CHEST FROM WHERE YOU STABBED ME.

Eve laughed picturing Abigail sprawled on her bed pretending to be injured.

E: I THINK MAYBE YOU MEANT THAT YOU RECEIVED A PAPERCUT AND ARE OVERPLAYING IT. LOL.

E: BUT, I CAN SEND OVER A BAND-AID IF YOU WOULD LIKE.

A: WOW. MY EGO WILL DEFINITELY NOT GET TOO BIG WITH YOU AROUND.

E: SOMEONE HAS TO KEEP YOU IN CHECK.

A: TRUE. SO, WHAT DO YOU THINK OF THE HORSEBACK RIDING IDEA?

E: I IMAGINE IT WILL BE FUN FOR EVERYONE. THEY SEEMED EXCITED.

A: YES, BUT DO YOU THINK IT WILL BE SOMETHING YOU WOULD ENJOY? THAT IS JUST AS IMPORTANT OR EVEN MORE IMPORTANT.

E: NEVER BEEN ON A RANCH OR AROUND A HORSE IN PERSON.

A: WELL, IF WE GET THERE AND YOU DECIDE YOU DON'T WANT TO, WE CAN DO SOMETHING ELSE. JUST KNOW THAT.

E: THANKS. WHAT TIME ARE YOU WORKING TONIGHT?

A: THAT WASN'T A VERY SUBTLE TOPIC CHANGE, BUT TO ANSWER YOUR QUESTION I AM WORKING 4P-CLOSE. I SHOULD BE DONE BETWEEN 11 AND 12. YOU?

E: I am working from 3p-9pm unless they need me to stay longer. I am doing a double tomorrow and I will be wiped out by the end of the night. Think I am going to try and get in about 45 more minutes of studying and then get ready for work. Talk later?

A: Yeah. Get some rest and be sure to eat.

E: You too.

Eve sat her phone down and tried to concentrate on her homework. In the end, all she could think about was her past and cursed herself for letting it stress her out. It wasn't like her friends didn't know she was raised by foster parents because she didn't hide the fact. There was something about it that made her feel like she was inferior for how she grew up. Who knew that a conversation about horses would trigger these feelings. She honestly was looking forward to getting out and trying something new. Plus, it didn't sound like everyone was an avid rider so that really should make Eve feel better. Deciding to push it to the back of her mind, she went to take a hot shower. There weren't as many people needing a shower right then and it was nice to simply bask in the steamy water for longer.

Once she was out of the shower and back in her room, she sat about braiding her hair. It is easier to handle in either a braid or a bun for work. Eve didn't care if it was wet or dry and not drying it would save her some time. She was dressed and out the door with plenty of time to spare to get to work.

The evening went well and she couldn't wait to tell everyone that one of her patrons proposed to his girlfriend. She hadn't ever seen anyone do something like that before and it was sweet. Thankfully, the woman said yes immediately, so there wasn't any awkward silence or ambiance afterwards. Those around them clapped and congratulated the couple.

She ended up having to work a little later and was tired, especially knowing that she had to be at work by eleven in the morning. She changed into her pajamas, sent a quick good night text to Abigail, and then crawled under the blanket and was asleep quickly. When she next woke, it was to her bladder hammering out an SOS signal and demanding to be emptied. Eve hurried and managed to make it before her bladder exploded like a gusher.

Once she felt normal again, she returned to her bed and went back to sleep. She was tempted to check her phone for a text message from Abigail, but she knew if she engaged her mind in something, it would be an hour or more before she could get back to sleep no matter how tired she was.

When she woke on Saturday morning, her phone was lit up from all the messages and notifications from different things. It looked like Katherine finalized plans for tomorrow and horse riding was a go along with a home-cooked meal there with her friends. They said everyone was welcome to go stargazing and asked if they would like to use the back of the flatbed trailer to lay on so no one was having to risk the cold ground and possibly end up sick. Looked like everything was settled and they would take two vehicles. Melissa could ride with Katherine and Logan while Eve, Abigail, Nori, and Jess would be in a different car.

Then Abigail messaged her and let her know that she managed to get back home around ten til midnight and was passing out herself, but would message her in the morning. Since Eve made decent cash tips last night, she decided to take herself out for breakfast before work for an omelet and pancakes. She was ready, out the door, and pulling into the restaurant for breakfast within forty-seven minutes. It had been a long time since she was excited to eat some pancakes, but this place had some banana walnut ones that were delicious and light. When she went inside, she was seated and ordered immediately. While she waited for her food to cook, she pulled out her phone and read some on her e-reader app. With all her studying and getting caught up on stuff, she hadn't had much time to read her book lately and she was at a good part.

CHAPTER 14

EVE

Sunday morning dawned sunny and chilly. Eve had checked the forecast the night before and was happy to see that the rain they thought might hit veered off more to the east of the city and so they wouldn't have to worry about clouds and possible rain. As long as it stayed that way during the day and night until they returned back to college. Eve wasn't sure what she should pick out to wear to go riding, but she decided to go with a pair of jeans based on what she had seen in several movies. After all, didn't a lot of cowboys wear them to do work on a ranch? It should be good for her as well. She dug through and pulled out a pair and then chose a t-shirt underneath a hoodie. It was only going to get up to around fifty-two degrees for the high so she didn't want to be cold. However, in case they were inside and she got rather warm, she could take the hoodie off and still be comfortable. Would today be a good day for her to wear Abby's hoodie? She better not since they hadn't told everyone yet, plus if something happened to the hoodie other than a little dirt, it would break her heart, especially if the hoodie was special to Abby. Maybe she was overthinking this.

Letting out a growl, she sank down to the floor and stared at the mess around her. Eve pulled out her phone and texted her friend.

Eve: I need help.

Nori: Uh oh. That witch didn't come back to your room did she? I have back up now and trust me, my girl is made of muscles.

E: No, nothing like that. What are you wearing today?

N: Clothes.

E: Smartass. Seriously. I am in over my head on what to wear. I don't want to be over or underdressed.

N: It is just us hanging out, unless there is some other reason or someone else joining us.

E: No. That isn't it.

N: Eve, jeans and long sleeve shirt and light jacket or hoodie. Layers. Wear boots or tennis shoes. Be comfortable.

E: Okay. Thanks. That is pretty much what I had decided on.

N: See. Trust yourself and you will be okay.
See you soon.

E: Can't wait to meet Jess.

N: She is excited and nervous to meet all of you.

E: She shouldn't be. Alright. See you all soon.
I am going to decide on an outfit.

Letting out a breath, she was glad that she messaged Nori because it helped to calm her anxious mind down. She ended up going with a shirt that said the path to this girl's heart is through the stars. Then she tugged on a plain-gray, zip-up hoodie over that. It was one of her favorites because it was really soft and warm.

Once she was dressed, she had a peanut butter sandwich while she unpacked everything from her backpack and then repacked it with only a notebook and pen to take notes, a couple of bottles of water, some granola bars, and a few apples. She shoved in an extra shirt and a pair of leggings in there, too. She had a mindset of always being prepared in case something happened. It was one of those life lessons she learned growing up and always moving about. Thinking about things, at the last minute, Eve also found a spot for a first-aid kit she kept in one of the drawers.

Her phone dinged and she looked to see who it was.

Abigail: Hey. Wanted to let you know I can't wait to see you.

Eve: My nerves are like a tangled bunch of Christmas lights.

A: I always wind mine back up and put them neatly in the box.

E: That is probably why your nerves are calm all the time.

A: You have no idea how much you have caused me to be twisted up over the past month.

E: So, I have caused chaos to enter your life?

A: In only the best and scary ways. 😂

E: Haha. I would say you haven't seen me looking scary yet, but well, you have seen me sick and at my worst.

A: Nori is knocking on my door and shouting for me to go. We will be over to pick you up in a few.

E: Meet you downstairs.

A: 😀

Eve slung her backpack on and double checked that she had her phone, wallet, and keys before locking the door and heading downstairs and outside to await her chariot. She had to admit she was nervous about the day. Because of that she was fidgety and shifting back and forth on her feet. When the red car pulled up, Abigail hopped out of the car to run around the back and hug Eve. Before pulling back, Abigail whispered in her ear, " Relax."

The door was magically opened by a stranger and she slid into the backseat on the passenger side. Well, she assumed the unknown person was Jess and that was quickly confirmed once they were all in the car with seatbelts on. Nori turned around and said, "You all can more formally meet later, but Jess, this is Eve. Eve, this is Jess.

"Nice to meet you, Eve," Jess twisted and held out her hand and Eve leaned forward to shake it briefly.

Nori turned, put the car in drive, and headed out of the parking lot. "We are going to meet up with the other three down the road. They left a little earlier so they could make a stop along the way. However, we aim to meet at the gas station off of Exit 645. From there, we will follow them. We can text them as we get closer to see how everyone is doing." They all fell into polite conversation with one another and Eve was grateful the attention was off of her.

"So, Jess, tell us what drew you to our darling Nori to begin with," Abigail asked.

"I am sure she told you how we met. It was one of those moments where you see someone across the room that you are attracted to. Something clicked inside of me and I knew that I wanted to get to know her more. So, when it was breaktime, I tracked her down and found her trying to wrangle two toddlers into chairs for a snack. Seeing how she reacted to that whole scene told me a lot about how good her heart was as if volunteering for a Christmas program on one's holiday from college didn't already allude to something. Anyway, after that I knew I had to ask her out."

"She did think that Ian and I were an item, though, despite being warned that we were only besties. Plus, technically, Ian asked you to join us for lunch the first time."

"This is very true. That man has no reservations about stating what he wants and going for it. I learned that very soon after meeting him. However, other than that, I did ask Nori out first."

"She was so nervous, though, and kept rambling and taking it back and rephrasing it, so I had a way to make an easy excuse if needed. It wasn't, though."

"No, it wasn't. However, the first date didn't quite go according to plan," Jess said.

"Babe, nothing about that holiday went according to plan," laughed Nori and then she lifted Jess's hand up to her lips and kissed it briefly.

"This is true," agreed Jess.

Eve was a little jealous that the two women were so relaxed and confident to be who they were together. She was so happy to see her friend glowing. She knew that Nori missed Jess since the two of them lived in different states. But, she hoped one day she had that level of ease with someone, specifically Abigail.

As if thinking of the woman conjured action on her part, Abigail slid her hand over and squeezed Eve's and then let it go. However, she left it resting in the middle of the seat near Eve's. When she looked over at the woman, Abigail mouthed, "soon" and Eve knew the day would be defining. While she knew her friends would be happy for the two of them, she was still nervous to reveal so much.

"So, Eve, when are you going to take Abby off the market?" Jess asked from the front seat. She craned her neck around

"Jess!" Nori hissed as she tugged on Jess's hand.

"What?"

Eve knew her face was flushed from embarrassment and she wasn't sure what to say. Thankfully Abigail answered, saving her once again. "Actually, I haven't been on the market for awhile now. I took myself off of it after a bad breakup. Never found the right person to risk things for again. I just let everyone think I am available."

"So, you aren't interested in dating?" Jess turned and faced Nori, "I thought you told me that... Ouch, woman."

"I swear I have rubbed off on you and I am not sure in a good way and we haven't even been dating long," Nori stated very matter-of-factly, "You are acting like me. Usually, I am the nosy one that isn't very tactful."

Jess twisted back and Eve could tell that the woman felt bad. "She is right. I apologize, Eve. I think my nerves and excitement at meeting you all has overridden my good manners. I am not usually like this. Please forgive me."

"All is forgiven." Eve decided that in an effort to save everyone from even more uncomfortable situations she would go ahead and tell them. Glancing at Abigail she lifted her eyebrows and pointed a little towards the front seat. Apparently understanding her meaning, Abigail nodded. "Actually, Jess, we were going to wait until later to tell everyone, but Abigail and I have decided to date one another."

The car swerved a bit in the lane and then righted itself. Eve had to brace one hand on the window and one on the seat to steady herself.

"What?" shrieked Nori from the front seat. "When? How? What?"

"Well, congrats, Eve, you have broken my girlfriend," laughed Jess.

"She might have a restart button on her somewhere, but I have no idea where," teased Eve.

"I would try and find it, but I have a feeling I might be putting our lives in danger if I were to search her."

"Yes, better wait until we pull over," Abigail joined in on the teasing. "She already had one hiccup. Next thing we know, we will be getting an error message in the form of a ticket from a cop."

All three girls laughed and eventually, Nori joined in. "Haha, you three. Seriously, though. How long have you been holding out on me?"

"It has only been a couple of days, Nori. I asked Abby and then we spent the weekend working. Not a big deal."

"Aww. You asked. I love that," crooned Nori. Eve caught Nori's eyes in the rearview mirror and rolled her eyes at her friend.

"Well, congrats you two. I am happy for you both. Here is to a car full of happy girlfriends. Wait, does that sound like we are all dating each other or all dating the same person?" asked Jess. "No offense, but I am not into sharing."

All of them echoed the sentiment. Talk shifted to relationships and different things. Eve sat back and listened mostly and commented here and there. She learned a lot from the other three ladies and it was nice to spend time away from school surrounded by people who genuinely liked her and wanted to hang out. Soon enough, they were pulling off the highway at exit 645.

ABIGAIL

Abigail knew that the whole conversation in the car was pushing all sorts of Eve's buttons, but she was proud of the way she took charge, made a decision, and then jumped in on the teasing of Nori. Eve had come a long way from the woman that first day at breakfast.

No sooner had they stopped when Nori jumped out of the car and rushed into the store in a hurry to go to the bathroom. "She must not have gone before we left," Abigail said as she unbuckled her seat belt at a more leisurely pace.

"Nope. She said she didn't need to go," replied Jess. "She better make sure to go before we saddle up if she doesn't want to be squatting behind some trees."

The other three ladies strolled in and by the time they got inside, Nori was headed back their way. "That was quick," Abigail stated once Nori joined them by the drink cooler.

"Thankfully, there wasn't a line. I was prepared to pay someone to let me go next if needed."

Jess hugged her girlfriend around the waist as she teased, "If you had tried to go before we set out, you probably wouldn't have been so bad off. You are like a child stating that she doesn't need to go and then fifteen minutes down the road, demanding to stop."

"Well, I waited longer than fifteen minutes." Nori stuck out her tongue causing the other three to laugh.

"See, like a child."

Jess kissed Nori's cheek as Abigail turned towards Eve. "Aren't they cute together?"

"Yes."

Then dropping her voice so only Eve could hear her, Abigail said, "That will be us soon I have no doubt, although I am not sure which one of us will be Nori in this situation."

"I don't think either one of us will ever step into Nori's shoes. She is definitely one of a kind." Eve laughed and then grabbed a cold bottle of water from the cooler.

"Darn straight, I am one of a kind. What were you two saying about me anyways?"

"That you keep us entertained and are a wonderful friend," supplied Eve.

That woman really could roll with the punches. Abigail would do well to keep her eye on Eve, not that it would be a hardship of any kind. It was harder to focus on something else besides the beautiful woman. A nudge on her arm brought her out of her musings. "What?"

"You ready or are you going to buy some of that chocolate you are staring at?" asked Nori with a quirk to one side of her mouth. She looked like she had no doubt that Abigail was not thinking about chocolate.

Not wanting to let her friend get the better of her, Abigail picked out five different king size bars for all seven of them to share. "Okay, now I am ready."

"I brought a few snacks in my backpack, but anyone that wants me to put something in there for later let me know. There is still room," Eve offered to the group. She was always thinking of others in that way and it was one of the reasons that Abigail has grown to care about her so much.

They thanked Eve and checked out then climbed back into the car and drove away from the door to give someone else the opportunity to park close. Nori texted the group chat to see where the remainder of their friends were. Melissa replied that they were about five minutes away. The four ladies settled down to wait and enjoyed their beverages.

Before long, a car pulled up next to them and everyone scrambled out of the two vehicles. Introductions were made again between Jess and the others. Then Nori let out a whoosh of air like a balloon releasing its air and revealed, "Guess what! Abby and Eve are dating now."

"Woohoo!" Katherine exclaimed.

"Were you about to bust before you could get that out?" Logan asked Nori as everyone chuckled. "Well, I am happy for the two of you."

"Guess I am the seventh wheel on this journey today."

Logan leaned over and ruffled Melissa's hair. "Your prince or princess will come along soon and in the meantime, we know you date around. Start bringing them on group trips if you want, especially if they are guys. I swear I am going to start bringing me a guy friend or two before I end up at the spa with you all having mud facials and seaweed wraps." All the girls laughed as Logan shivered at the image he must have gotten in his head.

"Thanks, man. And I wasn't really too worried about being the extra today. Just think there will be no seaweed wraps; however, if you take a tumble to the ground you might end up with some mud on your face, so that part is still up for grabs."

"I will be sure to keep my ass in the saddle and not on the ground," Logan commented. "Speaking of which, are you ladies ready to head out?"

A chorus of yes, yeah, and let's go was heard. They all piled back into the two vehicles and Logan pulled out ahead of Nori's.

"Hope he doesn't lose us," said Abigail.

"I have the address just in case he does. He said it is easy to find, but this way we can all arrive at the same time."

They continued down the highway for about five miles before they exited. Then they followed along for another twenty minutes until they arrived at a gate. It was black metal and had a logo for the ranch in the middle of it. Abigail watched as Logan clicked the buzzer and waited. Nothing happened.

"I hope nothing came up and they are only out," Nori said.

"This place looks fancy," Eve whispered. Abigail had a feeling her girl was ready to bolt so she reached across and grabbed Eve's hand.

She noticed Logan reached over to the little box and push several buttons. The gates swung open and both of them made it through before the gates closed behind them. They followed the path along and when they arrived at the house, Eve squeezed Abigail's hand harder out of reflex she would wager.

"Wow," Eve breathed out.

The structure in front of them was a two-story white house with a long porch that housed several rocking chairs, a porch swing, a couple of tables, and a rug or two. It looked like it could have appeared in a magazine. Abigail didn't think it looked fancy as much as it was really clean and spotless. It made her think of someone sitting out having a tray of sweet tea or lemonade served to them on a hot day.

The door opened and out rushed a young child followed by a woman that looked about the same age as Abigail's mother. The toddler ran to the porch rails and grabbed ahold of two of them with his little hands. Everyone but Abigail and Eve had gotten out of the car. "We might as well join them. It's going to be fine."

"Yeah, somehow this isn't what I was expecting. Not sure what I was picturing, but this wasn't it."

"I'm here for you." Abigail lifted Eve's hand and placed a soft kiss to the top of it.

By the time the two of them opened their door and gathered behind the others, a couple of new people had joined the party. There was a young woman hugging Katherine tight as the cowboy-looking guy next to her was shaking hands with Logan.

They turned around and Katherine introduced everyone, "*Rebecca, this is Melissa, Nori, Jess, Eve, and Abigail. Everyone, this is Rebecca, but most call her Becca, and her husband, Hunter, and that is their son, Wendell, and Becca's mom, Sarah."

Everyone waved and called out hellos. Becca smiled at each of them, "Welcome, please make yourselves at home. While the front here looks nice, trust me in that the whole place isn't this spotless. Don't let it intimidate you. Follow me and we can go around back.

Now do you all want something to eat and chat a bit or would you all like to get started with horseback riding?"

Katherine spoke up for them, "I think if we get started riding it might actually help everyone to relax. I appreciate you letting us come out."

"It is my pleasure. I miss seeing you so this will kill lots of birds with one stone. We are just as excited to have all of you here and do some star-watching tonight. I can't tell you the last time I laid back and enjoyed the beauty of the night sky. Sure, I have seen it plenty of times while outside relaxing or doing chores, but to take time out to stargaze hasn't been on the top of my priority list."

"You can thank Eve since this is for her class assignment."

Rebecca turned a big smile over at Eve and if Rebecca wasn't already married, then Abigail might have to worry what the woman's intentions were. "Well, thanks. So, you are studying astronomy huh? Do you know what you want to do?"

"No. I still am working on figuring that out. I might not even stay in the same degree program."

"But, no matter what, I thank the stars for putting Eve into my path," Abigail interjected.

"Well, good luck and anytime you need to borrow some country sky, you are welcome to come out here."

"Thank you, Becca. I will remember that."

They had arrived at the stables and there was a big aisle down the middle with stalls on both sides. Some of them had horses with their heads sticking out making noises. Abigail wondered if maybe they were talking to each other and asking who all the strange people were. Or maybe they were sizing up her and her friends and picking out who they wanted as their rider.

Hunter went up to the first horse and rubbed its neck. "This is Midnight. I will be riding him. Next to him is Harmony, who is Becca's baby. You all will each have a mount whose names are Soul Train, Happiness, Penelope, Cheyenne, Granny Smith, Cocoa Butter, and Lemonade. Some are named based on their coloring and others because of their previous owners or temperament. None of them are mean, but horses, like people, have bad days so you might get one that is a bit stubborn. You all can pick which one you would like to ride. They are each in a stall so go talk to them and see if you feel a connection with a particular horse."

Eve whispered to Abigail, or at least that was the objective she was sure. "Is he serious?"

Rebecca came up next to her, "Yes, he is. Have you ever ridden or been around horses before?"

Eve shook her head, "No."

"Come on and I will go with you. There isn't anything to be afraid of," Rebecca said.

Eve turned pleading eyes towards Abigail and she knew she wouldn't be able to tell that woman no very often. "Will you come with me?"

"Of course, darling. I had already planned on it." Abigail linked her arm with Eve's and followed behind Rebecca.

"Let's start down here at the end and work our way back. That way it is a little quieter here." Rebecca reached the last stall on the left. "This, here, is Lemonade. She is a pretty yellow color and reminds us of summertime. Plus, I think we were all having lemonade when she was born. It is funny because she doesn't like anything sour, but loves her sweets. Hold out your palm and let her sniff you."

Eve did as requested and the horse came over and nosed her hand around.

"She is looking for a treat. Here, we won't give them all something, but she can have something small. I am going to put it in your hand and just hold it out."

Rebecca dropped a piece of apple into Eve's hand and Abigail watched as her girl went stiff when Lemonade reached down and took it from her hand. But, no matter what, Eve didn't run away. Next, Rebecca showed her how to pet Lemonade and where her favorite spots to be rubbed were. After a few minutes, Abigail could tell that Eve was relaxing. She had a feeling no matter how the other horses were, that Eve would be choosing Lemonade.

Abigail stepped to the next stall which was only a few feet away. Inside was a pretty, light-brown horse. She looked at the nameplate and it read Cocoa Butter. "I bet I can guess how you got your name, beautiful." Abigail stood there watching as Cocoa Butter kept far away from the door.

"She is shy," came a voice to her right. When Abigail turned, she saw that Rebecca had moved over to stand next to her.

"That's okay. A little shyness never bothered me. Takes a little more patience and understanding, but after some time, I find they come around and make great companions."

"Are you talking about horses or people? It sounds like you have had your share of dealing with one or both." Rebecca clicked her tongue and Cocoa came over closer, but still stayed farther away. "Looks like she is being a bit more hesitant than usual. We might need to switch her out with a different one."

"Nah. Give me a bit and I will see if I can convince her to come closer."

"Are you sure?" asked Rebecca.

Eve joined them and spoke from Abigail's left side, "She won me over by being persistent and supportive so I believe in her."

"Alright then. I will leave the two of you for a few and go see how the others are doing." Rebecca moved down the line.

Abigail turned and grinned down at Eve, "So, I won you over huh?"

"You know you did. Now, can you do the same with her?"

"I am going to try."

"Tell you what, how about I go check on our friends so you can have some one-on-one time with Cocoa Butter there. She might warm up to you faster with no one around." Eve hugged Abigail before turning and leaving.

"Well, Cocoa, it looks like it is just me and you." Abigail rested her arms on the half door and leaned a little closer. "The others have gone on down the row. Tell me, do you like listening to people talk? I have a feeling you are a good listener and secret keeper. I have a sense about these sorts of things."

She leaned in a little closer and whispered. "I will let you in on a secret of mine, more like a worry. The girl that just left, her name is Eve. She is my girlfriend and it is new. I am worried I will do something to scare her off or push her too fast. I really like her, but she is kind of new to dating other girls." Abigail looked around to make sure no one was around since she was revealing personal stuff. "See, I knew you were a good listener."

As she was talking Cocoa Butter edged closer and closer to Abigail, which was a good sign, and Abigail kept on talking. "Do you prefer your full name of Cocoa Butter or just Cocoa? I can see you as both." A small neigh and another couple of steps closer was the response that Abigail received. "You are a good girl. If you come a little bit more I will rub your head and neck. We are here to go on a nice relaxing adventure with you and your friends. Then tonight we are going to lay underneath the stars on blankets and look up at the stars. Hoping the sky stays clear for us tonight so we can see all the tiny dots in the heavens."

Cocoa Butter had made her way all the way over and sniffed Abigail's hands. "See, I knew you would come over here and be my friend." She slowly with steady movements raised her hands up and rubbed the top of the horse's nose bridge and then when Cocoa moved another couple of feet, she moved on to massaging and petting Cocoa's neck. "Now, I think the others are about ready to ride, do you think you will let me ride you?" In response, Abigail got a little snort. "Good girl."

"Looks like you did it," Rebecca said, coming up to her. "Let's get her out and saddled up."

The two of them worked together and got both Cocoa Butter and Lemonade ready to go. Eve came back over and stood watching them. Rebecca described everything she was doing so Eve would know what was going on. Plus, she gave a few instructions on how to guide Lemonade once in the saddle.

Abigail climbed up into the saddle first so she could help out when Eve got up. Rebecca was assisting from the ground. They took Lemonade over to a mounting block so it would be easier for Eve to get up the first time. Abigail admitted that her girl was acclimating really quickly to everything and learning fast what to do and not to do. She was proud of her.

"Okay, Eve, now for this time, I will keep a hold of the reins. I want your focus to be on the movement getting into the saddle. Grab ahold of the horn and use it to help you balance getting into the saddle. Put one foot in the stirrup, grab the horn and swing your leg over it." It took a couple of tries, but then Eve was seated on top. "Very good. Now I am going to walk you a few steps and then hand you the reins." Rebecca helped to guide Lemonade away from the mounting block. "Okay, you are good now. I will ride with you today so I can help you."

Eve's face was scrunched up and Abigail could tell she was tense and called out in a normal voice, "Relax, babe. You are doing great. Lemonade is going to take care of you and Cocoa Butter and I are right here, too, aren't we, girl?" Abigail leaned over and patted the horse's neck.

"Thanks. I am a little nervous."

"It is expected. I see Becca coming over on Harmony. She won't let anything happen to you."

"Alright, Hunter is going to head out first and we will be towards the back. That way if you need to stop or get stressed out, we can take care of things. There is no hurry. Are you both ready?"

"Yeah." Eve's voice came out a little shaky and Abigail wished she could give her some confidence.

"Cocoa Butter and I are ready to go." Abigail nudged her horse with her legs and they started off.

About twenty minutes into the trip, Abigail could already tell that Eve might have been bitten by the horse-riding bug. She was having fun and smiling. It took a good five to ten minutes for her to relax more into the rhythm of riding and they were just walking today, but it was great to see her more carefree and laughing. Rebecca was keeping them entertained with stories of different things and it was a beautiful day. They took a trail that led them back into a pasture where some of the others who were more experienced could ride a bit faster and let the horses get more exercise. Abigail wanted to do the same, but she stayed back with Eve and a few of the others. They circled about and watched. It was a nice open area that allowed them to pick up speed a little on the walk.

Eventually, they all stopped for a break and slid down from their horses. Abigail went over to help Eve down. Thankfully, Logan also joined because the step down from the stirrup to the ground was a little farther since Eve was on the shorter side and Lemonade was a little taller. Logan was able to help ease Eve down on the ground.

"Wow, I feel like a kid having to be helped down by a parent," Eve said as she stood on the ground. "And my legs are a little wobbly. Is that normal?"

Hunter answered her question. "If you haven't ever ridden before or worked out using those muscles then yeah. You might be a little sore tomorrow."

"Good thing it is Monday and I am not going to have to wait tables. I might not make it through my shift. Definitely worth it, though." Eve turned towards Katherine and Logan. "Thank you both for the suggestion. I have really enjoyed this."

They let the horses wander around a bit and they all stretched their legs or sat around and chatted. After about thirty minutes, Rebecca said they should probably be getting back as dinner would be close to being done.

Nori spoke up, "Some of us should have stayed back and helped to cook. There are a lot of us to feed."

"Nonsense. My mother loves cooking and is used to feeding a crowd. Plus, my dad and sister will be there by the time we return and I am sure she will rope them into assisting her or entertaining Wendell."

Nori brushed off the grass from her jeans. "If you are sure."

"I am."

Abigail went over by Lemonade and clasped her hands together. She beckoned Eve over. "You can step here and I will help boost you up. Once you get your foot in the stirrup you will be able to swing your other leg around."

"Nope, I will hurt your hand."

"You will not. Up you get." Abigail squatted down a little and after a few minutes of looking between her and the horse, Eve let out an exasperated sigh and stepped into the foothold that Abigail made. "There you go." She watched as Eve grabbed the horn. Instead of standing straight up in the saddle and leaning towards the front middle of the horse to swing her leg around, she had her stomach laying across the saddle. "I don't think that is going to be comfortable riding back." Abigail chuckled and grabbed ahold of

Eve's butt and helped to push her around a bit. After a few minutes and Rebecca riding over to help, they got Eve sitting up and facing the right direction.

Abigail walked over to Cocoa Butter and got situated easily. All that did was cause Eve to pout and stick her tongue out.

"You know you are cute when you are mad and annoyed." Abigail shot a wink over at her girlfriend before nudging Cocoa closer. She watched as part of the frustration left Eve's expression and then a wicked smile replaced it.

"You know, one day being short will pay off for me."

They both followed after Melissa, Nori, and Jess. "I never said you were short, silly. You just happened to pick a larger horse to claim as your own."

"You're calling yourself a horse now are you? Plus, I think you might have claimed me first."

"Wait? What?"

"That was a good one, Eve," called back Nori. "Plus, you caused her brain to freeze so double points."

Eve laughed and then brushed her right knuckles along her left shoulder.

"I think something got into our quiet Eve. Did one of you put something into her water?" Melissa asked.

Abigail listened to them tease back and forth as her mind kept showing her all the ways that being short is a benefit. Several of them involved more of an advantage for Abigail, and she had no problems with any of those scenarios. Cocoa whinnied and shook her head bringing her back into focus. "Hey, girl, sorry about that. I got lost in my thoughts." Reaching down, Abigail patted the side of Cocoa's neck. "You are such a good girl and deserve a nice treat when we get back."

"Yeah, we will brush them all down and give them a treat when we return," said Rebecca as she rode up with the girls. "Any of you that want to help with that part are welcome to."

"Will you show me what to do?" asked Eve. "I want to learn anything I can."

"Of course. I am more than happy to. I know I have said it before, but you are welcome to come out whenever you all would like. Any friend of Kat's is good in my stable."

Until her stomach growled, Abigail didn't realize she was so hungry. She hoped that whatever was for supper there was plenty of it as she felt like she could eat a whole Thanksgiving meal by herself.

They went back partially in a different direction, but soon arrived at the stables as it didn't take as long to return as the first part of the trip did. Abigail slid off of Cocoa and then watched as Eve was able to swing herself off using the block that helped her to get up. One by one, they all led their respective horses back into their stalls. One of the workers came by with some apples and carrots for the animals while several others brought over the different brushes and combs to groom the horses. One took over Rebecca's horse, while she showed Eve what to do with Lemonade. Abigail hadn't groomed one in awhile, but once she began, the flow and memories came back to her. It was a soothing and melodic process and she just chatted with Cocoa Butter or hummed while she moved from one step to another. Everyone worked until a woman came out to let them know that dinner was ready.

They all stopped by the big sink and washed up before heading inside the house from the back porch. As soon as the door was opened, Abigail's stomach started growling and gurgling again. The aroma in the air was fragrant and smelled like peppers, onion, and garlic.

Wendell came running into the room and crashed into his dad's legs. Hunter swung him up in the air and then hugged him. "Hey, bud. Have you been a good boy for Nana and Papa?" In response the toddler just squirmed in his dad's arms. "Let's go show our guests where the dining room is."

"When it is just us, we usually eat at the kitchen table, but with so many guests, we are going to eat at the dining room table," Rebecca added as they walked through what looked to be a living room, into a room next to it that was a little more formal and had a table that stretched the length of the room. "You all have a seat and I will go help Mom bring everything to put on the table."

"Let us help," offered Nori.

"Nonsense. You are our guests. Plus, it will give you a few minutes to cool down and relax from the ride and grooming." Rebecca disappeared and everyone found a chair or spot on one of the bench seats.

Abigail, Eve, and Melissa shared one bench while Jess, Nori, Katherine, and Logan shared another one on the opposite side of the table. They left the individual chairs for everyone else. There was a highchair on the end between the head of the table, or maybe that was the foot, and one of the sides.

Abigail decided to pose a question that popped into her head. "How do you determine which end is the head of the table and what is the other end called? Everyone looked at her like she spoke a foreign language.

"That was totally random. Where did that come from?" Katherine asked.

"I was looking at everything and the highchair position and my mind went to the scholarly side of things. You always hear people talk about the head of the table, but that is all. Or at least that is all I have ever heard."

"This is true. I don't know. I wonder if the head is one end, if the other end is called a foot," Nori said and furrowed her eyebrows as she started pondering it.

Abigail saw Jess pull out her phone and soon answered, "According to what I see online, the head of the table is the furthest away from any entrances or obstacles." All of them studied the room and then pointed at the spot that was to the right of Abigail.

Eve then piped up continuing, "This said that the second host or hostess sits at the other end which is the foot. You were right, Nori. I found something about the head of the table sitting on the east side and everyone else sitting on the east, west, and north. It didn't mention the south, so not sure about that. That seems weird."

"I agree, Eve," added Logan.

While they were discussing this, Rebecca, her mom, and her sister came in and began setting down bowls and dishes on the table. Right behind them came Rebecca's dad, whom they learned was named Jim, and Wendell. "Well, in this house, anyone can sit wherever they want. It just happens to be that I sit in that spot over there and Sarah sits on the other end because she is always up and down for one thing or another it seems like. It is funny how we naturally fall into that line of seat placement without even thinking about it, though."

"Yes, sir, it is," Jess replied. "Even when it is just my grandparents and I, we have a tendency to sit like that. I don't know how they sit when I am not there and it is just the two of them. I never thought about it before."

Melissa pointed out, "It's a good thing we sit at a round table at the college, this way none of us have that position."

They all laughed. Abigail's mouth salivated at the sight of meatloaf, mashed potatoes, green beans, brown gravy, salad, and croissants. "This all looks so delicious. Thank you for the dinner. I miss home-cooked meals." Everyone echoed with their thanks.

Rebecca asked everyone, "What would you all like to drink? I didn't think about asking since we all drink sweet tea."

They all agreed that sweet tea worked for them, too. Once everyone was sitting around the table, Jim said a blessing over the food and then they started to serve themselves and pass around the dishes. Abigail was glad there were two big pans of meatloaf because it was something she really liked and she wanted a double portion of it. Once everyone had their food, she turned and saw Eve staring at first her plate and then Abigail's.

"What's wrong?" Abigail asked quietly in case something was up and she didn't want their host to hear.

"Where do you put all of that? I am jealous."

"I might be a little bit hungrier than usual and this might happen to be one of my favorite meals."

"Good thing we are eating after riding," Eve laughed.

"Why? You don't think Cocoa Butter would want a heavier me?"

"What? That isn't what I meant." Eve looked so appalled and Abigail winked at her to let her know she was teasing. "Oh you. I thought you really took offense." Eve waved her fork in the air. "That is why I don't talk much, I end up putting my foot in my mouth."

Abigail leaned over close and whispered low so no one else could hear, "I have something else you can put into your mouth."

A cough came from Melissa on the other side of them. Guess Abigail didn't whisper quietly enough.

"You okay, Mel?" Nori asked from across the table.

Melissa waved her off and took a drink of her tea. Once she had recovered, she shot Abigail a look and then answered, "Yeah, something just hit me wrong for a second."

Abigail smirked even as Eve's face flushed a tiny bit more than she already was from being outside. The remainder of supper went smoothly and was uneventful until a two-layer chocolate cake was brought out. "Anyone want some dessert now?"

Abigail groaned because she'd polished off all of her meal and now was comfortably carrying a food baby. "I think I am going to have to wait, but that looks like heaven."

Eve sat up straighter and raised her hand, "Me, please. I will take a big slice since Abigail doesn't want hers."

"Hey. I didn't say I didn't want any. I just don't think I can fit it in my stomach right now."

"You are passionate about meatloaf, I am passionate about desserts."

Sarah cut Eve a piece of cake and passed it over before continuing to serve cake to everyone else. It did look moist and rich and perfect. Abigail picked up her fork to take a little taste. Eve must have seen her because she shifted her hold on her fork to more of a grip position and aimed it at Abigail. "Ask Nori, I will hurt a girl over dessert."

Nori, of course, was right there agreeing. "It's true. She was in the hospital and threatened me if I didn't save her part of the dessert. I believed her then and more so now."

Eve grinned all innocently up at Abigail, "Especially chocolate. However, I am in a kind mood so if you ask nicely, I might share."

Deciding to play it up as much as she could, Abigail batted her eyelashes and posed with the top of her fingers under her chin in an attempt to look all innocent. "Babe, will you pretty please with a cherry on top let me have a bite of your cake?"

Rolling her eyes, Eve cut off a small corner and held the fork up for Abigail to try. She gave in and wrapped her mouth around the delicious forkful of chocolate heaven. She was right in that it was moist. It was airy and disappeared within moments of hitting her tongue. There was frosting in between the two layers that was the right ratio for the amount of cake. She was really tempted to go ahead and get a piece of the cake. Before Abigail could decide, a thin slice of cake was placed in front of her.

"I knew you would want more, so I had your own piece cut. What you can't eat, I will finish off for you," offered Eve.

"Thanks." She didn't need to be told twice and in the end, had no problem finishing off the piece of cake. "Guess I did have room for dessert."

Logan expressed his viewpoint. "I think dessert is like the illustration where someone puts marbles in a glass and asks the room if the glass is full and they say yes. Then the presenter pours in sand and of course there is room for the sand amongst the marbles. The presenter asks the question again once more if the glass is full and everyone says yes. However, the presenter proceeds to pour in water and that is absorbed and fills in the area in between the sand particles. In this situation, I think dessert is the sand. There is always room somewhere for it."

"Yes. I concur one hundred percent," Katherine said.

"Well said, Logan," Jess spoke at the same as Katherine did.

Eve added her own voice, "You are preaching to the choir."

Everyone laughed and this time when Nori offered to help with cleanup she wouldn't accept no as an answer. Both she and Jess volunteered to help Sarah clean up while Hunter and Rebecca showed the others where the trailer had been brought up towards the house and turned into a star lounging party.

CHAPTER 15

EVE

When they saw the trailer that Katherine's friend had set up for them, Eve was shocked. There were bales of hay at one end and halfway down one side of the flat bed trailer. Then a tarp and blankets were put over it to prevent people from being stabbed with the pieces of dried grass. But, this way they had places to sit on something or brace their backs against for support. Then the rest of the floor of the trailer had a couple of blankets to sit and lay on along with a few pillows and more blankets to cover up with. It was so cozy and over the top. Eve couldn't believe they used up so many items just for a few hours. They would be doing lots of laundry after this. On their way out, Eve grabbed her backpack she had brought along.

Everyone's amazement and comments floated around her over it all. Abigail climbed up on the trailer first and then held out her hand to steady Eve as she climbed the couple of stairs that had been placed at the end of the trailer. She knew she would be staking out a place at the end where there wasn't any hay when it came time. She wanted to be able to lay down flat and have the vastness of the sky above her be her huge screen. It wasn't quite dark enough yet, though. They still had about an hour until it got dark enough to really see everything.

Everyone settled down on the hay bales and chatted about different things. Eve sat close to Abigail and when her girlfriend reached out to hold her hand, she smiled internally at how right it felt in her own hand. While Eve knew she was among friends and none of them were going to think better or worse of her, she was still getting used to not only the beginning stages of dating, but rather dating someone of the same sex. All the little things that came with it that were probably natural to everyone else made her hesitate and overthink things. While she was stuck in her head overanalyzing things, she missed the fact that someone had turned on some music.

Abigail tugged on her hand, "You want to go dance with the others?" She nodded to where everyone was climbing off of the trailer and into the yard. A fast-paced song was playing and they were all moving to the beat.

"Sure. Why not." Eve smiled. She wasn't the best dancer, but she could hold her own.

"Let's go." Abigail swung her legs over the side of the trailer and hopped down.

Eve knew if she did that, she would probably fall to the ground. Instead she went down the stairs. Once she was on the ground, the five of them spread out and laughed as they swayed, jumped, twirled, and moved. One song ended and another one started up. They kept going.

The third song that came on made Melissa squeal. "Do you all know the dance that goes with this one?" Everyone shook their heads no. "I am going to teach it. Logan, go hit pause for a minute."

He rushed over and started it back at the beginning and then hit pause, so it would be good to go. About that time, Nori and Jess returned carrying a few thermoses and a container of something. They put it all on one of the hay bales before joining the group.

"You are just in time. I am going to teach them a line dance," Melissa said.

"Which one?" asked Jess. "I know a few myself."

"It is an oldie, but goodie. The Boot Scootin' Boogie"

"I know that one, so I can help if you want."

"Thanks, Jess. Okay, everyone, line up. I will walk you through the steps and then we will run through it a couple of times and then dance with the music."

They lined up in a row of two and then three with Jess at the back for when they turned around.

"Alright everyone, we are going to grapevine to the right and on the fourth count clap. Then you are going to do the same to the left. Let's practice that." Once they ran through that a few times, Melissa continued with the next set of steps of kicking, clapping, and twisting. On and on they continued first with the instructions and then practiced until they made it completely around all four directions once. "Awesome work, everyone. Logan, go start the song again and we get to do it to the music. If you get lost, look at either myself or Jess. Pick it up where you drop it and let's boogie."

Logan hit play and then ran back to his spot in time to start. Eve quickly picked up the steps and worked her way through focusing on what she needed to do next and tuning out everyone else. By the end, they were moving along like a well-oiled machine. The song ended and they all laughed.

"I think I either need a break or a slow one," Eve said as she headed to the trailer. The next song to start was a slow, country ballad and so she turned back around. Abigail was right behind her and the two of them ran into each other. "Ooph. Sorry about that."

"It's okay. Are you alright?"

Eve rubbed her nose, "Yeah."

Abigail cringed, "I was going to ask you to dance, but that kind of ruined the moment."

"Nope, I have one more in me." When Eve turned everyone was paired up except Melissa. Eve dropped her voice. "Actually, do me a favor, go ask Melissa to a friendly dance and I will sit out. I can tell she likes to dance and I will recover."

"Are you sure?"

"Yes."

Before she could prepare for it, Abigail dropped a kiss to Eve's cheek and then turned back towards her friend. Eve strolled back to the trailer and eased up on the end of it and let her legs swing back and forth as she watched everyone. A voice from the other side startled her so bad she almost fell off.

"You didn't want to dance anymore?"

When Eve turned, Rebecca was standing there leaning against the trailer. "Nah, I am not used to so much interaction with people. I am more of a private person and could use a few minutes."

"Is that the only reason?" Rebecca seemed to be more perceptive than Eve would have thought.

"Plus, I thought it more important for Melissa to feel a part of everything right now."

"Ahh, yes. You are a good friend. I wanted to come check on you all and see how you were doing."

"You and your family are welcome to join us, of course. You all have been the best hosts. I feel bad that you have gone to so much work for us, though." Eve motioned at everything around her.

"It truly is our pleasure. I think Hunter and I will be out shortly, but my parents will stay inside and keep a listen out for Wendell. It will be his bedtime before long."

"He is really cute. I love his enthusiasm for things." Eve smiled remembering parts of dinner.

"Yeah. He is a sweetheart, but also exhausting. I wish I had his energy all day long." They both laughed and then Rebecca pushed back from the side of the trailer. "I will head back inside and see all of you shortly. Come on inside if you need the bathroom or anything else."

"Thanks."

With that, Rebecca turned back towards the house and mosied inside while Eve returned her attention back to the six people in the yard laughing and having fun. When the slow song ended, another faster-paced one started up and they were all dancing around again to it. Eve had a feeling that maybe all of them needed this time away from studying and working to relax and have fun. Of course, Eve had to remind herself that this trip wasn't just pleasure for her. She grabbed her backpack and pulled out her laptop before powering it on. She wanted to review what she wrote the last time so she could focus on the same points. After a couple more songs, they called it and came to collapse on the trailer.

"Man, I'm thirsty and tired!" Logan exclaimed.

Nori pointed to the two thermoses, "We brought hot chocolate out here, but I don't think that is going to help us right now."

"No, we need something to cool down and quench our thirst first. Hot chocolate will be good soon. I am going to go see if I can round us up some bottles of water or a jug and some plastic cups," Katherine said as she trudged towards the house.

Eve decided to have a little mercy on them, "I brought a couple of bottles of water if you all want to share them." Eve pulled out the water she had stashed in her backpack at the college.

Melissa grabbed two of the bottles, "You are our hero. This will help until Kat gets back. Logan you can down about half and then I will drink the rest. Nori, Jess, I assume you two are okay sharing a bottle."

"Yep. I am grateful. I know I still have some left over in the car, but that is too far to go."

Eve handed over one to Abigail, "Here you go. You can have some first. I am not as hot and in need of relief as much as the rest of you."

"You look pretty hot to me." Abigail's voice was all husky and deep. That alone made Eve melt some on the inside.

"Haha. Thank you, but not what I meant." Eve watched as Abigail twisted the cap off and then chugged down a good portion of the water before letting out a deep sigh of satisfaction. "That good, huh?"

"Well, there are better things out there to taste, but since I can't have the other right now, this will do," Abigail winked before hopping up on the end of the trailer next to Eve. "What are you doing?"

"I am looking at my notes from last time, or I was using my phone's flashlight."

"Very studious are you."

"Yes, I am, Master Yoda." They both laughed and then turned when Logan called out.

"Here comes my heroine to save me from this drought. Alas, she has brought company with her."

Melissa punched him lightly in the arm. "Are you sure you aren't a drama major because your performance is a little over the top?"

Logan wrapped his arm around Melissa's neck and then ruffled up her hair. "You take that back. My performance was top notch."

"Fine, fine. You are worthy of an Oscar," Melissa said. As soon as Logan released her and she had moved back a few feet, she added, "An Oscar the Grouch award."

Katherine had arrived by then and rolled her eyes as Rebecca and she set down a cooler of water. "You both are children. I swear Wendell behaves better than you two ."

Rebecca joined Katherine. "Hunter will be out in a minute. We decided to fill up the water cooler we use for ranching with ice water for you all so you could have plenty."

Nori sat upright as if she had remembered something. "Oh and Sarah sent Jess and me out with a container of cookies earlier when we came out. She figured we might want a snack at some point."

"That's my mother, always wanting to feed people. This is why having you all for dinner wasn't any big deal. She enjoys it."

Eve laid back and rested her head on one of the small pillows. This wasn't like a movie or something that had to begin at a specific time. She was the only one that was actually required to look up at the stars for research. Plus, she didn't even need for it to be peaceful for that. She enjoyed listening to the mild chaos around her as she focused on all the brilliant holes in the sky.

After a couple of minutes, someone laid down next to her and whispered, "How's it going?"

"Abby, hey. It is going well. I really enjoyed today. Not only what we did, but spending time with everyone. It wasn't about rushing to class or the library or trying to mash schedules for a movie or game time."

"Yes, it is nice to get away from the college and our jobs. Plus, I got to spend more quality time with you in a way that allows us to get to know one another on a different level."

Eve reached out with her left hand and found Abigail's right to clasp. Abigail rolled on her side and kissed Eve's shoulder. It felt like they were in their own little bubble for a moment and it was nice. Of course, with seven other people around them, it wasn't going to last long. In the meantime, Eve was going to enjoy every second of it.

"Tell me what you see out here that differs from the city for your assignment."

"First off, probably the biggest difference is that there are no city lights to hinder the view of the stars. Out here, you can see all the big bright stars, but you can also see lots of dimmer and smaller stars. The vast numbers just perplex me and I am in awe. Moments like this make me realize how small we are, both on this planet and in space."

"It definitely gives you pause to think about things, doesn't it?"

"Yes, it does. Plus, you can see some of the constellations easier or I like to make up my own. Some people look at the sky during the day and see shapes in the clouds, I do it at night with the stars."

"I used to do that as a child. When we were driving, I would look out the window and see big, puffy clouds. Those would turn into trees, animals, waves, or objects around the house. Sometimes I would watch them change as we drove and they would morph."

"Yeah, precisely. Except with stars, they don't change as often or quickly. Depending on the sky, you can see the same images each night."

Abby laid quiet next to Eve and then she propped herself up on her elbow. "I never thought about that. So, show me something tonight."

Laughing, Eve pointed, "First off, you have to actually be looking up."

"But, you are more beautiful to look at and I love observing you while you are in your element."

"Charmer." Eve pointed up and found a group of stars. "You know it is harder to point out something that is so small. I will have to show you with a telescope one day."

"Deal, but still, humor me. Please."

Eve couldn't resist and it gave her something to share and expand the moment. "Look at that star right there and then move over to the right and then up to the next one and connect the line. From there, trace your line down to that one and across." Eve continued outlining the image and then at the end she said, "When you get back to the starting point, you have a cut gem. It could be any kind you want it to be."

"Hmmm. Let me try and find something." Eve's heart melted a little that Abigail was taking an interest in something that was important to her and maybe not something that Abigail would have done otherwise. After a few minutes, Abigail pointed to a selection of stars over to the left of them. "Over there I see an elephant."

"An elephant, huh?"

"Yeah, you can see the wide body from the side and two of the legs on that side. Then there are two lines that go down representing part of the legs on the other side. Then there is an ear and a long trunk stretching up. This is fun."

Eve grinned next to her. "Let's find another. Also, are you going to name your elephant?"

"His name is Oliver."

"Why Oliver?"

Abigail shrugged, "I don't know. Just something that came to me."

After they each pointed out something else, they heard a voice coming from above them, "Hey, girls. What are you two doing?"

Eve spoke up louder so she could answer Nori. "We are finding objects in the stars."

"Oh that sounds like fun. We want to join in," exclaimed Nori.

Eve felt the trailer shift as footsteps crossed the length of it. "Come on. There is lots of open space above and down here." Eve tilted her head back and saw that Nori and Melissa had settled down and stretched out with their heads near Eve and Abigail's. "Hiya."

"Hey there. Are we taking turns or just all going at once?" Nori asked from inches away.

Eve answered, but her eyes were hurting from trying to focus on her friends in a weird position. "We were taking turns, but whatever works is good for me."

Melissa asked from beside Nori, "Who's turn is it first?"

"You can go, Mel," Abigail said. "Eve and I have gone a couple of times. We can go around. Where is Jess, Nori?"

"I'm here. Sitting next to Nori reclined back against the hay."

"Okay, let me see. Oh, I found a banana," Melissa squealed as she pointed up.

Nori laughed and asked, "Is it next to a peach? Because then we would know where your mind was at."

"In the gutter," Both Abigail and Nori replied at the same time before bursting into laughter.

"Haha. No it isn't. Although that isn't a bad idea. Maybe I can make one appear."

"A banana or a peach?"

"The peach in the stars; oh wait, maybe both."

Once everyone calmed down from laughing, Nori proclaimed, "It is my turn." She took her time all the while humming. Eve was about to hurry her friend along when she finally stopped and went, "Got it." Nori waved her hand up above as if magic was to appear. "I see a house next to a lake with a mountain in the background."

Eve turned her head one way and another, but still never saw it. Then again, it really was hard for two people to see the exact same thing so far away and with so many dots. Plus, even psychology proved that the same two people looking at the exact same set of dots will see two different things. One of the things that made humanity great was the imagination and the way the brain worked.

"I don't see it," Melissa vocalized the same thought out loud.

"You don't have to. I would wager none of us really see the same precise thing. Even if you saw a mountain and house, it might not be the same mountain and house as I see. Jess, babe, it is your turn."

Jess jumped into the game with both feet, uh eyes. "I see a baby cradle. The old-fashioned ones."

Eve asked, "You been thinking about babies, Jess?"

At the same time Eve asked her question, Nori added, "I bet it is made out of wood. You should see the pieces Jess has made."

"I have only been thinking about babies because someone asked me if I could make a small cradle for a child to use with her dolls."

"Told you," Nori said. "Eve, it is your turn."

They went around and around and eventually, the other four joined them and they were one massive group. At some point, they all stopped for some fresh hot chocolate and cookies and all sat up against the hay to enjoy their snack as they cuddled under blankets.

When they were done, Eve announced, "I have everything I need for my assignment whenever you all are ready. I figured it was about time for all of us to get going since we have a little drive to get back to the college."

Melissa seconded the notion and they all helped to gather everything up. Rebecca showed them where to drop the blankets in the house and then everyone hugged each other while good-byes were exchanged. Within fifteen minutes, everyone was loaded up in the car and they were pulling out and pointing back towards the school.

Chapter 16

ABIGAIL

Monday morning dawned early and Abigail wanted to sleep in. However, she knew better and had to get going. If she missed anything today and Eve found out, her girl would blame herself and the excursion the previous day. So, Abigail gathered up her clothes and went into the bathroom to shower and dress for the day.

When she got out of the shower, she had a text message on her phone. It was from Eve.

> E: Good morning. I wanted to say again how much fun I had with you yesterday and how much it meant to me. I hope you aren't dragging too much. I feel like I need extra strength caffeine since I stayed up for a while last night writing on my assignment. Have a great day in class and talk soon. 😊

Abigail smiled even as her hair dripped water onto the towel slung around her neck. She sent a quick reply.

> A: Good morning. ❤️ Have a great day yourself. I will swing by the library tonight if I don't talk to

YOU BEFORE THEN.

After her afternoon class, Abigail went by the cafeteria to get a late lunch and then headed over to the library. She didn't want to bother Eve while she worked, but she was hoping to catch her on a break at some point during the night. There were two tests that week that she needed to study for, so she had more than enough to keep her occupied for the evening. She set up camp in her favorite area of the library. Diving into studying, time passed by quickly. When Abigail looked at the time, she couldn't believe that it had been two hours since she moved. She stood and stretched in an attempt to get the blood moving in her body and to keep her body nimble and not sore.

As she was standing up from bending over, there was a body standing in front of her. She almost jumped, but prevented herself from doing that. There stood Eve with a cart full of books smirking.

"Nice view."

"Eve, you scared me."

"I bet. I have walked by here a few times and each time you were engrossed in what you were working on. With that kind of focus, I wasn't going to bother you. I had decided if you were still in the same position as before, I was going to demand that you get up and move for a few minutes. But, it looks like you took care of that yourself."

"Yeah. I have a chem test I am studying for. Do you have a break coming up?"

"I can take a few minutes to sit."

They both sat down and Abigail realized the one disadvantage to her corner. "There should be a couch over here. That way we could actually sit next to each other."

"Yeah, but this way you and your baggy shirt can tease me about what I had a glimpse of while you were bent over."

Abigail could feel her face heating up and that wasn't like her. She looked down at what she was wearing and then thought about her previous position. Taking back control of her thoughts and actions, she leaned over closer to Eve and asked, "Did you see anything you liked?"

That, of course, caused the blushing to transfer from Abigail to Eve. "Maybe. Plus, I was teasing you. I didn't really see anything. You are wearing a tank top underneath your sweater."

"Well, darn. Guess next time, I will have to keep it off to try and tempt you into some naughty thoughts."

"Who says I don't already have them?" Eve said. She sighed and stood up. "Guess I better go file more books away."

Abigail patted Eve's butt as she walked by, "Nice pants. I bet they would look better off of you, though."

Eve's eyes widened and she coughed as she said, "Behave. Get back to your chemistry."

As Eve kept walking, Abigail said, "Trust me, there was plenty of chemistry going on." She beamed as Eve misstepped and then shook her head. However, Abigail did what she needed, and turned back to work on studying for her exam.

Abigail ended up hanging out until Eve got off work and walking back to the dorms with her. When they reached the main doors, Eve turned towards Abigail, "You don't need to climb those stairs just to have to turn around and come back down. I appreciate the company on the walk, though. However, who is going to make sure you get home safely?"

"I will be fine. It isn't much farther. You want me to come up and hang out for a bit?" Abigail leaned in closer to Eve.

"I would love to relax and chill, but I need to get some homework done and will not make good company."

"You are such a responsible woman." Abigail gave Eve a quick kiss on the cheek. "I will take my broken heart back to my room and mend it."

Eve rolled her eyes, "Go on and text me so I know you made it. I will see you in the morning for breakfast."

Abigail stepped back and waved. The temptation to do more than press a chaste kiss to Eve's cheek was there, but Abigail was proceeding with some caution. She didn't want to rush Eve for more. However, now that they were together, she needed to find some time for them to go out so she could get in a bit more makeout time or some one on one study time in Eve's room would work.

She thought about that all the way back to her room and by the time she arrived she was in desperate need for a cold shower. Ever since that first day, Eve unintentionally found a way to burrow underneath Abigail's skin and settle in. It seemed like she had known Eve forever instead of a couple of months. Before she hopped into the shower, she sent Eve a text letting her know she arrived safely back.

The next morning, Abigail arrived at the breakfast table exhausted and in need of some major caffeine. All night she tossed and turned and couldn't settle down to sleep. She wasn't sure why she had a hard time sleeping as she felt confident in her knowledge for the test she prepared for. No matter, she grabbed a large cup of coffee and a muffin and collapsed into one of the chairs before letting her head drop onto the table.

"Bad night of sleep?" Nori asked.

"Yes. Can you all wake me before class if I fall asleep."

"What kept you up? Was Alex too loud? Do I need to give her a piece of my mind?" asked Melissa.

"I am sure that isn't all you want to give her," Katherine smarted off. Abigail, long ago, figured out that Melissa had a crush on Alex even if her friend didn't want to admit it. Apparently, she wasn't the only one to have reached that conclusion.

"Shut it," was the only reply that Melissa came back with.

Abigail wanted to smile and laugh, she really did, but that simple act would have taken up too much energy and she had to conserve what she had left. She was wondering where her fair beauty was when the woman appeared in her sights. She looked like she was refreshed and bubbling with energy.

Eve sat down next to Abigail and said, "I knew I shouldn't have let you go back to your room alone. A zombie or alien snatched you up along the path and replaced your normal self with this catatonic bag of flesh. You need to eat something." Abigail pointed at the muffin and Eve shook her head no. "Come on, woman. That is not going to help you. We have a class that takes energy this morning. You can't sign with your head on the table. Here. Eat." Eve sat half of her banana in front of Abigail along with some scrambled eggs and cheese. "Don't make me have to threaten you. Why didn't you sleep last night? Did something happen after you texted me or did you end up staying up far too late studying? You know that is my thing, not yours."

Abigail patted Eve's leg that was within easy reach. "You are chatty this morning."

"I was about to comment on the same thing. Not that it is a bad thing," Nori hastened to add when Eve's face started to fall. "I just meant you are usually the quieter one of the group."

"Well, I stayed up too late last night studying so I might be a little sleep deprived. Plus, I have already had two cups of coffee this morning. However, mine is manifesting itself in chatty hyper energy and not that." Eve pointed at Abigail and Abigail wasn't sure how she felt about being referred to as 'that.'

Logan stroked Abigail's head, "Poor Abby, she is getting picked on by everyone today." He dropped his voice down into a form of baby talk and continued, "Want me to beat everyone up for you and tell them to stop being bad?"

Abigail flipped her head over to glare up at Logan before bracing both hands on the table and shoving herself to sit more upright in her chair. "No. I can take care of my own dirty work. Hopefully this coffee will help." She took a long swig that turned into more of a chug of the cooled liquid. She downed over half of it in one drink. Everyone sat there staring at her, some of them with forks of food part-way to their mouths. "What? I seem to be everyone's entertainment this morning." She grabbed the half of a banana and took a big bite to give her mouth something to do so it didn't spurt grumpiness at everyone.

"Was that still hot?" Eve asked in amazement.

"No. I mean it was warm, but it wasn't burning hot. Go back to eating or I am going to take my muffin and coffee and leave. You all are making me feel like a baboon scratching his butt at the zoo. Everyone has to stop and observe."

"I never understood the fascination with watching animals scratch themselves," Eve said.

Logan chuckled, "Oh I love when you catch them doing something more naughty." Katherine elbowed him in the side for that comment.

"Ouch. That hurt. You will have to kiss it better later."

"Men! Fine, I will kiss your boo boo better tonight when we are back home."

"Darn straight."

Katherine raised her eyebrows and pointed her fork at Logan, "Watch it or else you will be having another injury that won't be kissed better."

"Yes, dear." He leaned over and gave her a big, loud kiss on the side of cheek.

Giggling, Eve said, "I bet he doesn't stay in trouble very long does he?"

Katherine ran her fingers through Logan's hair, "No, he learned long ago how to charm himself out of trouble."

They all laughed, including Abigail. Taking a page from Logan's book, Abigail lifted up Eve's hand and kissed the top of it before eating the eggs that Eve had slid in front of her. After that she ate her muffin. By the end and after the remainder of her coffee she was starting to feel more human. It helped that everyone left her alone while they discussed the fact that in the next few weeks they all had midterms or regular exams. Soon, everyone was cleaning up their mess and heading off in different directions. Abigail and Eve left for their ASL class.

"Hey, Eve, I need to detour and grab another cup of coffee."

"Sounds good to me. I could probably use another as well. Although after that, I better stay with water or I am going to be even more jittery today."

When they got to the front of the line, Abigail paid for both of their drinks.

"Thanks, Abby."

"My pleasure. Hopefully, we both sleep better tonight."

"Cheers to that." They clinked the paper cups together as they strolled to class.

In class they broke off into groups of three and practiced being at a restaurant ordering different things from a menu. They had been learning food signs lately and this would give them an opportunity to practice. One person would be the server and the other two would be the guests. Abigail, Eve, and their other table-mate, Donald, were in a group together. Abigail figured that out of the three of them Eve had the best practice at being a server since that was one of her jobs. Abigail mostly stuck with acting as a host. So, as such, Eve was nominated to be the server first.

Eve turned and signed, "Hello. I'm your server. My name is Eve. Welcome to Michelangelo's. What would you like to drink?"

Donald motioned for Abigail to go first, so she signed, "Sweet tea, please."

Eve and Abigail turned towards Donald and he smiled before signing the word for beer.

Eve didn't miss a beat, she just asked to see his ID. He actually pulled it out and showed Eve his license. He indeed was twenty-one years old last week.

"Thank you and happy birthday," Eve handed his license back and then paused letting them choose what to eat. "Here is your tea and beer. Do you know what you want to eat?"

This time Abigail looked up and signed, "Do you have a recommendation?" She had to refrain from laughing when Eve rolled her eyes.

"I like the shrimp pasta or the hamburger with blue cheese."

"The shrimp pasta looked good. I will take that. Thank you." Abigail winked up at Eve and saw it made her blush a little.

Donald placed his order saying, "I would like a steak, baked potato, and green beans."

"How would you like the steak cooked?"

Donald fingered spelled medium.

"I will place these orders."

Once that was done, they all switched roles and practiced different food and drinks each time until the session was concluded. The class came back together and discussed what was hard or easy about the practice session. Next, the professor asked them all to think about what to do if they didn't have a server that signed and shared their responses. That led to their assignment for the week.

"Each of you needs to go out to eat somewhere, it could be fast food or a restaurant and pretend to be deaf. No talking out loud. If you want to put earplugs in to help with this, then you can. You can't hear the other person talk, either. If you have the capability to read lips, this is acceptable. Then write up a brief essay on your experiences. This will be due in one week. Okay, class dismissed. See you next time."

Eve and Abigail left class and naturally fell into step and headed towards the library as was their custom for the early afternoon post class. As they strolled, Abigail brought up their assignment that was issued. "Eve, I know it might be a little unorthodox, but what do you think about us going out to eat for our assignment and making it a date? This way we get to enjoy one another's time while accomplishing something for class."

"I think it sounds good. Would you prefer to do something early on Saturday or Sunday evening? I am picking up a lunch shift on Sunday afternoon and won't be done until probably three."

"If we do Sunday evening and you take the entire night off, would that interfere with your studying?" Abigail asked as she began to think up a plan.

"No. I will work hard to get a lot of it done Friday and Saturday before work."

"How about I come and get you at 5pm from your dorm. Then we can go out to dinner and then maybe to a movie in a theater. I haven't been since before the semester started. It will be fun and cozy."

"Five sounds good to me. It will give me time to get back, take a shower, and dress. This way you aren't taking a smelly person out all night."

"Somehow I imagine you would still be the best smelling and most beautiful woman around." Abigail winked and held open the library door as Eve walked in laughing.

"Laying the charm talk on thicker today, I see."

They made their way across the first floor and Abigail watched as Eve waved at a few people. It was good to see her open up more and feel more relaxed and comfortable than when she first arrived at campus. They settled into their seats and opened their computers up to do work.

Abigail enjoyed the easy routine they had gotten into on Tuesdays and somehow knowing that someone she cared about was sitting next to her studying helped make the topic more interesting. However, she still wanted to cram for the exam she was due to take. While she knew she was prepared and it wasn't a last minute thing, she always felt like there was something she was forgetting or wasn't remembering correctly. It was definitely a flaw of hers. Apparently, her agitation was showing because Eve spoke up from next to her.

"What gives? You have sighed like seven times in the last ten minutes?"

"Sorry. It is this test. I am over stressing about it."

"Do you have any kind of questions or note-cards? I can quiz you on what you need to know and maybe that will help."

"What about your own work?"

"Everything I am doing right now can wait until later. Let me help you."

"If you insist."

"It is either that, or I am going to gag you with a dirty sock to keep you from sounding like you would rather climb a cactus naked than sit next to me."

Abigail laughed at the ridiculous idea. "I didn't sound that bad."

"You weren't the one listening to you." Eve took the notes that Abigail handed over and scanned through them before beginning to ask her questions.

By the time they made their way through the group of questions, of which Abigail only messed up a couple of them, it was time for each of them to leave for their next class. Outside they separated and went in two different directions.

Chapter 17

EVE

By Sunday afternoon, Eve was simultaneously looking forward to her date with Abigail and wanting to call it off to veg in her room. She was exhausted from working all weekend. Friday and Saturday night at Michelangelo's was busy per usual; however, normally Sunday afternoons were a little slower. Not today, though. Oh no! Today, she ended up working a lunch shift because there were two parties scheduled in the restaurant. The first was a birthday party celebration for a group of twenty-three people. The reservation was for 11am, but of course the entire party didn't finish arriving until closer to eleven-thirty.

After they all left, she had to quickly clean up and prepare for an engagement party. Another waitress was supposed to work that party, but ended up calling out sick which left Eve working the second event. That one was only for sixteen people. One would think less people would be easier than the first group. Not a chance. It was so much worse. The alcohol flowed freely amongst them. Plus, they were all very demanding and picky about every little item. Eve wouldn't finish fetching something for a couple of people before another set of people needed something else. Her feet were killing her and she was exhausted.

She already had texted Abigail to change their date time to 6pm because she got home later than she planned and she desperately needed a hot shower. However, despite the delay in time and the rushed preparation, she was ready to go on time in a mid-thigh length dress and a pair of flats. Not even Abigail being taller than her was getting her in heels that night. Her stomach was growling and she hoped that it didn't embarrass her and growl too loudly before they had a chance to eat.

Eve waited downstairs in the community room for Abigail's text, letting her know she had pulled up out front. As soon as she received the message, she waved bye to a few people and went in search of her date. Abigail was standing outside of the passenger side door and as Eve approached, her girl opened the door and held out her hand. "Milady."

"Why thank you, kind ma'am." Eve grinned as Abigail tried to hold together her expression at being called a ma'am. "Okay, how about, kind miss? Because you aren't a kind sir unless you are hiding something from me."

"No, no. I am all woman." Abigail leaned into the car and gave Eve a quick kiss. "As I will show you soon enough. But, for now, we behave."

"Yes, kind woman." Eve made sure to emphasize the last word.

"Sassy tonight, I see." The door shut, cutting off Eve's laughter from Abigail. She was glad she didn't cancel. When Abigail had circled around the car, opened her own door, and slid in, she asked Eve, "So, long day at work?"

"Yes. But, I don't want to bore you with my drama. Tell me, where are we going? You didn't ask me what I wanted to eat."

Abigail started the car and pulled out of the parking lot. "Since we don't have as much time, I was thinking maybe over to the Greek restaurant by the theater. What do you think about that?"

"Sounds good to me. I have a question, though. Are we both going to pretend to be deaf or only one of us?"

"Since we both have to do the assignment, I was thinking both of us would be," Abigail said. "But, if you want to do dinner now and then dessert after the movie or breakfast in the morning, we can take turns and add that part into our paper, too."

"Here is something I just thought of. What if our server or someone else there is fluent in sign language? We don't know enough to fake our way through that conversation." Now that Eve had the thought, it was rolling around in her head.

"True. I hadn't thought of that. Maybe at that point, we just reveal our assignment and go from there."

Letting out a sigh, Eve prayed that scenario wasn't the one that they encountered. "How about this time, I am the one who doesn't hear. I don't know if I will be able to stand to wait until later and have this hanging over my head. At least if something goes awry you can go out alone or with one of the others tomorrow night. I have to work."

"Deal. Although, you have nothing to worry about. I am actually going to let you take the lead if you want."

When they pulled up to the restaurant, it didn't look too busy. Eve was busy rubbing her thumb along her finger in a nervous fidgeting gesture. Abigail got out and walked around the car in an effort to be a good date Eve was sure. However, before Abigail was in front of the car, Eve had opened her own door and stood up. She looked at Abigail and signed. "Ready." Then she shoved a pair of ear plugs into her ears.

Abigail extended her arm and they walked into the restaurant holding hands until they got to the hostess stand. Eve saw the hostess move her mouth and was able to make out the words hello and how many. Holding up two fingers, Eve smiled at the woman. Eve wasn't sure what the lady said next because she had turned, but she had menus in her hands and was walking, so the two of them followed behind. When they sat down at the table, Eve noticed that Abigail wasn't smiling any longer and said something towards the hostess. Eve wasn't sure what was happening, but smiled and tilted her head down before signing "Thanks."

As soon as the lady went away, Eve signed, "What's wrong?"

"Rude woman."

"This is hard."

"Here comes the server."

Eve was surprised by the number of phrases they actually knew and were able to communicate. Eve had a pad of paper and pen in her purse. Plus, they had their phones out that allowed them to communicate more easily with longer conversations.

The server walked up and greeted them both. Eve read her name tag as Emily and decided to test the waters. She signed, "Can I have water, please?"

The girl was surprised, but her smile became bigger and then she started signing a little herself. "Hi. I'm Emily. I know a little ASL." Well, at least the girl wasn't fluent in it. "I am happy to be your..." She paused and then fingerspelled. "Waitress."

Eve grinned and showed her the sign for the word.

She saw the girl say, "This is exciting." Abigail chuckled a little and Eve saw Emily's cheeks pinken before muttering something. The two of them exchanged a few words and Eve caught some of them. She could read lips somewhat, but she wasn't a professional. The ear plugs were helping to mask most of the words, but she still had to continue to remind herself that she couldn't hear anything and to tune everything out. Deciding to look at the menu, she zoned out. After all, it wasn't important for her to stare and wait for someone to talk to her.

She looked up when Abigail tapped her menu. "You okay?" Abigail asked.

Nodding her head and smiling, Eve motioned at the menu before signing, "I don't know what I want to eat. You?"

"I think I'm getting the moussaka." Abigail had to fingerspell the name of the dish and it took Eve twice of her spelling it to finally understand what dish she indicated.

"Sounds good." Eve was about to point to what she was thinking of when Emily returned with their drinks. "Thank you."

"You are welcome." Emily spoke and signed at the same time. She seemed really respectful and Eve appreciated that. As an assignment, she had different points of view to write about with this dinner out. She looked from one to the other and then signed a few words. "Know what you want to eat or need more time?"

Deciding to just get what she was thinking about, she pointed to the dish on the menu that was a filo pastry filled with beef, carrots, peas, and mushrooms. Emily nodded and wrote it down. Then she turned to Abigail who did, indeed, order the moussaka. Once the food was ordered, Abigail picked up her phone and waved it at Eve. Waiting a second, she then saw a text come through.

A: GLAD OUR SERVER IS NICE. WANT TO SPLIT PART OF OUR DINNERS WITH EACH OTHER? I DIDN'T WANT TO TRY AND FIGURE OUT HOW TO SIGN ANY OF THAT.

E: DON'T BLAME YOU AND I TOO AM HAPPY SHE IS NICE. SOUNDS GREAT ON THE FOOD. THINK THIS IS WEIRD THAT WE ARE BOTH JUST TYPING AWAY ON OUR PHONE TO EACH OTHER WHILE SITTING AT THE TABLE TOGETHER?

A: IT IS EITHER THAT, WE BOTH STUMBLE THROUGH TRYING TO SIGN THE FEW WORDS WE KNOW, OR WE WRITE WITH PEN AND PAPER.

E: TEXTING IT IS. WHAT TIME DOES THE MOVIE START?

A: 7:50. WE HAVE PLENTY OF TIME AND OUR TICKETS ARE ALREADY BOUGHT ON THE APP. SO, EVEN IF WE ARE A FEW MINUTES LATE, WE HAVE OUR SEATS.

E: AT LEAST THERE I WILL BE QUIET BECAUSE THE MOVIE IS PLAYING AND NOT FOR AN ASSIGNMENT.

A: TRUE. BET YOU WILL BE READY TO EXPLODE AFTER WE LEAVE HERE.

E: IT ISN'T TOO BAD NOT TALKING. I NEVER WAS A BIG TALKER. IT IS THE NOT HEARING SIDE OF THINGS OR THE PRETENDING TO NOT HEAR. EVEN THOUGH I CAN STILL HEAR SOME THINGS WITH THE EAR PLUGS IN, THE NOISE IS CONSIDERABLY LESSENED.

A: WE ARE BLESSED INDEED.

The two of them continued texting back and forth until their food arrived and then exchanged a few words while enjoying their dinner. After they had paid, Eve waited until they were in the car and heading over to the theater before pulling out her ear plugs. "Wow. I feel like everything is in surround sound now."

Being silly, Abigail lowered her voice and asked, "Does this mean you want me to speak quietly?"

"Not at all. We are going from a quiet dinner to a loud movie theater. I need some acclimation and you are it."

"I didn't think of that. Do we need to skip the movie?" Abigail reached out and held Eve's hand.

Eve squeezed Abigail's hand. "Nope, I am adjusting back rather quickly. Plus, I am looking forward to this. It is a nice break from the constant assignments and working."

They were at the theater in minutes and made it to their seats with about three minutes until the movie started. The theater was about half full and no one was sitting immediately on either side of the two girls. They lifted the arms between them and reclined backwards until their feet were raised up. Since they had just finished eating, they skipped the concession stand and snacks. The theater went dark and Abigail tugged Eve closer and snuck her arm around her. Eve cuddled next to her beautiful date and enjoyed the movie from her cozy spot.

After the movie, it was about ten-thirty, so they opted to go back to the campus so they could both get a good night's sleep. When Abigail stopped in front of the dorm, she tried to park and walk Eve to her room, but Eve wasn't having it.

"There isn't any reason to, Abby. Message me when you get back."

Abigail growled a little and then pulled Eve into a big hug. "Fine. You win." Then before Eve could turn to open the car door, Abigail tugged her closer and kissed her slow and passionately. She took her time and had the woman tried to plead her case at that moment, Eve would have given in and demanded that Abigail just stay over for the night. However, that wasn't the wisest of choices, so when the kiss ended, Eve went inside the dorm and up to her room alone, thinking about the next time.

CHAPTER 18

EVE

"You need to ask for the night off so we can all go together and have fun," Nori whined.

Eve wasn't sure if she wanted to or could even take off the time. Nori found a place where there was a huge bingo night that was played every Monday and demanded that they all go to celebrate passing their midterms. Of course, Eve had been putting her friend off for weeks now, saying she had to work or study. However, Nori wasn't taking the hint and instead, she was becoming more persistent. Finally, to silence her, Eve gave in.

"Fine. I will send an email or go by later and ask since I don't return back to work until Monday. But, I can't promise it will be this next Monday since it is only a couple of days' notice."

"I will settle for that. What is one more week after the months you have tortured me?"

Everyone laughed and Katherine piped up, "Dramatic much."

"I am restless. Plus, the cash prizes per game isn't too bad, either," informed Nori.

This had Eve's interest piqued. "Like how much are we talking?"

"Everything is over a hundred dollars a game and a couple of them are five hundred or higher."

"Yeah, but how many people are playing and what are the chances of any of us actually winning a game?" asked Abby.

"It depends on the night, but I heard this bingo hall is rather large and people take food and drinks inside. So, we could grab some pizzas and sodas and make it a fun time. Plus with six of us, our chances go up as we have more opportunities to play. What do you think?"

"I'm in!" chimed in Melissa. "Sounds like a riot to me."

"Count Logan and I in."

"Oh Logan, if you want to invite some of the guys, too, feel free. Any of you can add people to this bingo party. The more the merrier!" Nori's voice rose as her excitement escalated.

Eve looked over at Abigail and mouthed, "wow" out of sight of Nori. However, Melissa saw her and started laughing. Knowing her friend would want to know what was funny, Eve cut her off before she even had a chance to ask by introducing the one subject that was known to make Nori forget about everything around her. "Hey, Nori, how is Jess doing?"

"She is good. Even talking about coming down soon. Thinking maybe I can talk her into coming down for our bingo night. Oh and I should invite Ian. That boy hasn't been here this semester and he is long overdue."

"I would love to meet Ian in person," Eve said, knowing it was true. Sometimes when Nori and she were studying he would call and the two of them together was hilarious. It made her wonder what it would be like to have a friend that long. It made her sad at times when she thought of it, but then she reminded herself that she had friends and a girlfriend now. Or at least she had friends as long as she had a girlfriend. If they broke up, she would be alone again because all of her friends were closer with Abigail. Plus, she wouldn't ever make them choose between the two of them.

She must have slipped into her own rambling mind because Abigail nudged her and in a quiet voice asked, "Are you okay? You look suddenly sad."

Eve attempted to put on a smile and reassure Abigail, "Yeah. I'm fine. Just thinking about something, but it isn't anything important."

"Are you sure? Your happiness is important to me." Abigail leaned over and kissed the side of Eve's head.

Of course, that gesture made Eve want to cry after what her brain had been thinking, so she did what she was good at. She escaped. "Hey, guys. I need to go to class. I will talk to you later." Was that a wobble Eve heard in her voice? It didn't matter, she needed to bolt. Swinging her backpack on her shoulder, she gathered up her barely-eaten lunch and tossed it into the trash before exiting and arrowing straight for her Trig class.

On Thursday, the group usually met for breakfast, but today it so happened that they could meet for lunch. Now Eve was happy she had classes for the next six hours so she didn't have to worry about ignoring anyone as she had a legit reason as to not message anyone back. She imagined back before cell phones, it was a lot easier to avoid people when one didn't want to explain how one was feeling or why all of a sudden the realization of how fragile the world was pieced together fractured one's soul into shards. Guess she was being the overly dramatic one now instead of Nori. Rationally, Eve understood she was getting hurt and offended by something that hadn't happened yet nor was there any indication of it ever occurring. Her heart wasn't listening to that logic and instead arrived to class twenty minutes early and to an empty room.

She took her normal seat and pulled up the notes from the last session. Within a few minutes, a few other students trickled in and before long, Peyton was standing in front of the class lecturing on the topic of the day. Everything slid away as she focused on what was happening in the class around her. Once it was concluded, she hightailed it over to the science building for her astronomy class. At the beginning of the semester she wasn't sure if she wanted to pursue Astronomy, but Professor LeForge really made the class interesting and she thought she might stay on this particular path. It wasn't until class started that she remembered they had a lab of sorts after the lecture. With that, she wouldn't be back to her room until close to midnight.

Once Eve made it back to her dorm room, she was done. Exhausted. Wiped Out. At least she could sleep later in the morning. She dropped her bag to the floor and forced herself to go down to the bathroom to brush her teeth and wash her face. It was only by habitual motions that she managed to complete the tasks. However, that was as far as she went. She didn't take a shower nor did she change into pajamas, but rather just stripped down and grabbed a t-shirt. She didn't care how much of her body it covered because she lived alone in her dorm room right now. There was no one there to look or care. Her eyes closed as sleep claimed her within a couple of minutes of pulling the blanket over her.

Eve came awake to the sound of knocking on her door. She rolled over and slapped the pillow over her head to tune out the sound, but it didn't work. There was silence for a few moments and then the knocking resumed, but this time, it sounded like fists meeting the door rather than mere knocking. Throwing her legs over the side of the bed, she got up and marched to see who was interrupting her sleep and why.

Flinging open the door, Eve forgot her state of undress in her annoyance until the person on the other side paused and dropped her gaze first downward and then quickly back up. When Eve looked down at herself, she turned around and went to find the first pair of bottoms she saw that wasn't jeans. It just happened to be a pair of gray sweatpants and that was fine with her. She left the door open allowing her visitor to either retreat or come in. There was a quiet click of the door shutting and then the sound of the desk chair being pulled out. Guess Abigail chose to come on in then. Eve, however, wasn't going to be the first to speak. Nope. Rather she sat on her bed and scooted up against the wall and sat with her legs criss-crossed and waited. She didn't have long to wait, though.

"You always answer your door looking like that?" Abigail asked. When Eve raised her eyebrows and went to say something, Abigail shook her head and kept on speaking. "Ignore that. I know better. It shocked me. I apologize for the insinuation of the question. I think that picture will be firmly one I remember for a long time to come."

Despite Eve's tiredness and annoyance, she gave Abigail a half smile. "What was with all the banging? I am surprised half of the floor didn't wake up and flog you alive."

"I was worried about you. After you left lunch yesterday, none of us heard from you despite several messages. Usually even if it is late, you will reply back. When I still didn't have anything this morning, I came over to check on you. I thought maybe you had gotten sick again or someone bopped you over the head after your last class."

"I am fine. I haven't even looked at my phone after I left. It was a busy second half of the day. When I got back here last night, I passed out immediately and didn't wake until you banged on the door."

"Oh."

Eve nodded and then knowing she was being weird and kind of rude without any cause, gave more of an explanation. "I appreciate the concern. Sorry I worried you and the others. When I got to my astronomy class I remembered we were scheduled to use some telescopes last night for an assignment. I didn't get back until late."

"It's fine. I mean, Nori might say otherwise, but you aren't required to report on every movement you make. We aren't your parents, we are your friends."

"I know. And that friendship means a lot to me."

Eve watched as Abigail scooted closer to the bed and leaned in to rest her arms on those long legs of hers before speaking. "Is there anything wrong? I know I asked yesterday and you said it wasn't important. But, I don't believe you. You know you can talk to me about anything right? Big or small."

Eve nodded and knew she couldn't share her irrational thoughts and worries. "I promise everything will be good."

"Now that I woke you up early, do you want to go get some breakfast?"

Breakfast sounded good, but honestly, she didn't want to take the effort to get up and get around. Eve opened her mouth to reply, but Abigail cut her off.

"Actually, forget that idea. I have a better one." Abigail sat straight up, "I will go get breakfast and bring it back to you. Then you can have breakfast in bed and we will lounge while watching a movie. How does that sound?"

"I am amenable to that, but I can't promise I won't fall back to sleep."

Abigail shrugged, “Maybe I will fall asleep, too. Who knows?” Abigail stood up and stretched. “Anything in particular you want?”

“Pancakes.”

“Then I better make sure to rush back so they will still be warm for you.”

Eve watched as Abigail left after blowing her a kiss. Then she slid back down to the bed and closed her eyes. A nice little nap until Abigail returned would be heaven.

ABIGAIL

As she closed the door to Eve’s room, Abigail thought back over the last twenty-four hours and had no idea what happened to cause Eve to close herself off from Abigail and the rest of the gang. However, the fact was there that something was wrong and off. Hopefully breakfast and hanging out would help whatever was resting heavy on Eve’s mind.

Since Eve requested pancakes, Abigail decided to go to a nearby diner instead of just grabbing something from campus. She drove a few miles away and ordered when she arrived. Knowing that they both needed more than just pancakes, Abigail ordered a stack of buttermilk pancakes, a stack of banana nut pancakes, a veggie omelet, a side of bacon and ham, and some hash browns. She might be a little hungry, and they could warm up leftovers.

While she waited for the pancakes, she sent a text off to Nori.

Abigail: Morning. I went by Eve’s room and woke her up. She is alive.

Nori: Uh oh. Are you alive after waking her and why did you go by so early?

A: Because I was worried and I couldn’t wait in case she was sick or something.

N: You have it bad, but don’t smother her. She will run. Speaking of which, did you find out if something was wrong?

A: She said there isn’t, but I can tell there is.

N: Give her some space.

A: Well...
N: Let me guess, you made an offer she couldn't refuse so you can stay by her side and see if she opens up.

A: Maybe. But, honestly my only goal is to hang out. I am giving her space with the emotional stuff. Just getting pancakes and vegging in her room. I won't bring anything up the rest of the day.

N: Don't make me hit you with a rolling pin for hurting our girl.

A: Never. Do you even have a rolling pin?

N: Not the point. I can find something.

A: No doubt. Okay. Food is here. Text later. Love ya.

N: 🩶

Abigail grabbed the bags with the food in it and headed back to the dorms. This time when she got to Eve's room, she knocked quietly and more normal-like. When there was no answer, Abigail had a moment of wonder if maybe Eve decided to agree to the food and movie simply to get rid of Abigail, but then she realized that Eve wouldn't do that. She twisted the doorknob and found it was unlocked so she eased it open with caution. She found her girlfriend curled up on the bed asleep. She would leave her alone and let her sleep, but while the food was hot, she wanted Eve to be able to taste it.

Setting the food down on the desk, Abigail crossed over and sat down on the edge of the bed and whispered as she gently shook Eve awake. "Eve, hun, you want to wake up and eat your pancakes? I have warm syrup to go with them."

Eve muttered something unintelligible and rolled over, melding along Abigail's leg and hip.

"Hey, babe. Wake up for a bit to eat."

This time Eve must have roused from her sleep a bit more because she sat up and looked around. When her eyes settled on the sacks, she smiled. "Pancakes."

Abigail laughed and went to unload everything. "Yep. I wasn't sure what kind so we have plain and banana nut. If you are interested in both, we can split them. Plus, we have other stuff as well. Full breakfast for you."

"You didn't have to get all the extra stuff."

"I wanted to. Now, what would you like?"

Eve yawned, "A little bit of everything."

"Coming right up." Abigail shifted food around until she had a container with some of each of the food in it before handing it over to Eve. Then she fixed her own plate and settled in on the bed next to Eve where she had already logged into her streaming service and pulled up the menu. They ended up choosing a competition show to start watching together as they dug into their food.

Four hours later, the food was demolished, they had binged four episodes and had to forcefully stop what they were watching. Neither of them fell back to sleep. "Do you have any favorites to win?" Abigail asked.

"I kind of like either the one guy with the accent or the woman that had the glasses. What about you?"

"I like those two as well, but I am also rooting for the one that almost was sent home in the last episode."

"Yeah. Me, too. Speaking of being sent home," Eve said.

"Subtle. Very subtle. But, I get the point. We both need to start getting ready for work."

"Yes and I will need a shower first."

"I will be sad to miss that." Abigail winked over at Eve and then grinned at the small blush that crept up her face. Climbing off of the bed, Abigail tossed all the trash in the bags. Eve had joined her to help clean up. "Come here." She tugged Eve close to her and gave her a long hug before tilting her face up and placing a light kiss on her lips that grew into gentle nips and sucking on Eve's bottom lip. "Have a great night at work. Text me when you get back tonight if you can."

"You do the same. On both the good night and the texting."

"Will do. I will drop the trash down the chute as I leave. Later, babe."

Abigail left and thought that the morning might not have started the best, well guess that depends on one's perspective, but it ended on a positive note. Tossing the trash, she hustled down the flight of stairs and to her car to head to her dorm to prepare for her own night at work.

CHAPTER 19

Later that night at work, she was returning back to the hostess stand when a guy carrying a vase of flowers walked in. It wasn't often that someone arrived with flowers outside of Valentine's Day, but it did happen. The gentleman approached the hostess stand and Abigail sent him a big smile. "Welcome to Fahrenheit 212, how may I help you?"

"I have a delivery for Vanessa Perkins."

"Oh wow. She has stepped away for a moment if you would like to wait."

"Uh, sure. That is fine."

The man stepped back against the wall to wait. It was only a few minutes and Vanessa joined Abigail at the hostess stand.

"Hey, Vanessa, there is a guy here with flowers for you." Abigail pointed where the guy was standing.

"Oh wow. I wonder who they are from."

The male must have seen her gesture at him for he walked over towards the two of them.

"Are you Vaness Perkins?"

"I am."

"I have a delivery for you." He handed them over and then turned and left.

Abigail watched as Vanessa pulled out a card and read it.

"They are from my boyfriend. He was missing me and wanted to surprise me at work."

"That is so sweet." Suddenly that gave Abigail the idea to send over flowers to Eve. But would that embarrass her or would she enjoy them. Ugh. Trying to figure things out could be really difficult. Deciding to risk it, she pulled up a site on her phone and ordered them. However, she had them set up to be delivered tomorrow night since it was already late that evening.

After the flowers arrived, Vanessa was all gooey and anxious to get off work. Once it was approved by their manager, Abigail worked until close and let Vanessa take her early departure time. Once she finished her close process, she jumped in and helped some of the others since they were slammed all night and short a server. She was tired when she made it back to the dorms, but not too worn out to message a certain female and see how her evening went. Before she left her car, she sent a text out to Eve. Maybe if she was lucky, Eve would be up for grabbing a bite to eat at an overnight restaurant or continuing watching the show they'd started earlier.

Abigail: Hello, beautiful! How was work? Did you get off already?

As soon as Abigail sent the message she realized how that last question sounded. Hopefully, her girlfriend's mind wasn't in the gutter like Abigail's was. A ding on her phone as Abigail shut the car door had her pulling it out to look at it.

Eve: Hey yourself. Work was the usual madhouse of customers, but no big catastrophes this evening. I am off work, yes.

Winky face? What does that mean? Was she just being flirty or did she catch the accidental sexual innuendo in that last question.

Abigail: You up for company? I could come over and see you.

EVE: I'M NOT AT MY DORM YET AND NOT SURE WHEN I WILL ARRIVE. WANT ME TO TEXT YOU WHEN I GET THERE?

A: OF COURSE. I NEED TO KNOW YOU MADE IT HOME SAFE.

E: SO PROTECTIVE YOU ARE. WHERE ARE YOU? SNUGGLED IN YOUR BED?

A: NOPE. WALKING INTO MY DORM BUILDING NOW.

E: QUIT TEXTING SO YOU DON'T TRIP AND FALL.

A: YOU KNOW I GOT SKILLS.

E: SO, YOU KEEP TELLING ME.

A: BETTER WATCH YOURSELF.

E: SERIOUSLY, MESSAGE ME ONCE YOU ARE INSIDE YOUR ROOM.

A: WILL DO.

Shoving her phone in her pocket, Abigail laughed as she opened the door to the building. She had to squeeze by several people that were hanging out to get to the stairs. Once she got into the stairwell, it became quieter for a few minutes until she arrived on her floor. There seemed to be a kind of party going on. She barely made it to her room door and was thankful that the noise level reduced the closer to her room she crept. When she opened the door, Abigail kind of poured herself into the room even as she dropped her purse and keys on the shelf as you opened the door.

"Took you long enough to get here."

Abigail shrieked as she saw Eve sitting in her desk chair. When her heart calmed down she looked at the woman slouched down and asked, "What are you doing here and how did you get in?"

For an answer Eve pointed over to Alex's side of the room. "She saw me sitting in the hall waiting for you and let me in the room. She was worried I might get mowed down. She seems to think I am small and will be squashed like a bug."

"Well, the small part might be correct, especially when compared to Alex."

"I was going to say I am a perfectly normal height. But, you are correct. Alex is definitely taller than me, as are you."

"Not that I am unhappy to see you, considering I messaged you about me going over to your room. Smooth texting since I didn't suspect anything was up."

"I wanted it to be a surprise."

"It definitely is."

"I hope it is a good one. Here, this is for you."

Abigail took the package that Eve handed her and opened it. Inside was a container that had one of the pieces of chocolate goodness that Abigail loved so much. "It is so beautiful. I hate to disturb its purity with my fork. Part of me wants to eat it tonight and part of me wants to wait until tomorrow. Or I guess it would be later today since it is after midnight."

"Pull it out and see what else is in there."

When Abigail did, she found a container with some mashed potatoes, asparagus, shrimp, and lobster. "Dude. What the heck?"

"I am not a dude."

"Dudette. What the heck?

Eve laughed even as Abigail found a fork and popped open the container. She bit into one of the shrimp and her mouth was doing a happy dance. If life was like a cartoon, her teeth would have been growing a pair of legs suddenly and dancing.

"I don't even care that it isn't hot. This is delicious. I might need to switch jobs if this is what you get to eat all the time."

"No, it isn't. I wanted to do something special for you tonight. That is all."

"What about you?" Abigail asked even as she took a bite of the potatoes. They were so creamy and flavorful.

"I have my own food."

"Good, because I wasn't wanting to share, but willing."

“I have something different. A simple pasta with a garlic sauce and vegetables.”

Abigail fell in love with everything she put into her mouth. “That sounds delicious, too. I didn’t get a chance to eat much tonight so this is wonderful. You win the prize for best girlfriend.”

“With chocolate cake and cold leftovers? You are easy.”

Grinning as she swallowed her food, Abigail then spoke, “You have no idea. Want me to show you?” She purposefully licked her finger slowly and she watched Eve’s face heat up. She loved how she could make Eve change color in part embarrassment and hopefully part arousal.

“Umm.” Eve coughed and then looked around the room. This caused Abigail’s smile to broaden.

“Come here.” Abigail sat the food to the side on the desk and pulled the chair Eve was sitting in over to the edge of the bed. Then she leaned over and cupped her girl’s cheek with one hand and she pushed back a lock of hair with the other. “You can tell me to stop anytime,” whispered Abigail. Then in a slow descent giving Eve all the time to call a pause, she lowered her head and brushed her lips against Eve’s. She pressed harder and then spread open her own mouth to lick at the entrance and ask for permission to enter. When Abigail felt Eve open up, she hardened the kiss to claim her mouth with more passion. Sliding one of her hands into Eve’s hair and the other around her back, she tugged her closer to the edge of the chair causing Eve to have to spread her legs apart.

As Abigail continued to kiss Eve and felt the response of Eve’s body under hers she, without paying attention, moved Eve to straddle atop her lap. Their kissing moved on from lips crashing into one another to mouths finding cheeks, jaws, and necks to nibble along. Abigail made her way down Eve’s neck to the place where it met her shoulder and nibbled there. She was careful not to leave any lasting marks. Then she moved back up to nip at Eve’s earlobe and whispered, “Are you okay?”

EVE

Was she okay? Heck no, she was not okay. She was on fire. Of course, she and Abigail had kissed before, but nothing like this. This was setting her insides alight. She felt like she was a mass that was about to explode and be made into a star. Every kiss and caress from Abigail was branding her and creating this pressure to remake her.

But, she wasn't about to stop what they were doing to say any of that. In fact, if she spoke like that then it was most likely going to ruin the mood. No, she was keeping her mouth shut and nodding. Well, that was the plan at least. Her mouth, of course, decided to intervene and blurt out, "More!"

More? Where did that come from? More was not in the plans. As she felt Abigail's hands move from holding her tight over her clothes to sliding up inside her shirt along her back, *more* became the primary objective of the plans. Those hands were molding and breathing even more life to the fire. Of course, fire needs oxygen and the next thing that happened gave the fire in her body plenty of oxygen. Abigail grabbed the hem of Eve's shirt and pulled it over her head.

Jupiter and Venus, was she an inferno! The cool air hit her skin and fanned the flames. Eve found herself digging at Abigail's shirt because she wanted to see her woman's body, too. It was only fair, right? Abigail allowed Eve to take it off and she threw it over her shoulder to land somewhere. Then all that soft, smooth skin was there for Eve's perusal. She wanted to touch it, but wasn't sure what to do exactly.

Abigail reassured her, "Eve, babe. You can do whatever you want and we will stop whenever you say. Explore away." Then Abigail turned them and she laid back on the bed while Eve still straddled her.

Eve was still nervous and cautiously ran her hands down Abigail's arms and then placed them on her stomach. The woman shivered beneath her and she wasn't sure if that was good or not.

"Ticklish. Keep going. Feels good, see."

Eve was going to, but then Abigail reached up and touched Eve's stomach and side and she melted into a pile of goo. Leaning over she kissed Abigail again and caught herself on her arms. Abigail must have figured out that maybe she didn't want to be the explorer because Eve found herself flipped over and laying on her back on the bed.

Fine with her. Abigail took charge again and began the slow torture of kissing Eve everywhere her skin was exposed. She worked her way over Eve's clavicle licking right along where the bone laid underneath her skin. Oh this would make a great exercise for an anatomy class. Before Eve got lost in that thought, her girlfriend was making her way down lower and placing kisses all over her stomach.

"I am going to kiss the constellations over your skin," Abigail said as she began placing kisses over her stomach. "And then connect them with my tongue." And immediately did just that.

The entire time Eve wanted to laugh at the silliness of her fellow nerdy girlfriend while also moaning at how good it felt and how aroused she was getting. Not knowing what to do with her hands, she reached out and held onto the sheets around her.

Abigail had made her way back up and was lying beside Eve with their arms wrapped around one another when there was a knock on the door. Instantly the liquid lava in Eve's veins turned to hardened rock and she was immobile. Abigail jumped into action and tossed a random shirt on to go to the door.

Eve watched as Abigail cracked open the door and spoke to whoever was on the other side. She found her own shirt and slipped it back on. It was only then she realized that her shoes were still on. For some reason that amused Eve. She settled her back into the chair and focused on calming her heart rate down and getting some regular non-fire-feeding oxygen into her lungs. She grabbed a bottle of water and guzzled it down. When Abigail glanced over her shoulders, Eve gave her two thumbs up. In reply, Abigail just chuckled and opened the door farther. In walked Alex. Oh my goodness. If Alex had simply walked into their room instead of knocking, she would have caught Abigail and her shirtless and making out heavily.

"Eve, breathe, you have gone white," Abigail ordered.

Hell yes, she went white. The realization of what happened just hit her.

"Hi again, Eve. Was Abigail surprised when she got home earlier?" Alex went over and collapsed down on her bean bag and cracked open a can of Dr. Pepper.

Somehow that normal behavior helped to soothe and reassure Eve. She relaxed and laughed. "Yeah, I swear she jumped so high, I thought her head was going to hit the ceiling."

"Sounds like her. You both want to watch a movie or play cards or something?"

"I would love to, but I think I better head back. I am afraid if I start watching something, I will pass out. However, let's set up a time and you can teach me one of the games you like to play."

"Definitely," Alex tipped her drink towards Eve in a salute before taking a swallow.

"I will walk you down," Abigail said as she put her shoes on.

"You don't need to do that. How about I message you when I get to my dorm?" Eve proposed.

"Are you sure?"

"Yeah. We are both tired and no use in you climbing all of those stairs unnecessarily." Eve gathered up her stuff and went to the door.

When they got there, Abigail leaned in. "Are you okay? With everything."

"I promise I'm not running away or anything. And we can talk."

"I am trusting you." Abigail reached out and pulled Eve into a quick kiss that turned into a longer slower one.

"Good night, Abby."

"Night."

Then Eve turned and left, knowing she was sort of running away and mostly not.

CHAPTER 20

EVE

Sunday morning arrived and Eve dragged her butt out of bed even earlier because Nori sent the group a message last night insisting that everyone join her for breakfast. Eve didn't want to get up earlier and she was a bit cranky because she needed sleep. However, at least it was for a good reason.

The previous evening while she was at work, a bouquet of flowers in a vase arrived at Michelangelo's for her. There was a sweet note attached stating that Abigail wanted her to receive something beautiful and special since she was that in Abigail's life. Everyone in the restaurant ooh'd and ahh'd and asked her who they were from. So, she told them all about Abigail. At first, Eve thought they were sent because of what happened Friday night, but when she reached out to thank her kind girlfriend, Abigail informed her that she had already arranged to send them Friday early before their heated late night.

Now the flowers were sitting on the edge of the desk where Eve could see them constantly. They really were beautiful with the various types of flowers and colors mixed together. She would have to try and look up the flowers to see what kind they were as that was one area she was not the slightest bit knowledgeable in.

While Eve was tempted to lure Abigail over to her dorm to continue what they started Friday night, she knew she needed to get some studying done before going to sleep. However, in between working on homework, she was texting Abigail, so it took longer than normal to get anything accomplished. Thus, she didn't get to sleep until after two in the morning. Now it was seven-thirty and she had to be awake and getting dressed. This meant a long hot shower in an effort to wake herself up. Then she had to dress and drive to the diner where they were meeting for food. Abigail offered to come by and pick her up, but she refused, stating that she would do a few errands afterwards, if there was time, before going into work.

As she pulled up, she noticed that Katherine and Logan had parked two down from her and were getting out of their car. She hurried and joined them.

"Good morning, Eve!" Logan called out and embraced her.

"Ugh. It is too bright and sunny out today," Eve replied as she hugged Logan back.

"Have any idea what Nori is up to?" Katherine asked.

"Nope. I just want my coffee."

"Didn't get enough rest, did you?" asked Logan as he held the door open for the two ladies to go in before him.

"Nope." Seems Eve's vocabulary for the day was holding strong and intelligent.

"Hopefully, the caffeine will help," Katherine tried to reassure her.

Eve hoped it did, too. They went to the hostess and told them they were there meeting some friends. The woman showed them over to where five people were already sitting. Eve was not expecting the group that awaited her. Looked like Jess made it down and was that Ian? Eve recognized him.

All at once everyone started exchanging hugs and shrieking in happiness. Suddenly, Eve was being engulfed in a huge, tight hug. "Girl, I recognize you from the video chats with our Nori. You look as fabulous in person as you do on camera. Come and sit down right beside me, Eve. This way I can tell you all the dishy secrets about everyone."

Eve felt like she had been strapped into a seat on a rollercoaster without her permission and the ride began without warning. When the waitress came over to ask them if they would like something to drink, Eve motioned for the girl to lean down and then spoke as quietly as she could. "I will give you a $5 tip for coffee alone, if you will bring me some now before getting the rest of their drink order."

The waitress beamed and winked at her. "Will do, hun. Be right back." Then she hurried off.

Nori looked around and asked. "Where did our server go?"

Three pairs of eyes looked at Eve and busted out laughing. She didn't care. She was desperate. Her dear Abigail saved the day since she was on the other side of Eve and heard what she said.

"Eve, here, bribed the waitress to forget about the rest of us for a minute to express deliver her some caffeine."

"It's your own fault, Nori. You know I don't get up this early on the weekend."

"Hmmph." Nori play pouted for a minute and then bounced back into her cheerful self. "I was excited since Ian and Jess both made it in last night."

"And we couldn't have waited until 11am?" Eve grumbled.

"Cranky girl, no. We are going to have breakfast and then I thought we could go do something fun before you have to go to work. Tomorrow we have class and then Bingo! You were able to get off right?"

Eve banged her head on the edge of the table before a hand reached to grab her forehead. "Girl, don't do that. You are going to ruin that beautiful mind of yours." Ian let loose.

Eve looked up and wanted to cry. The past several days have been so emotionally wrecking for her. "I forgot. Between everything going on, I simply forgot to send off the email."

A pair of arms from her left squeezed her even as a cup of coffee was set down in front of her with a carafe placed in the middle of the table. Once more it was Ian that was providing comfort. She could see why Nori loved the man. "We have all been there, girl. You just fix up that coffee how you like it and everything will work out."

"Do you think–?" Nori started to ask a question, but was quickly interrupted.

Jess asked, "What do you think sounds good to eat this morning?"

Eve saw Jess wink at her and was so grateful for the woman right then. Everyone started talking about the different options which allowed Eve to pour some creamer into her coffee and take a sip. Deciding it was cool enough that it wouldn't give her second degree burns going down, she took a big, long drink. Then she turned her interest back to the menu and hopefully the rest of the group would keep talking around her and allow her to stay in the background.

She heard her name being whispered and looked at to see Abigail trying to get her attention. "Would you be interested in splitting some blueberry pancakes if I added them to my order? I want some, but don't want all of them," Abigail asked.

Eve smiled and nodded. She really didn't want to offend and take out her mood on everyone. She cared about her friends and it wasn't their fault she was crabby. Well, it wasn't anyone's but Nori's fault. To be fair, it was only partially hers. "Sounds good. I think I am going to have a breakfast bowl."

"So, a breakfast burrito minus the tortilla?"

"Exactly." Eve placed her menu back on the table and gulped down the rest of her coffee. She refilled the cup and poured more cream into it. She was starting to feel a little more normal. It was then that she noticed the others had received their drinks and were beginning to pour coffee out of other carafes. No one touched hers, though. Guess they didn't want to cross that line. She felt bad and didn't blame them but wasn't going to venture back over that line, so she kept her mouth shut and listened as everyone talked over one another while laughing and having a good time.

"No one thinks less of you for being cranky," Abigail whispered as she leaned over and laid her head on top of Eve's head. The woman simply had this sixth sense about when Eve was upset or worried.

"I hope not. I will have to apologize."

"Let it go for now. You can bring it up later." Abigail kissed the side of her head.

Eve did exactly that. All of them placed their orders with the server before continuing to discuss what they were going to do next.

ABIGAIL

After breakfast, everyone drove over to the mall to shop for a couple of hours. While they were enjoying their food they had made a plan to do one of those painting party things. The kind that is advertised as a wine and paint kind. However, none of them were drinking age, so they were going to have a soda and water painting party. They pulled up the website for a couple of locations and debated on which one they wanted to go to based on what image was on the calendar for that day. Ultimately, they chose the studio that was painting a bright moon behind a tree. There were a couple of other good options, but neither of the guys wanted to do those as they were a bit too girly in their opinions. Abigail could see why as one was all glitter and jeweled out with high heels and dresses. But, the moon and tree one was beautiful and Abigail knew it would be a great addition to her dorm wall or if it turned out nice, she would give it as a gift to her mom.

Since they had a few hours to kill before they had to be at the studio, they, by that Abigail meant everyone but Eve, decided to do a little shopping. Personally, Eve declared she would rather take a nap. In fact, she even tried to get everyone to let her drive to the parking lot where the studio was located and take a nap in her car until they arrived. No such luck. Nori insisted, nay demanded, that Eve took her grumpy, fed butt with them. Nori was going to force Eve into having fun whether she wanted to or not.

Abigail, trying to be a mediator and a good girlfriend, promised Eve a present if she went along.

"I can keep my mouth shut, nod, and smile when it's required to appease Nori and earn my bribe. Let's be honest because we both know that is what the gift is," Eve had said when they were getting out of the car. They dropped Abigail's car at the studio and rode over to the mall together.

After going into a few stores, Eve saw a store she wanted to check out. It had different incense, holders, figurines, crystals, clothes, some books, and other things. It was quite an eclectic sort of shop. Eve dragged Abigail into the store.

"I want to get my present from here."

"Okay, pick something out," said Abigail.

"Don't give me carte blanche. I need to know what my limit is." Eve picked up a scarf that was laying on one of the shelves and stroked it.

Abigail really didn't care how much money Eve spent. She knew her girl was frugal and even if she went a little overboard this one time, it would be a rarity and one that Abigail would indulge her in. However, she had a feeling that Eve wouldn't get anything if Abigail didn't throw a number out. "How about forty dollars?"

Eve's head whipped around, "Seriously?"

"I can go higher if needed. What were you thinking?"

Eve's voice squeaked out a little when she replied, "Higher?" She cleared her throat and the next words came out more in her regular voice. "I was thinking like ten, fifteen max."

"You are having a bad day and I can afford to spoil you a bit. Go on and get you something you would really like. I promise I can afford it." She pulled Eve to her and wrapped an arm around her shoulder. "Please get a few things you wouldn't buy yourself. Let me pamper you and shower you with a couple of gifts."

"The flowers last night were more than enough."

"They will fade. If you don't pick something out, I will buy the most expensive thing I can afford whether or not you might like it."

Eve laughed and nudged Abigail in the side, "Fine you win."

"That's my girl."

Rolling her eyes, Eve edged away and over to a shelf on the wall to look at some of the reverse smoke incense burners. Nori stepped up next to Abigail and almost scared a life off of her. "You startled the heck out of me. Where have you all been?"

"The boys stopped at a video game store and we had a hard time pulling them out of there."

"How did you get them to leave?" asked Abigail.

"We told them if they didn't leave, we were going to paint their nails and put makeup on them while they slept. Then we would take pictures and share them on our social media accounts."

"NORI!"

"What? It worked and they were about to leave after that. I saw you two disappear into here and decided to follow after you. How is Eve feeling?"

"She isn't the best, but our girl is strong and she is going to push through. But, I wouldn't nettle her any more without a reason that you can tell her."

Nori agreed, "Fair enough. I had already decided to behave. We don't need a grumpy Eve going to work. Her tips would suffer and pay the consequence for her mood."

"She is shopping here, so hopefully that will help elevate her spirits. I guess I better go check on her. Are you meeting us back in here or do we have a meetup point?" Abigail looked around the store locating Eve in the corner.

"How about on the benches right outside this store in about ten to fifteen minutes? Then we can head on over to the painting place after that."

"Sounds good. I will go give a countdown to Eve. See you in a few."

"Good luck."

Abigail had a feeling that she might need it. If Eve was in good spirits now, she really didn't want to rush her. When she approached, Abigail noticed that Eve had a little baggie and was filling it up with small incense cones. She watched as Eve occasionally lifted one and sniffed it before putting it back down with the rest or now and then it ended up in her bag along with a few others like it.

"What are your favorites?"

"It is hard to decide. I like the rose ones, but there is one that is supposed to smell like rain that smells good. I picked out a holder in the shape of a dragon. Thought I would get that and some cones for it, if you are sure about this?"

"Of course, I am or I wouldn't have offered. I am going to go look at a couple of things while you finish up. Nori said we are to meet her in about ten to fifteen minutes. Will that give you enough time?"

"Yep. I will be ready to go."

"Have fun."

Abigail left Eve in her happy glow while she crossed the store to where she saw some dreamcatchers hanging up. She thought she would buy a couple. One for herself and one for Eve. However, while she was looking she found a really pretty one that her sister would like and her birthday was coming up. Picking out the three items, she strolled around seeing if anything else caught her attention.

On one of the shelves was a necklace that had a telescope charm on it. She carefully took it and added it to her collection. She had to be sneaky about buying it, though, because she was going to save that for a special night. She saw some stone bracelets and grabbed one for everyone. They were masculine enough for the guys to wear also. Knowing she was done, she turned and found Eve almost skipping over to her. All traces of the grumpy girl were gone. Abigail would have to remember this for the future when Eve was irritated.

"All done picking out your cones?"

"Yep. I am set for quite a bit now."

"Do you want or need anything else?"

"Not today. Looks like you have found several things yourself."

Abigail nodded, "Yeah, picked up some gifts while I am here, but I am done also. Let's go check out and then we can go see if the rest of the gang has made it to the benches,"

The two of them were second in line, so it didn't take very long for them to be waited upon. They each set their purchases up on the counter and the store associate began ringing them up and asked, "Is this all together?"

"Yes, but can you put these items in a separate bag? This way we won't have to separate it back out."

"Will do," the guy reassured her.

"Hey, Eve, go on out and find the group and let them know I am about to check out." She was trying to keep Eve distracted so she didn't accidentally see what Abigail bought her.

"If I must." Eve dragged herself away and Abigail had to keep from laughing at her grumpy cat. For some reason seeing this side of Eve highly amused Abigail.

When the young man told Abigail the total, she swiped her card and then collected their purchases before heading to the benches.

When Abigail arrived, Eve, Melissa, Ian, and Logan were sitting and chatting with the other three girls nowhere in sight. "Where are the others?" Abigail asked.

"Oh they went off to get some pretty panties. I wanted to join them, but Nori told me that I would scare all the women away if I were to start holding them up to myself, even if I was just teasing." Ian pouted.

Eve busted out laughing. "I think I might pay to see that."

"Let's go, hun, and I will show you for free."

Abigail pointed, "Too late, I'm afraid. They are almost back here."

"Oh, pooh. That Nori is ruining all my fun."

"You stick with me, Ian, and we will pay her back." Eve linked her arm with his tight. "Maybe we can find a way at our next location."

"You got it."

Abigail covered her face to hide her smile and laughter.

Melissa spoke up from where she was sitting cross legged, "Those two together are trouble. I thought he and Nori were always quite the pair, but those two tag teaming it against Nori will give her a run for her money."

"Give who a run for her money?" asked Nori as they approached.

Ian answered before Melissa could say anything, "No one. You girls ready? My moon awaits me."

Abigail couldn't contain her laughter as he started to skip away and Eve had to hustle to keep up with him since their arms were still linked together.

"I have a feeling I missed something," Nori said as the rest of the group followed behind in a more leisurely fashion.

"You did, but nothing to worry about. Be glad everyone is in good spirits," said Abigail.

"And bonding," added Melissa.

Jess spoke up from next to Nori, "I will get Ian to tell me the details later. He likes me."

"Good. Then you can tell me what is going on," Nori said.

"Not likely. I have to keep something from you, but you are free to try and coax it from me all you would like," Jess teased.

They made their way outside then split up into the individual cars. However when Abigail reached Eve's, she found Ian was waiting in the backseat. Abigail opened the passenger front door. "You riding over with us?"

"Yep. Sticking with my girl here."

"Well, let Nori know so she isn't waiting for you."

"I already texted her."

"Let's go then."

Eve pulled out and they drove back over to the studio for an afternoon of creativity. Abigail hoped that nothing went wrong. She had her work clothes with her because she was going to change and head straight over after they finished up for the afternoon. She guessed that Eve had the same plan for her job.

Chapter 21

EVE

Monday night, everyone piled into two cars and headed out. One car went over to the place that Nori found to play Bingo. There was a line already forming at the door and down the front of the building. Logan, Katherine, Abigail, and Eve were the chosen ones to go stand in line while Melissa, Nori, Ian, and Jess went to pick up pizza and cold drinks. They divided and conquered so they could get great spots for everyone and have hot food to eat. Logan said some of his friends were going to join them and Abigail invited Alex. She wasn't sure if she would be able to make it, but they were going to hold a chair for her until they heard if she couldn't attend or until they were forced to give up the spot.

The doors opened an hour before it kicked off and the four friends made their way through the line. Once inside the room, Eve's mouth dropped at the number of tables and chairs everywhere. Abigail tugged her sleeve and they moved over to the side of the room to claim sixteen spots. The four of them spread out and added some items to the table in front of chairs to make it look like people were there, but not at the table currently. This way it was less obvious that the group was saving spots. There was a zip-up hoodie on the back of one chair, a purse on the table in front of another.

Abigail laughed when Eve plopped down her backpack in front of another seat and there was a loud thunk.

“Please don’t tell me that you actually have your textbooks in there, Eve.”

“Then I won’t tell you that.”

“Were you planning on studying in between daubing the numbers on the page?”

Eve rolled her eyes, “Of course not. But, I have learned to be prepared for any circumstances.” That was mostly the truth, but she still occasionally had a hard time not having her possessions with her at times because when she was growing up, there were a few times when something didn’t get packed when she had to change homes or she wouldn’t be allowed to take things.

“Well, if someone attacks us for winning, then we can use it as a weapon it sounds like.”

Logan joined them from where he and Katherine ventured off to find the bathroom, “What is being used as a weapon and why? Do I need to rough someone up?”

Katherine ruffled his hair, “I will rough you up, later.”

“Kinky. But, not what I meant. Abby and Eve were talking about weapons.”

Katherine glanced between both of the other two as she asked, “How did that topic come up?”

Letting out a sigh and sending a glare over at Abigail who was trying to hold in her laughter, she sank down into her chair and explained, “Apparently, the fact that I have textbooks in my bag today is amusing your dear friend. She stated that if someone attacked us, she could use it to fend off the individual.”

“I didn’t say which of us would be rendering it as a weapon, just that one of us could.”

“This is true. She didn’t indicate which person would be operating said blunt object,” Eve agreed.

“I love you girls!” Logan gave each of them a hug. “You all keep me entertained.”

“Notice he says that before his boys arrive.” Katherine pinched him in the side. “Oh, look, there are Garrison and Ford now.”

Eve turned and saw two tall and wide guys heading their way. Since she had mostly hung out with her group, she didn't pay attention to most of the students around her. She leaned over and whispered to Abigail, "If someone attacks us, then I think they will be brandishing the weapon of themselves."

Eve watched as Abigail almost spit her drink all over the table. Logan looked over at them and quirked his eyebrows. "Do I even want to know?"

Eve shook her head as Abigail worked on maintaining her dignity and swallowing her drink without choking. She would apologize, but she wasn't sorry. The muscles just made her think that a toy car could drive over them like hills.

When the guys made it over to them, Logan made introductions. "Garrison and Ford, I would like you to meet Eve and the one that is coughing and trying to regain her composure is Abby." Eve stood up and held out her hand as Logan continued. "Ladies, these two guys are obviously Garrison and Ford. They both play football for the school."

"Nice to meet you both," Garrison said as he shook Eve's hand. His voice was deep and rich and she almost swooned despite being very committed to Abigail.

Ford was next to shake her hand and he was just as polite. "It is a pleasure to meet you both. I used to go with my grandma to play Bingo back home. She and the ladies she played with were very serious players. Thanks for inviting me. I am looking forward to this as I haven't played since the last time with her."

"I haven't ever played other than in school or something. Never in a setting like this," Eve shared with the group. The two guys sat down and even when they were seated, Eve barely topped their height. Before she could say much more, three more guys showed up and one of them brought his girlfriend, too. Eve looked around and wondered if they would need more chairs. Before she could think anything of it, Alex came through the door with another girl.

Abigail waved at them from where she was standing next to Eve to catch her attention. Alex must have seen because she waved back.

"Hey, Alex. Who do you have with you?" Abigail asked her roommate.

"This is Esmeralda."

Abigail held out her hand, "Hi. Welcome to our mashup tonight. I am Abigail, but everyone calls me Abby."

"Abby is my roommate I was telling you about."

"A pleasure to meet you all. Thanks for allowing me to crash your group tonight," Esmeralda said as she looked around.

About the time that all the introductions had been done, Nori came walking in with Ian, Jess, and Melissa behind her. Ian had all of the pizzas in his hands and the guys quickly stood up to help everyone with the items they carried.

Eve was watching when she saw Melissa's face change expressions. Her eyes widened and her mouth opened in shock. What surprised Eve the most was the fact that Melissa dropped what was in her hands. As quickly as all of that happened she saw another emotion cross her friend's face. Anger. Uh-oh, apparently one of the new people here was someone that Melissa was not prepared to see tonight nor was that person a welcomed visitor. Eve wondered who it was. The people in the area that Melissa was staring at were Garrison, Alex, Esmeralda, Victor, and Victor's girlfriend. Eve didn't know enough about any of them to be sure of what was going on.

Suddenly, Ian saved the moment even if he wasn't aware of it. "Girl, good thing you weren't carrying the pizza. I would have been sad for all the cheese to be on the lid of the box. But, I can't blame you with all of these yummy guys around." He bumped her hip and she laughed.

Eve glanced around to see if anyone noticed what she did, but no one else seemed to be aware of the little glitch in Melissa's behavior. She let it go to ponder about later.

They all grabbed seats and put some of the pizzas at each end of the table and in the middle of the group. Then they all started passing things out and chatting. The noise in the room was growing louder and louder. Nori stood up and started to go around grabbing money from everyone. When she got to her side of the table, she bent down between Ian and Eve. "You two come and help me buy the bingo cards."

Eve pushed her chair back and then when Nori had everyone's money, followed behind her to the line. Nori split it up between herself, Jess, Ian, and Eve. This way they each had four people to pay and collect bingo cards for. When they got to the front, Nori went first and asked for four. She paid the first lady, gathered four sets of papers from the second person, and rules from the third. Jess, Ian, and Eve followed behind and did the same thing. Once they were back to the table, they all handed them out randomly.

As soon as she arrived back at the table, Abigail reached out and hugged her. "What was that for?"

"Just felt like giving you a hug."

"Aww. Let's eat because there is only about thirty minutes before everything gets started." Eve was tired of smelling the food and wanted to enjoy tasting it. They all had finished up and had trash thrown away when a lady came on the microphone, "Ten minutes until we start, everyone." She went over the rules and told anyone that needed help finding a seat to come up to the front and they would help.

Nori pulled out a bag and opened it to reveal lots of daubers. "I had a feeling no one would remember to bring any, so I went to the store and bought several. Pass around the bags and pick out a color or style that you want, there is a variety."

Everyone thanked Nori and started scrambling. After Jess handed Ford one of the bags, he stood up and went down to the other end and instead of handing it off, poured them out in the middle of the people. Ian saw what he was doing and repeated the process on his side of the group.

Eve didn't care what color she received, but when she saw a Wonder Woman one, she grabbed it. Turned out the ink was red, so that worked for her. Ian, next to her, grabbed a glittery label and when he opened it, he frowned, "Now, why did they have to get my hopes up about some sparkle only to give me plain purple ink. Boo." Everyone near him laughed at his disappointed expression. Abigail grabbed a regular blue one.

Ian's face lit up and Eve knew he must have come up with something. She wasn't wrong. "You know, we might have all the colors of the rainbow and could just organize all of us to have the colors in order. Then together we would make a pretty rainbow."

"Why not just assign a different color to each row and make it even more complicated?" Nori asked.

"I think that is a little drastic. Besides, I might get distracted and we need to win!" In reply, Nori just threw a chip at him. He picked it up from the table and popped it into his mouth.

Eve looked around the room, "I can't believe how many people are all crammed into here."

"Yeah, at first when Nori said we were going to bring in pizza and snacks, I thought she was crazy and we would stand out, but not at all. There is a group over there having a birthday party," Abigail nodded her head over a couple of rows.

The same lady as before spoke into the microphone. "Hello, everyone. We are about to begin. The first game is regular bingo. Shout out bingo when you have it and then make your way to the front of the room. Good luck and have fun." An older gentleman climbed up into the chair and pulled the first ball. "N45."

Everyone around them hushed down and Eve looked over her cards and found that out of the nine boards on her page, four of them had that number. She quickly marked each of them as the next number was called.

After about 10 numbers, she heard Ian mutter, "B15, I just need one more."

The announcer called, "I19."

From somewhere in the room, Bingo was shouted and all of them deflated. Three other people joined the first person at the front of the room to confirm the numbers were correct. As soon as they were, the sound of papers being torn or crumpled was heard. They moved quickly into round two. This time it was the caller's choice and he chose to make a baseball diamond shape. So, none of the numbers in I or N were needed. Eve looked over and saw that Abigail had missed one of the numbers and pointed at it. "Oh thanks. I am trying to only mark the ones that we need to win, so I don't have random marks everywhere to distract me."

"That is a good idea. I will have to do that next time," said Eve.

No one from their table won that round or the next two. After the fourth, it was time for a ten-minute break before they started again with the next set. There were three sets of four rounds and the stakes grew as the night went on.

On break, they all stood and stretched a bit. A couple of the group wandered off, but mostly everyone stayed put. When they were seated again, Nori leaned in and spoke quietly as if she was about to reveal her secret underground society, "I think for this next set, we should guess how many numbers it will take to be called before someone calls bingo. It will add a little additional fun."

"You are such a math nerd, Nori," Logan said. "I am game; I like a little friendly competition."

"I am a math nerd, yes. But, you don't have to be one to join in and guess."

Jess studied the page with the rules. "For the first round, it says it is regular bingo. So, my guess is twelve."

Nori added, "Mine is eleven."

Ian thought, "I will take fourteen."

Eve didn't have a clue and took fifteen.

Abigail tilted her head to the side, "Do we all have to have different numbers?"

"No, if you agree with someone else, then you can choose that number, too," confirmed Nori. After all, it was her little game.

"Then, I, too, will choose twelve."

Down the line everyone began guessing and the last person finished when the session began again. As soon as the twelfth ball was drawn and announced, someone called Bingo. Jess, Abigail, and Victor were also happy because they were the ones that guessed correctly on how many numbers would be drawn.

They did the same thing with the next card, but this time, the goal was to make a checkerboard pattern. Again, all sixteen of them guessed how many balls would have to be called out before there was a Bingo. However, this time, Alex and Ian were correct. Eve knew that the group was enjoying their little side game as much or more even than the actual bingo game.

There was another intermission break and then the last set of four games would be starting. Eve took the opportunity to go to the ladies room. The bathroom was so small and the stalls were tiny. She opened the door and there was like ten inches between the open door and the toilet seat. Eve had to almost straddle the toilet seat to get the door shut. But, she made it work. Once she was done, she washed her hands and returned to her chair.

In eight games, no one from her table had won yet. Several people came really close, but no one had won.

"Anyone need more snacks?" Nori called down the row.

A few of the guys raised their hands and so everyone passed down food. Eve grabbed another slice of pizza. Soon, they were all immersed again in that anxiety rollercoaster of wondering and hoping that the right numbers would be picked before another person bingoed.

It felt like they were at a baseball game with twelve innings and they had all been struck out for eleven of them. However, all they needed was one hit and they would be happy. It all came down to the final round. It was a coverall round. Every single square had to be covered up. These were the rounds that took the longest to have a winner proclaimed.

Eve was focused on the numbers and lulled into a tense autopilot state, so when Abigail poked her, she almost screamed in startlement. However, she kept that noise inside. Apparently, Eve didn't respond fast enough because Abigail screamed Bingo loud and then pointed at Eve's board. She had managed to achieve a Bingo. She was stunned and everyone had to cheer and push her up to go claim her reward. When she got up there, they looked over her board and sure enough she had won. No one else called it out so she got the entire prize to herself. She just won $700. She wasn't sure what to do really. When she got back to the table, everyone was clapping and hooting. They were all really happy for her. She was stunned into silence.

Abigail wrapped her up in a big hug and squeezed her tight. "I am so happy and excited for you. Congrats, babe!" Garrison and Ford each gave her a big bear hug and told her they would walk out with them when they got ready to leave.

Everyone helped to gather up trash and leftovers to carry out to the cars. There wasn't much left after that many people had devoured it, but there was a little. When they were back in

Katherine's car, Logan asked her, "What are you going to do with the money?"

"Well, I think I am going to give everyone their entrance money back. Logan, if I give you the guys', do you think you can return it to all of them?"

"Yeah, but why wouldn't you just keep it? They aren't going to care about that."

"Because it was luck of the draw on which of us would end up with the papers that had the winning combination on it. Then I am going to give some to Nori to cover all of the food. I think after that, there won't be too much left. Maybe I will treat everyone to ice cream."

"Oh, I am down for that tonight," Logan said.

"I wasn't thinking tonight, but sure. If you message the other car, we can all meet up and go have ice cream tonight."

Abigail was already on her phone before Eve had finished talking. "Okay, Melissa said they would stop at the place closest to the campus and meet us there."

"I texted Garrison and Ford and they are going to meet us, too, if that is okay," Logan said as he waved his phone in the air to emphasize the point.

"Definitely, then I can give them their money back," Eve said. She wasn't sure, but she would have sworn she heard Logan say "good luck." Well, she would insist.

CHAPTER 22

ABIGAIL

What Eve didn't realize is that no one wanted part of her Bingo winnings. All they wanted was for her to be happy and enjoy it; but, she knew her kind girl thought it would be fair to split it. Abigail let it go and let someone else be the one to lead that battle. When they parked, Abigail hurried out of the car and ran around so she was there by the time Eve shut her door. She linked her arm with Eve's and took off for the front door.

Logan hollered out behind her, "What's the rush?"

"We need to get our ice cream before you boys go through the line and eat it all," Abigail called over her shoulder. She had neared the door by that point and heard Katherine laughing.

Next to her, Eve admonished her, "That wasn't nice. There is more than plenty of ice cream."

"Yeah, well, he is fun to pick on and one time we went somewhere late and there was only one piece of a certain type of dessert left and Logan got it. Since then, I like to beat him to get dessert, especially ice cream."

The two of them got in line and saw everyone coming in through the front door. Looked like everyone arrived within a few minutes of each other.

"What are you going to order, Abby?"

Abigail scanned the menu and then the open containers to see what flavors were out and available. "I can't decide if I want a hot fudge sundae or a double dip with two different flavors."

"Why not get your sundae with the two flavors? That way you can have both."

"You are genius! What are you doing?"

"I think I'm going to get a sundae also. Treat myself."

The line moved up a couple of people. Nori came up behind Eve and gave her a big hug. Abigail watched as Eve blushed a little, but she squeezed and patted Nori's arms.

Garrison's voice carried from where he stood back a few people. "This is awfully nice of you to treat, Eve, but unnecessary."

"Nonsense. Y'all get whatever you want. My treat."

Ford's smile lit up his entire face. "Don't tell a couple of guys that, we can put away a lot."

"No doubt. But, seriously, even if you want something other than ice cream. I'm not able to do this often, so please allow me the pleasure tonight."

Well, darn. When Eve put it that way, there was no way that any of them were going to be able to squirm out of letting her buy. Although, Eve was wrong that she wasn't able to be nice when it came to food. She was always bringing leftovers from the restaurant to them.

"As you wish, Eve." Garrison nodded his head in thanks.

They moved up and Eve ordered a brownie sundae with peanut butter cup ice cream and marshmallow topping. Abigail went with her hot fudge ice cream with cookies and cream and rocky road. Garrison, Ian, and Logan ordered banana splits. Katherine was going to eat part of Logan's. Ford ordered a large order of fries since he wasn't feeling like ice cream. Melissa had a strawberry shake while Jess had a cookie dough one. Last person to order was Nori and she was having a hard time deciding.

"Choose, Nori, or I am ordering both things for you," Eve threatened

"Fine, give me a snickers candy sundae, please."

They all got cups of water to wash the sweetness from their mouths. After they ordered, the guys and a couple of the girls went to put some tables together for the ten of them while everyone else finished and Eve paid. Then those left helped to carry everything over.

Abigail took a spoonful of her ice cream and loved the warmth of the hot fudge and the coldness of the ice cream mixed together. She listened to everyone around her chatting.

"I still can't believe one of us won," Ford said.

"Definitely, congrats, Eve. Are you going to do something special with the winnings?" asked Garrison right before he stole one of Ford's fries and popped it into his mouth.

"Actually that reminds me." Eve bent over and took her wallet from her bag. "I decided in addition to treating everyone tonight, that I am going to give everyone their entrance money back and pay for the food at the event."

Abigail watched as several people's mouths opened and she couldn't help but smile. She didn't say a word and only watched the show that was about to occur while enjoying her sundae.

"Before any of you start to argue, hear me out," continued Eve. "Nori took everyone's money and we all grabbed four sets of pages. Who knows who would have ended up with the winning set of the group if we were all individually in line. I figured this way, the pot money was used to pay everyone back and no one is out anything. Plus, there is no reason I can't do that and pay for all the food that I helped to eat. I also thought maybe I will find something that would benefit all of us so it was like everyone there had a hand in winning. Kind of like when you have a group of people that pool their money to buy lottery tickets. They split any winnings that were earned. This is the same way."

Abigail was impressed, she had to hand it to Eve, before anyone could object, she addressed most of the arguments.

Nori raised her hand for a moment before speaking without being acknowledged. "I understand your reasoning and applaud you for it and thank you for the generosity you want to bestow upon all of us. However…" Nori paused for a moment and Abigail knew it wasn't going to be over so quickly. "This isn't more like a lottery drawing numbers as much as if we used all of the money to buy lots of scratch off cards, hand them out, and tell the winner he or she keeps what they win. If you are gifted something you aren't going to pay the person back for that gift."

"There is some debate on that whole philosophy. Sheldon on Big Bang Theory has a whole theory on gift giving that I partially employ myself," Ian piped off from next to Nori with his next spoon of banana on the way to his mouth.

"Don't get me started on Sheldon. I swear that man is your role model," Nori teased.

"Intelligence is sexy," was all Ian had to say in response.

"My point is that it isn't necessary for you to pay any of us back," insisted Nori.

"I have decided and you aren't going to change my mind." Eve's confidence and boldness was chart-topping that night. Abigail cheered on Eve internally. It wasn't everyday that she put herself out there as much.

Nori held her palms up in surrender. "Fine. I will find a way around your rules."

Katherine leaned in close and said, "You should have been a lawyer instead of studying to stare up at the sky."

Shaking her head, Eve dug back into her ice cream. Then as Abigail quietly observed, Eve passed around money to everyone for their entrance fee and handed extra over to Nori for pizza and snacks.

No one said a word, but Abigail had to school her face when to the right of her, Jess tapped her leg and handed her a wad of bills. She didn't even look down, but just shoved it all in her pocket. Now she only had to find a way of returning the money to Eve. She wasn't sure if it was everyone's or just her couple of friends at her end of the table.

While she knew no one was bothered by the loss of the money, she cared about her girlfriend and if she wanted to do something that would allow the cash to be used for everyone, she would help organize a small get together or a movie night out or something to make Eve feel better. Then maybe next time they all went, they could figure out some ground rules for instances like this.

The topic at the table easily shifted to school and classes and Abigail learned that Ford had a couple of the same classes as her, but they were taking them at different times. They arranged a time to study for final exams that would be coming up in the next few weeks. Garrison was a Junior and a computer information major. He had an internship lined up with NASA for the summer. Abigail wasn't sure what she thought his major was, but a computer nerd wasn't exactly it. He kind of reminded her a little of a character that made a short appearance on *NCIS*. She needed to look him up later and ask her group if they agreed. He was a sweetheart.

Once they were finished with their dessert, they all tossed the trash and put the tables back into their original positions. In the parking lot, they all exchanged hugs and Abigail hid her smile as both Garrison and Ford wrapped Eve up tight and gave her a kiss on the top of the head before they took off. Abigail knew Eve didn't realize she'd just made herself two new brothers. They all had fun, but it was Monday night and Tuesday morning classes would be there before too long. Katherine dropped Eve and Abigail back off at their dorms. She wasn't sure about anyone else, but Abigail had the goal of getting in some schoolwork for the night before calling it quits.

Once she arrived at her room, she saw Alex hadn't made it back yet. Her roommate must have had a post game date, too. Taking advantage of having the room to herself, she grabbed a towel, some pjs, and her toiletries and took a shower. If she didn't force herself to take one immediately, she knew that she wouldn't get one in before bed. When she walked out about a half-hour later, Alex was sitting on her bed cross legged with a computer in her lap. Waving, Abigail tossed her dirty clothes into the hamper and climbed up into her own bed. She didn't feel like sitting in a desk chair this late at night.

Alex waved back and removed her headphones. "Hey, Abby, have you been back long?"

"No, only long enough to shower and put on pjs. We stopped for ice cream afterwards."

"I wanted to thank you for inviting me along. I had a lot of fun. I hope it was okay that I brought Esmeralda with me."

"Of course," Abigail replied as she tugged the towel off of her hair and began to brush it out before weaving it into two braids. "Did someone say something?"

"No, but Melissa kept glancing over while we were playing and I saw her send a couple of not happy looks towards E."

Abigail paused for a moment thinking she had a feeling that it was less about the woman herself and the fact that she was with Alex. However, she wasn't going to share that with her roommate. "I will have a talk with her and see what was up. I don't know of any reason that Mel would have an issue with your friend as they didn't act like they knew one another. But, I could be wrong. It has happened before."

"You sure about that? I have been rooming with you for a long time and haven't seen you admit to being wrong about something before."

"Haha, smartass. Speaking of Esmeralda, were you two on a date? Not a very romantic one if so."

Alex puckered up her lips and tilted her head back and forth. "Sort of. I mean, it was and it wasn't.

"What does that mean?"

"I invited her specifically to go to Bingo. It wasn't like I asked her out on a date and then said, 'Hey, how about joining a bunch of people for Bingo.' It was more like I was thinking of going and she was there and so I thought, why not see if she had an interest. Plus, it is a nice casual way of getting to know someone without all the extra pressure. Know what I mean?"

"Yeah. So, what did you think? Did you all go do something afterwards?"

"Tonight went well and didn't set off any red flags. I will probably see if she wants to go do something else later on."

"I swear you go through the women of the campus."

"I can't help it if they like my charms. Plus, those that want to experiment know I am available for fun and not trying to tie someone down. As long as they aren't in a relationship, why not?"

"This is why I haven't ever been weird with you. I want commitment and you don't. Neither of us judge each other."

"Plus, you like having someone to solve your computer issues for a roomie." Alex smirked.

Abigail couldn't resist throwing a pillow over across the room. "It was one time."

"Look, you were correct earlier. You are wrong occasionally. It was more than one time. There was the time last semester right before your paper was due when it crashed and you were afraid you lost everything, even though I kept telling you to back up your documents somewhere. Plus, the time when you spilt water all over it by accident.

"Okay, two times."

"See, two is more than one. I'm right."

"You are smug is what you are. You sure the females fall for this?" Abigail teased.

Alex, in response, flipped her off.

"Love you too, Alex."

"I know! I'm magnetic."

"Shut it. Go back to listening to your music. I am going to try and get in some studying before passing out."

"You might check out your messages. Your phone kept buzzing while you were in the bathroom," said Alex as she settled her headphones back over her ears.

Abigail grabbed her phone and textbook and reclined back against the wall. She had two missed calls, a voice message, and seven text messages. Sheesh. She decided to see who called and left a message first before getting to the text messages. It was her mother, "Hi hun, sorry I am calling so late, but thought you might still be up. Wanted to let you know before you heard it from someone else that grandma fell and broke her ankle. She will have to have surgery on it, but she is doing fine. We are leaving the hospital and heading home. Call me tomorrow if you have time. Love you!"

Abigail wanted to pack her bag and head home, but she knew that wasn't reasonable, especially this close to the end of the semester. She sent her mom a quick message letting her know she would call tomorrow and sorry she missed her call.

Next she checked her messages. Some were from the group chat letting everyone know they all made it safely home and would see everyone in the morning for Tuesday breakfast. Then she had a separate one from Eve.

EVE: THANKS FOR A GREAT NIGHT AND SUPPORTING ME WITH MY CHOICES.

EVE: YOU MUST BE EITHER IN THE SHOWER OR ALREADY PASSED OUT. I WILL BE UP FOR A BIT WORKING ON AN ASSIGNMENT. SWEET DREAMS IF YOU ARE PASSED OUT. ALTHOUGH, I GUESS IF YOU ARE ASLEEP THEN YOU WON'T SEE THIS UNTIL THE MORNING SO REALLY IT SHOULD BE GOOD MORNING AND HAVE A GREAT DAY.

ABIGAIL: YOUR TEXT MADE ME LAUGH. I WAS IN THE SHOWER, SO THE SWEET DREAMS ARE STILL APPLICABLE.

E: I JUST GOT BACK FROM MY OWN SHOWER ADVENTURE.

A: IT WAS AN ADVENTURE HUH?

E: FEELS LIKE IT AT TIMES.

A: THE JOYS OF SHARING BATHROOMS.

E: YOU ARE LUCKY THAT YOU DON'T HAVE TO SHARE WITH VERY MANY. OKAY. I AM OFF TO STUDY. SEE YOU IN THE MORNING?

A: DEFINITELY.

A: OH, AND IN RESPONSE TO YOUR FIRST TEXT, I WILL ALWAYS HAVE YOUR BACK.

E: MUAH AND STUDY WELL.

Grinning wide, Abigail settled down to study until she started to fall asleep.

Chapter 23

EVE

The next day, Trig class went over a few minutes since so many of the students were having questions about the upcoming test they had on Thursday. Professor Edison stayed as long as the students could stay to go over as many as she was able to. Eve decided to stay up until the moment she needed to get to the library so that way she could listen in and test herself on if she knew how to solve them herself or not.

So, she was running late for work when her old nemesis stepped into her path. Eve tried to avoid her and go around her, but Bentley mirrored her actions and kept her from progressing. With nothing else to do, she stood her ground and gave in to the fact she was going to be late. But, if she could hurry this altercation along, then she might still make it.

"Well, well, well... look who stumbled upon our path. It is whiney pants Eve."

"What do you want, Bentley? We both got what we desired months ago."

"I heard all about what you got, or rather who you got."

Eve smirked and knew she should keep her mouth shut, but for some reason, when it came to the female in front of her, she always failed. "Are you jealous? I am beginning to think the lady protests too much." Eve dropped her voice, "Maybe all these barbs towards me are really your way of acting out because you can't be the person you secretly desire to be on the inside."

"Why you little –"

"Hello, Eve! It is nice to see you again so soon. I had a great time last night." Eve looked over and saw Garrison had approached the altercation Bentely was attempting to cause. When he reached her side, he gave her a hug.

"Hi, Garrison. It was definitely fun."

Eve had to hold in her laughter when Bentley's voice dropped to a sugary sweetness. "Hello, Garrison, how are you doing today? You are looking quite handsome."

"Where are you heading, Eve? Can I accompany you as I have a couple of questions I need your assistance with?" Eve watched as Garrison bluntly ignored Bentley and her friends.

"What could you possibly need her help with? I would gladly help you in whatever you need. It would be my ultimate pleasure." Bentley reached out to touch his arm, but Garrison casually stepped away. It was in a manner that looked like he was unintentionally avoiding her, but Eve knew better.

Eve took a page from Garrison's book and ignored Bentley. "I am heading to the library for my shift there."

"Great. Let me escort you as I need to head that direction myself." Garrison finally turned and looked at the others. "If you'd excuse us, I need to borrow Eve for a bit. I apologize for stealing her away." He turned his attention back to Eve and held out his arm. "Shall we?"

Eve bit the inside of her lips and nodded. What else could she do? She grabbed ahold of his arm and let herself be led away. When they were out of hearing distance, she let out a small laugh and said in complete honesty, "Thank you so very much for that. I owe you big time."

"I saw what happened and I hate bullies. You don't owe me at all. It is my pleasure to save a pretty woman from the snatches of an evil villain." He gave an evil laugh before he turned serious and asked, "What is her problem with you anyways? If you don't mind me asking, that is."

Eve loved that Garrison slowed his step to match her shorter stride so that they could talk with ease and she wasn't huffing and puffing to keep up. "Oh I don't mind at all. We were roommates at the beginning of the semester. We are vastly different types of people in what we are wanting to gain from our college experience. I didn't object overly to what she did, but she did cross the boundary a few times. However, then she turned to acting like an ass and harassing me for my friends and when I started dating Abigail."

"You are right. She is an ass."

"As much as I appreciate the save, the best part for me was the way she kept trying to flirt with you and you ignored her. That made my week."

"It is only Tuesday and you won money last night," expressed Garrison.

"My statement holds true. You have no idea what life was like and to see her not get her way was the best."

"It is my pleasure to help you out."

"Now, since we are almost to the library doors, did you really need my help with something or were you just saying that to rile Bentley up?"

"Mostly the latter, but I would be interested in getting together with you all to hang out."

"Yes, I will see if we can plan something soon since the semester is coming to an end. Thanks again for seeing me to work. Have a great night."

"Bye, Eve!"

"Later, Garrison."

Eve opened the door and disappeared inside to apologize for her tardiness. Thankfully when she explained what happened in class, they didn't have a problem with it. Eve didn't share the run in with Bentley and her crew as she didn't want to come across petty in any way, especially after what happened the first time. There was no need to add additional drama to her work life.

The rest of the night went smoothly. Eve was anxious for most of it wondering if Bentley would come into the library and cause some kind of commotion and get her almost fired again. Except this time, she had no doubt that she would be let go. Afterall, what employer wants to keep someone on who is going to bring disturbances constantly.

Her wonderful Abigail stopped by late in the evening to study and then escort Eve back to her dorm. It was on that trip when she shared about what happened earlier.

"I knew I liked Garrison for a reason. I would be worried he might whisk you away if I didn't know you were smitten with me," Abigail teased.

"You have no reason to be worried or jealous. I think he sees me more as a little sister or something, and I do mean little. He is just a big teddy bear and I have only known him for two days."

"This is true. Some person is going to be lucky to date him, I think."

"Speaking of which, but not really, are you coming up to my room to study or do you need to get back to your room?" Eve asked.

"Is that study as in actual homework or as in code for getting some making out?" Eve shot her a quick glance as she drove. "Gotcha. The boring definition. Yeah, I have some stuff I can work on. You never know, I might convince you to actually do the other kind once I am in your room."

"This is very true. I mean, World Geography and English are hot subject matters and I might be tempted to rip my clothes off."

"Woman, the visual of that sends chills down my body. You aren't playing fair. Besides, where you are concerned, even the mundane topics can't keep me from being turned on. Intelligence is sexy."

Eve laughed to hide the effect that Abigail's words had on her. She parked in a spot and both girls headed up to Eve's dorm room hand in hand. Over the many weeks, Eve had grown more comfortable with the physical affection of hand holding or causal touching. It had taken her a while to not feel like everyone was staring at them each second or like they were a form of entertainment. No matter what happened between them, Eve would always be grateful for the time with Abigail as it had helped her confidence grow.

Up in the room, each of the girls grabbed a snack and sat down to work on what needed to be done. After a couple of hours, Eve started to nod off and she knew it was pointless to continue because it was after midnight and she had an early class.

Eve watched as Abigail stretched and put all of her stuff in her bag to leave. Before she realized what she was saying, Eve suggested, "Why don't you stay here tonight with me." Not sure where the words came from, but not only did it surprise Eve, it must have shocked Abigail by the expression on her face.

"Are you sure?"

"Yeah. Unless you just want to go sleep in your own room."

"No. I would love to stay here with you. Want me to take the other bed?" Abigail asked hesitantly.

Eve knew she was offering it so if Eve didn't intend for what it sounded like, she could take it back.

"Only if you want to. But, I was thinking maybe we could try sleeping in the same bed and cuddling. I have an extra t-shirt or pajamas or something for you to sleep in."

"A t-shirt or tank top would be perfect."

Eve scrambled over to where she stored them and held up a couple of options and Abigail chose the simple red tank top. Now what Eve was going to wear, she wasn't sure. She ran through all the warring emotions in her mind as she searched. When a hand appeared next to her and grabbed a pair of pink shorts and a tank pj set, Eve fell back on her bottom from where she was knelt down.

"Sorry about that. I think you should wear this."

"Alright. That works. Let me grab you a toothbrush so we can go down the hall and prepare for bed."

When she stood up, Abigail grabbed ahold of her and gave her a tight hug and a light kiss on the lips. "Relax, babe. Nothing is going to happen. We are both too tired. I am surprised we haven't done this before now. In comparison to most couples, I am sure they think we are turtles. I am not pushing you faster than you want. I love our pace and am not going anywhere."

"Except to the bathroom?" Eve smirked.

Abigail's smile was all the reassurance Eve needed. "Yes, except for there."

They both raced down the hall for no other reason except for fun. Once they were done brushing their teeth they did a breath test on one another.

"You smell so minty fresh now," Abigail grinned.

"You smell the same. Hmm. I think you might be copying me."

"Or I used the same toothpaste."

"See, copying me."

"Silly."

Eve winked and pulled Abigail back down the hall. She might have been a little giddy and nervous. When they were back in the room, Abigail and Eve changed into their pajamas. Eve crawled in first and slid up next to the wall. Then Abigail crawled in and faced her.

Once they were in the bed, Eve reached over and turned off the lamp. However, as she went to settle back down on her side, Abigail stopped her and pulled her down to lay across her chest before kissing her long and slow. It heated Eve up and she was glad she didn't opt for the warmer version of her pajamas.

They stayed like that for several minutes exchanging slow and lingering kisses before breaking apart.

"Wow. That was, umm, yeah," stammered Eve.

"Glad you approved. I am enjoying sharing a bed with you."

"You say that now. Wait until we are asleep and I hit or kick you. You might choose to go make camp on the other bed."

"Nah. I will just wake you up and make you kiss my boo boo." Abigail laughed and gave Eve one last kiss before pulling her in her arms.

Eve laid snuggled against Abigail and they fit together nicely. It was one benefit of being shorter than your girlfriend. Snuggling was really comfortable. She wasn't sure if she would be able to fall asleep easily, but once she relaxed and sunk into the comfortability of things, she slid off into slumber quickly.

CHAPTER 24

ABIGAIL

It was the last week before cram week for finals and Abigail wanted to take the opportunity to plan a special date for Eve before all the chaos began and then school was out for the summer. There really wasn't a good time, but the one night that Eve had off from both the library and the restaurant was Thursday night. Eve had astronomy class until nine, but after that she was free. But that time worked perfectly because Abigail wanted it to be dark for their date.

While Abigail knew that Eve would enjoy what she had planned, she was still nervous. For some reason her palms grew clammy everytime she thought of it. She kept trying to reassure herself that it wasn't anything big and majestic but rather simple and hopefully romantic; however, her brain wasn't firing the right signals to the rest of her body, thus the doubt and anxiety. She hadn't even managed to make a date yet. Abigail knew that was one thing she could tackle and mark off her checklist.

Picking up her phone, she tapped on Eve's number and waited for it to ring. Then she hung up before it connected. Maybe she should text because that is what they normally did. Would calling and asking her out be weird and give away that something different was up? Switching over to the messaging icon, she started to type.

ABIGAIL: HELLO BEAUTIFUL. I WAS THINKING ABOUT YOU AND WONDERING IF YOU ARE UP FOR A DATE THURSDAY NIGHT AFTER CLASS?

Wait, should she just come right and ask or be more casual and lead into it? She backspaced and tried again.

ABIGAIL: HELLO BEAUTIFUL. HOW HAS YOUR DAY BEEN?

That sounded better right? Ugh. Before she could drive herself even madder, she hit the send button. Then she waited and waited and waited, staring at the phone the entire time. Why did people think that someone was instantly going to reply back when a message was sent? Eve was probably busy and would return the message when she had free time. Abigail needed to chill out. Maybe a run would help.

She sat the phone down and was bent over grabbing a pair of socks when the phone dinged. The sound caused her to jerk up fast and hit her arm on the edge of the door. What she got for being on edge. She rushed over and collapsed on the bed while picking up the phone.

EVE: DAY HAS BEEN BUSY, BUT GOOD. SAW YOU TRIED TO CALL. I DIDN'T HEAR IT RING. EVERYTHING OKAY?

Darn it, the call did connect, she guessed. Nothing to do about it now, but what to say.

ABIGAIL: YEAH. I CALLED, BUT CHANGED MY MIND AS I THOUGHT YOU MIGHT BE BUSY SO HUNG UP ON MY SIDE BEFORE IT EVEN STARTED TO RING. SORRY. 🙁

EVE: ALL GOOD. WHAT'S UP?

ABIGAIL: CAN'T A GIRL JUST WANT TO TALK TO HER GIRL?

As she was watching the bubble at the bottom move indicating that Eve was typing, her phone rang and the jarring noise caused her to fumble it to the floor. She leaned over the side of the bed and retrieved it before answering. However, due to everything, her voice came out panting, "Hello."

"Hey. You okay? Have you been running?"

"Umm. Not yet, I dropped the phone on the floor. Although I was about to get dressed and go for one."

"I swear I still don't know how you run so much. I am not a fan of it."

"That is okay, you are great just the way you are."

"Aww. Aren't you sweet! I thought if you were wanting to talk to me, then I would call and chat."

Abigail laughed and hearing Eve's voice helped to calm some of the worry in her mind. "What are you doing?"

"Sitting here trying to keep my sine and cosine from throwing a tangent. Get it?"

"You are horrible, but that is funny."

"Thank you, I will be here for a couple more weeks. Feel free to book me for a show."

"Actually, speaking of that–"

Eve interrupted, "I am not doing any comedy routine."

"Not that, booking your time."

"Thank goodness, carry on then."

"How would you like to get together Thursday after class is over?"

"You know class isn't over until nine right?"

"Yep."

"What did you have in mind?"

"That is a surprise. All you have to do is show up."

"Okay. I am game. Do I get a hint? How will I know what to wear?"

Abigail rubbed her forehead a little. "Woman, do you think I am going to make you wear a ballgown or something? Your attire is all very similar. Wear something comfortable and come as you would to anything else. The clothes don't matter outside of the fact that you have some on. It is your presence that is important."

"Fair. Although, I am tempted to wear pajamas just to be ornery, but alas I will behave. Okay, Thursday night around 9pm, destination to be determined. Where am I to meet you or are you picking me up?"

"You will receive instructions."

"Will it be in an envelope with an audio message that says I have a mission should I choose to accept it that will explode about thirty seconds after I read it?"

"Now you are being silly," Abigail said.

"And you are being too serious." Eve's voice dropped, "Is there something I need to be concerned with? Are you breaking up with me?"

"What? No! Not even close." Abigail wanted to stare at the phone in disgust.

"Well, your tone has me concerned about what is going on."

Abigail forced herself to take a deep, slow, quiet breath and think about all the times they laughed and joked around. "I promise you dear, that everything is positive. I want to throw you a surprise date is all."

"I trust you."

"Good. Now tell me about your assignment."

Abigail listened to Eve talk about her homework and they moved on from there to other topics including both of them looking forward to hanging out at Katherine and Logan's place the following Sunday. A few extra people were coming over for a last celebration before tackling studying for the next week.

By the time they got off the phone, it was time for Eve to go to work. Abigail had the day off and, in fact, decided she would still take that run around campus.

The week flew by and every day closer to Thursday tightened the strings running through Abigail's body. By Thursday morning at breakfast, all of her friends were sending her glances and not engaging in long conversations with her. She didn't want to tell them what she was planning because it would add even more pressure to what she was already feeling. She sat at the table and ate her granola and yogurt while everyone else giggled and chatted.

Eve walked up and sat a chocolate, chocolate chip muffin in front of her before kissing her on her head and sitting down next to her. It seemed that the roles had reversed on this day and it was Eve trying to take care of Abigail and relax her while being comfortable with everyone around them. Abigail's heart melted even more as she bit into the muffin. It was even warm which meant that Eve stopped by a microwave to warm it up a bit. The chocolate helped her to feel a bit more normal and she even joined in the conversation a few times. However, mostly she mentally went through her checklist and double checked she had bought or ordered everything she needed for the night.

One night, Alex saw her unloading items from a bag and asked if she was preparing for them to lose electricity and she shared that she was trying to show Eve a romantic end of the semester date. Alex gave a few suggestions which Abigail gladly accepted. But, now that it was the day of, she was worried something would go wrong.

When breakfast was over, Abigail and Eve strolled silently to their sign language class. It seemed as if Eve knew she needed the quietness and wasn't bothered by it or asked what was worrying her or anything. Once they entered the class, Abigail was able to switch over to her student brain and focus on what was in front of her. She shoved everything else aside and concentrated on the exercises. That day in class, the teacher was having them break into groups of three or four and practice the presentation part of the final next week. Each of them had to do a small solo piece and then a conversation exchange piece. Then there was a written exam. By the end of class, Abigail was energized and tired at the same time.

As they were departing class, Eve grabbed her arm and instead of heading them towards the library, Eve tugged her over to the courtyard where there were several benches. She plopped down on one and straddled it and then tapped the seat next to her. Abigail gave in and mirrored Eve's position. She didn't have to wait long before finding out what was up.

"So, I haven't asked you or inquired as to what is going on, but now that it is only us and class is over, I am going to. Want to tell me what has you in this mood? Because I have been excited about our date tonight, but if we need to cancel it so you can take care of—or work on—whatever is stressing you out we can. Talk to me."

Abigail grinned at how Eve was starting to sound like Nori in a way by talking and asking questions and not taking a breather to let the other person talk. "We are not canceling our date. I promise that by tomorrow things will be better," *or worse depending on how the night goes,* Abigail said that last part inside her own head.

"Are you sure? Is this stress something I can help with?"

Abigail rubbed her thumb along Eve's cheekbone, "No. But, you being with me helps. It is simply I am all up in my head and I will admit, I might be a little nervous about our surprise date."

"Oh, I should have put two and two together. Trust me, whatever we do, I will love it. I enjoy spending time with you. We can hang out and watch reruns of Star Trek and I would be happy."

"I know and that is what is great about you. But, that isn't what we are doing. And before you ask, I am still not going to give you a hint, either. Okay, one small, tiny fraction of a hint." Abigail held her thumb and forefinger a quarter of an inch apart. "We will have food, so come hungry."

Eve beamed, "We better have food. I am always starving after class on Thursday. Between going from Math and rushing to Astronomy, I have to carry granola bars in my bag. Neither Peyton nor LeForge let us out early. I'm definitely getting my tuition money worth in their classes."

"My poor girl. Well, that is your one clue. You will be fed. Not telling you what or where."

"Ahh darn. Come on, I really could use the visualization and think about it all day."

Abigail shook her head, "Nope."

"Fine. I would eat now, but I am usually still full from breakfast. However, by the time I am thirty minutes into staring at numbers, my stomach is ready for more nutrition."

"Thus the snacks."

"Exactly. When I found out that walnuts are good for the brain, I buy them now and then in the hope it will help with the mental stamina needed."

"You know, you are starting to make me hungry. How about we go grab a snack now before you have to battle the terrible tricky trig."

Eve rolled her eyes at Abigail, "Haha. I never said it was terrible. I enjoy Peyton's class."

"No doubt. She is a great professor. Let's go."

They ambled towards the cafeteria to see what they wanted to eat.

Abigail had a hard time focusing on her afternoon class, but it was a review session and she didn't want to miss out on any hints or suggestions on areas to concentrate studying on. This was going to be one of her harder finals for the semester. The moment the professor dismissed them, Abigail hustled over to her dorm to start packing up everything. She had several hours ahead of her, but it would go by quickly.

She took the picnic basket and box of stuff down to her car and then came back upstairs to take a quick shower. She debated on wearing a sundress, but knew what Eve was wearing and she didn't want Eve to feel underdressed; plus, they would be laying down for part of it so, practicality won out. Instead, Abigail chose a nice pair of jean shorts and a loose, purple tank top since it was almost May in Texas after all. She braided her hair in a simple braid that fell down the middle of her back.

Once she was dressed, it was off to the store and then to Michelangelo's to pick up dinner. This was one of the ideas that Alex gave her. She suggested treating Eve to one of her favorite dinners. She remembered one time that Eve mentioned beef wellington. However, to make sure, she called the restaurant and asked to talk to the chef. Then she explained who she was and what she wanted. Carlos immediately jumped on board and said to leave it in his hands and he would prepare dinner for them. She asked that he include the famous chocolate cake for dessert and he readily agreed.

Before she went to get the food, she went by the store and bought some strawberries, grapes, cheese, and little crackers. She didn't think they would need anything other than the dinner, but she wanted to make sure if they needed something to nibble upon, she had it. She grabbed some ice also to keep things cool. She was going to put ice in a cooler around a rack she set up inside. That way she could sit things on top of the rack, but the air inside the cooler would keep the food from melting or warming up, well the food that didn't need to be hot that was. She had never tried this and only thought of it so she was curious if it would work.

When she arrived at Michelangelo's, she knew she wasn't dressed in the normal attire of the patrons of the restaurant. She could definitely tell by the look that crossed the hostess's face before she regained control and politeness. "Good evening, how may I help you?"

"Hello, my name is Abigail. I called and spoke with Chef Carlos about an order for pickup."

"One moment and I will check on that." The woman, whose name was Trisha according to the nametag, meandered away leaving Abigail to check out the part of the restaurant she could see. A few minutes later, Trisha returned. "Come this way, Chef insisted that I bring you back to him." By 'insisted,' Abigail had a feeling that Trisha had warned Carlos that Abigail's appearance reflected that of one heading to the beach.

He must not have cared, because Trisha swished open the door leading to the kitchen and beckoned Abigail to follow her. Once back there, they headed to the right and to a small office. Abigail saw a man sitting and typing on the computer. When she entered, he turned around to face her.

"Ahh. The famous Abigail! It is a pleasure and delight to finally get to meet you. Please come in and have a seat. I will be but one moment." He stepped back out and strode off. She heard a bit of loud talking and then a few seconds later, Carlos returned. "Sorry about that, dear, I have to keep my staff preparing for tonight's guests."

"I understand. I don't want to keep you from your duties. I was only here to pick up the dinner."

"I know, but I wanted to meet the girl that has captured our dear Eve's heart." Carlos sat back and brought his hands and fingers together in a temple. "You know that Eve doesn't have any family, right?" Abigail only nodded, anxious where this may be going since Carlos's voice was a bit more stern than when he first spoke with her. "Well, my wife and I have sort of adopted Eve since she started working here and while she may or may not think of me as such, I feel like she is a cross between a daughter and a sister to me. I care about her very much."

Abigail continued nodding not knowing what to say at this point, but tried, "I know that Eve cares about you both very much. She has said so on several occasions."

"Has she now? That is wonderful to hear. Thank you for telling me. It is hard to get that girl to open up." He relaxed more in his chair and then leaned forward resting his arms on the desk. "You seem like a good girl yourself, Abigail, based on what little Eve has shared and the fact that you are trying to do this special thing for her tonight." Abigail's muscles relaxed at those kind words. "However..." Great, now they were tense again. "I wanted you to know that I don't want to see her hurt. I am not doing any of the mafia, 'if you hurt my daughter, then no one will find you' stuff. But, I do want you to know that she has people that care and love her very much. She has a makeshift family here in this restaurant. Now, that is all I have to say. Have fun tonight and lastly, don't bother trying to pay for this food as there isn't a price listed on it. Take it with my blessing."

"Wow. Thank you, I would attempt to argue, but I have learned from Eve how stubborn you can get. May I say one thing before I leave?" At his nod, Abigail continued, "I am glad she has you looking out for her. Eve is very special, not only to me, but to the group of friends we have at the college. You might not string me up for hurting Eve, but they gladly would. Just know that there are others who care about her and welcome her into their hearts just as you have with yours. And I appreciate what you have done for me tonight."

"You are welcome, Abigail. I have a feeling I will be seeing more of you. I will grab your food." Carlos disappeared again and returned carrying not one, but two large bags.

"That looks like way more than I asked for."

"Just take it and good luck." He grinned and handed over the bags.

Abigail left and despite wanting to look immediately in the bags, she waited until she drove to her destination.

Her plan was to have a cozy dinner outside under the stars. Most of the steps they made in their relationship happened under the stars, so Abigail thought this moment would be best under the night sky, too. And luck was showing her kindness as it was a beautiful, cloudless, and, more importantly, rainless night. She was going to execute it in the same place as one of the first nights, but the idea that anyone could walk by and interrupt them or just stare bothered her, so she might have offered up a few favors.

At first she thought of the football stadium, but that was way too big. Then she thought of the top of one of the buildings which was a viable option, but she didn't want to haul everything up and down several flights of stairs. In the end, she decided that the baseball field would work. She was thinking about it one day when she and Ford got together to study and she asked him if he knew of a good secluded place to stargaze. Then she went on to explain her idea and the different areas she had thought of. He suggested the baseball field and even reached out on her behalf. There was some begging and lots of promises on her part and threatening on the other people's part, but she was granted access. Plus, it wasn't near all of the buildings so it was even better.

Abigail showed up and was let into the gate. Doug shut it and reminded her, "Don't forget to call me when you are about to leave so I can come and lock up."

"I promise. I appreciate this and will owe you one."

"Yes you will. But, Ford spoke highly of you, so I will trust you."

"Thanks, Doug."

He waved and trudged off while Abigail got to work. She carried the box out and decided to keep it at a spot close to the gate. First thing she pulled out was a big soft blanket. She spread it over the ground between the pitcher's mound and home plate.Then she took all the LED candles and placed them around the blanket so it was all lit up. She had a couple of battery operated lanterns in the middle so they would have more light to eat by.

This next part she wasn't sure about. She bought some fake flowers to spread around, but since they were outside, she thought she better not in case they blew away. However, she did use a vase and put some fresh flowers she picked up in it. Abigail placed two pillows down on the blanket next to each other along with a smaller blanket in case it was needed. Once that was all set up, she went back to the car and brought the cooler out along with the bags Carlos gave her.

Now that she was working and putting together everything, it helped keep her mind occupied, but the closer it got to 9pm, the more her nerves got the better of her. She knelt down on the blanket next to the bags and opened the first one and found a cushiony bag inside with a note on top.

~Dinner is inside. Leave until ready to eat so it will stay warm longer. Have fun. C~

When Abigail opened the second bag that was just as heavy as the first one she found several things and began pulling things out. The first thing she noticed was laying down on top in the middle there was what looked like a bottle of wine. However, when she pulled it out, she found it was non-alcoholic sparkling wine with a note. ~Chill me~ Abigail simply laughed and opened the cooler and shoved it inside the ice. What she would have done if she didn't bring ice she wasn't sure.

The next layer that was inside were two salads and a couple of different dressings. She sat those on top of the cooler for now. The remainder of the items were real forks, cloth napkins, plates, and two wine glasses wrapped up carefully. Carlos did not go half measures on anything. Abigail was beyond impressed and would have to do something to thank the kind man. She tugged it all out and organized it all into two settings like at a dinner table in front of the picnic basket. Guess she didn't need half of what was in there now. Lastly, from the bottom of the bag she pulled out a large pan with a lid on it. Again, there was a note taped to the top of it.

~You can have Eve return all the dishes to me when she works next. I thought you all needed more than cake. C~

Abigail couldn't resist peeking inside, but before she managed to, her phone went off alerting her that Eve texted her.

EVE: CLASS IS OVER. WHERE AM I GOING OR ARE YOU COMING HERE?

ABIGAIL: I AM WAITING ON YOU. GO TO THE BASEBALL FIELD EAST OF CAMPUS AND GO UP TOWARDS HOME PLATE.

E: INTERESTING. NOT SURE WATCHING A GAME IS IN THE TOP TWENTY OF WHAT I WOULD HAVE GUESSED, ESPECIALLY THIS LATE.

A: THE GATE IS OPEN FOR YOU. COME THROUGH THERE AND YOU CAN'T MISS ME.

E: ON MY WAY. DO I NEED TO BRING ANYTHING?

A: JUST MY GORGEOUS GIRLFRIEND.

E: WHERE IS SHE AT? I CAN PICK HER UP.

A: SMARTASS.

E: YOU KNOW IT.

Since Eve was on her way, Abigail sat the dessert on the rack in the cooler and hoped nothing inside would be ruined by the chillness. Then she scrambled and packed everything she didn't need inside the box and moved it over against the fence. Once all of that was done, she glanced over it all and was happy. She only prayed that Eve was surprised and pleased. There wasn't anything else she could do now.

CHAPTER 25

EVE

All day, Eve knew something extra was up with the date that night. Abigail was acting weird and definitely not herself. At first, Eve thought maybe she was about to get dumped when she was asked about getting together without any details, but when she inquired about that, the shock and outrage from Abigail had Eve quickly tossing that idea.

She had left Abigail alone in her planning and her mind. Now that the time had arrived, Eve was a little nervous herself. What if she didn't act with the appropriate amount of excitement Abigail was expecting with such a hush-hush event. Eve even asked Nori if she had any idea what was going on and Nori didn't know what she was even talking about until Eve explained about the secret date. Of course that made Nori pout for a minute that Abigail didn't include her until Eve reminded her friend that she couldn't keep a secret and would have blabbed the whole thing ahead of time by accident.

As soon as class was nearing the end, Eve texted Abigail to find out where she was to head. When Abigail replied back with the baseball field, Eve was really confused and had no idea what was up. She had thought once the location was divulged she might have a guess, but she was as in the dark as deep as the vastness of space.

She approached the baseball field and there weren't a lot of lights, so she had to turn on the flashlight of her phone at one point. She was starting to get worried and decided to call Abigail. The other woman picked up on the second ring.

"Hey, babe, everything okay?"

"Yeah. It was getting darker and it didn't look like the ballfield had the big lights on so wanted to make sure I was going to the right place."

"Dang it. I didn't think of that. I drove over here and have been getting used to the dimming light. Need me to come meet you along the way?"

"No. I am almost there."

"Well, stay on the phone with me until you get here. So, how was class?"

Eve chuckled, "Still keeping the mystery going. Alright then. Both classes went well. Trig wasn't terrible contrary to your teasing earlier. We had a review session today over the last couple of week's material before our big exam on Tuesday. Same for my Astronomy class. I know we have the group party on Sunday, but other than that, I think I am going to be hitting the books hard this next week."

"You and me, both."

"Okay, I see the fence. I am crossing the grass and heading to the gate."

"I see you."

Eve saw Abigail leaning against the opening in her shorts and shirt. She waved and Eve smiled at that small gesture. Behind Abigail, Eve could tell there were little lights. She heard a click and realized Abigail hung up the phone and was rushing towards her.

"Hold on. I thought of something last minute. Close your eyes and put your hands over them," Abigail instructed.

Eve did as requested, trusting Abigail wouldn't let her trip.

"Alright then, I am going to take hold of your arm and lead you."

"Okay. If I fall, I am not going to forgive you easily. I don't want to explain why I ended up in the ER. Again."

"I won't let you fall. It isn't far anyways."

Eve felt Abigail wrap her palm and fingers around Eve's bicep and then gently tug. The first few steps that Eve took were hesitant, but once her body relaxed, it became easier.

"Just a few more feet. Okay. Stop, but don't uncover your eyes quite yet."

Eve paused until she heard Abigail say, "Now." Then she dropped her hands and opened her eyes. Immediately her hands raised back up to cover her mouth instead. The picture in front of her was so beautiful. It was all lit up and magical. Never had anyone done anything like this for her, ever. "It is so, wow." Eve felt something wet on her cheek and wiped away a tear.

"You like it?" Abigail was rocking on her feet and Eve grabbed the woman around the neck and brought her head down for a long kiss.

"Yes, of course. Abby, this is just wow. Amazing. The flowers, candles–"

"Which aren't real, the candles that is."

"Even better. There are pillows and plates? Those aren't paper ones."

"No they are not. There is a story there. Come on over and have a seat. We have dinner."

Eve walked over and dropped her backpack on the edge of the blanket and then took off her tennis shoes before stepping on the blanket. "Where do you want me to sit?"

"In front of either place is fine. Let me grab things." Eve watched as Abigail opened a cooler she hadn't even noticed and brought out two salads and a bottle of something to drink. "I wanted to give you a nice romantic dinner out, but cozy and for just the two of us. I called your workplace and spoke to Carlos about making you some of your favorite things."

"No, you didn't!"

"Yeah. I kind of let him know part of my plans. When I arrived this afternoon, he handed me two bags that were closed off. When I opened them there was so much more inside than I asked for. He said to bring the dishes back with you when you work next."

"Of course."

"He included this bottle of something to drink, non-alcoholic, of course. Do you want some now, later, or never?"

"I am flexible," Eve had no idea what was planned, so she didn't want to influence the night.

"Let's put it back on ice for a bit longer and let it chill. We can have some water in our fancy glasses for now."

"Sounds like a plan to me."

"How about you pour us some water while I grab the salads."

Eve took the two water bottles and used about one and a half of them and then downed the last half. The walk over had her thirsty.

Abigail handed one of the salads over and held up some salad dressing options. Eve chose ranch as did her date. "I was going to have us put the salads on the plate, but then I thought we should save that for the dinner portion. What do you think?"

"This is your orchestra, I am here for the music."

"You know, sometimes you are a nerd."

"True." Eve wasn't going to deny that.

"But, you are my nerd," Abigail whispered as she leaned over and kissed Eve lightly on the lips.

"As you are mine." Eve raised her glass of water. "Here is to great girlfriends who surprise you with delicious food on a beautiful night."

"Cheers."

Eve clinked her glass with Abigail's. "I have always wanted to do that."

They chatted while eating their salads about what all was going on in their day and about the preparations that went into the night. Then when they finished their salads, Abigail put the containers back into the cooler until the end when she would throw everything away.

"Next up is the main course. I will admit, I know what I suggested, but I actually don't know what Carlos made. This is a surprise for us both."

Eve watched as Abigail reached into a bag and brought out an insulated bag. "That man thought of everything."

"Yeah, there was a note to not open until we got ready to eat." Abigail placed the bag between them and Eve rubbed her hands together. She really did love all the food Carlos made.

When Abigail unzipped the bag, and pulled out a dish, Eve let out a squeal. "It's little beef wellingtons!" In the next container there were oven roasted potatoes and asparagus. "One day, I will have one of these right after it is cooked. I imagine it tastes so much better than after it is reheated or at room temperature."

"Well, I got it as late as I could because I didn't want it cold."

"Woman, I don't care how I get to eat this. Hand me one of the containers and I will split up the food on our plates."

"I can serve you. This is your time to be dined."

"I appreciate it, but it's faster to split the job," Eve pointed out. She heard Abigail sigh and knew she won the battle. "I promise your intentions are well received."

This time while they ate, Abigail turned on some quiet music and Eve had to keep from moaning at each bite of food. It was still magically warmer than she thought it would be. And the potatoes were heavenly. She was going to bed a happy woman tonight.

After Eve did everything but lick the plate, she finished off her water. "That was so delicious. I think I might need a nap before hiking back to my dorm room."

"Well, my car is here, so you get to have a ride and we aren't going anywhere immediately."

"No?"

"You don't think I put together this lovely environment for us to not luxuriate in it do you? Plus, we have the best course still to indulge in. Dessert."

Eve's hand dropped to her stomach. "Okay, I appreciate that, but I think that I am going to need to wait a bit."

"No problem, I have several reasons I brought you out here other than feeding you."

"And what are these reasons?"

"Well, one of them is right above us. I knew we would need to relax and thought having our favorite chaperone would be a great way to enjoy the night. I tried to get a spot dark enough where we could see more of the stars. Plus, I brought us pillows and if for some weird reason one of us gets chilly, there is a blanket."

"Mmmm, I like the sound of that. And the other reason?" Eve asked.

"You will have to wait and see."

"Tease." Eve didn't really mind. She liked surprises sometimes and so far, everything that Abigail had shown her tonight was wonderful. "In that case, I vote we stretch out on this pillowy ground and listen to the sounds around us." Eve crawled over to where the pillow was. "What happens if we fall asleep? Are the sprinklers going to turn on and soak us or will we be found in the morning by people walking by or worse, people showing up for practice?" At the beginning Eve was simply being fanciful and silly, but by the end she was really starting to freak out. She did not want to be found sleeping in the middle of the field. That totally had the makings of something that would haunt her for years to come.

"Relax. I set two alarms for that reason. Although, I doubt we will fall asleep."

"That makes me feel better. Thanks."

"Of course. Now lay down and let's see what kind of story the stars tell us tonight."

Eve scooted close to Abigail so they were touching along their sides. "First off, there is Ursa Major, you can see part of it." Eve pointed up, but she knew that it was like pointing at a big wall of dots and expecting a person to know which one you are looking for.

"Isn't that the one that has the Big Dipper in it?"

"Yes, it is. But it has more than that. However, you can use the end of the ladle part of the dipper to draw a line up to the North Star."

"I find it fascinating that sailors and other people used to know where they were going simply by looking up at the night sky and recognizing the same stars."

"It definitely makes you think. If people were to not have a GPS or a compass on their phone and get lost, not sure how many would know where they were heading and not run around in circles."

"Which is why I will have you with me. You and your stars can keep us pointed in the right direction."

"You put too much faith in me, Abby."

"Go on and tell me more about the stars."

"Well, this isn't entirely about the stars, but about the sky in general. We will be having a full moon right before we have finals."

Eve heard Abigail mutter, "Oh great. Time for everything to go crazy is when I need things to be calm."

"You are one of the most put-together persons I know. But, you will also be able to see the Eta Aquariids Meteor Shower."

"What is that?"

Eve turned her head and found Abigail on her side observing Eve. It was oddly turning her on and that flustered her.

"Umm. What?"

"What is Eta Aquarius?"

"Aquariids."

"Yeah, that."

"It is when Earth passes through the dust debris of Halley's comet. It happens in May and October."

"Oh, cool. You are so sexy when you speak about this."

Eve squeaked out, "I am?" She cleared her throat and repeated, "I am?"

"Yes, you are." Then before she knew it, Abigail was leaning over her and kissing her. When she sucked on Eve's bottom lip, Eve was glad she wasn't standing up or her legs would have collapsed.

On their own accord, Eve's hands wrapped around Abigail's back and pulled her tight against her. She was lost in the sensation of the moment and the weight of Abigail half laying on her. It felt so right having her in Eve's arms and letting their bodies and mouths express what neither of them had yet to say out loud. None of that mattered and Eve knew she was chicken anyways.

Abigail pulled apart, panting, and Eve wanted to ask her why she stopped. "This isn't what I had planned for tonight."

"I don't care. I think it is a rather pleasurable unexpected perk. Now, kiss me again."

Abigail smiled a saucy grin and did exactly as Eve requested. Mouths melded back into a slow and passionate embrace, time suspended, and Eve worked to focus on the feelings of what she was experiencing and hoping that Abigail was as aroused as she was.

Before Eve knew what was happening, Abigail had shifted slightly and was running her hand up and down Eve's body under her shirt and every touch was once again setting her on fire. At this rate, the sprinklers would need to turn on to keep them from setting the blanket ablaze.

Eve was panting hard and was that a moan or groan she made? The minute Abigail's hand slid under the waistband of Eve's pants, she froze. Was she going to? Did she want her to? Her body screamed out a very loud *Yes*!

"Eve, look at me."

At first, Eve couldn't figure out where the voice was coming from. Then she realized Abigail was talking to her. She opened her eyes and straight into the dilated pupils of her girlfriend.

"There you are. You want me to stop?"

"No. I don't think so."

"You sure? Because you have a rather tight grip on my wrist."

"Sorry." Eve let loose.

"Nothing to apologize for." But instead of Abigail continuing, she pulled her hand out and laid her palm on Eve's chest right over her heart. "That was quite intense."

"The kissing or my grasp on your wrist?" Eve wasn't sure at this point. Her brain was all muddled.

"The kissing, of course." Abigail sat up.

"Come sit up with me for a minute."

"How are you so damn calm? See, I told you the full moon wouldn't faze you. I am a molten mess and am about twenty seconds from combusting. If I was a guy, I think I would have blue balls that would be frostbitten right now. Do you think they might be called blue breasts on women? Because if so, that is what I have." Eve stopped her rambling when Abigail began laughing. "What is so funny?"

"You, my love. I love this side of you."

"I don't. I feel crazed and all logical mindset has been tossed into the wind and carried far far away."

Abigail kissed her again, probably to shut Eve up. This time, however, it was simply a closed-mouth kiss that pressed both of their lips together. After a few moments, Abigail pulled back and

Eve realized she had dropped down from a twelve on the crazy horny scale to more of an eight or even a seven point nine.

"Better?"

Eve just shot Abigail a look. "Not really, but you are safe from having your clothes ripped off."

"I don't think either of us wanted our first time together to be in the middle of the baseball field," rationalized Abigail.

"Perhaps not. But, now I feel all twitchy and like my mood is off."

"How about some chocolate?"

Eve's face instantly lit up. "Yes, my stomach is ready for dessert now. I swear I am not going to eat for two days after tonight. That will be just in time for the party at Kat and Logan's."

"We both know you will eat tomorrow."

"This is true, but you could let me have my moment," Eve pouted.

All Abigail did was smile and open the cooler to pull out a dish with a lid on it.

"What is inside?" Eve asked.

"I am not sure. Again, this is a surprise. But, if it doesn't appeal to you, I have grapes and strawberries along with cheese and crackers. I don't know how long I thought we would be out here, but I guess I thought I would need to feed you multiple times."

"Oh, let's have the sparkling stuff that Carlos sent us, too."

"Perfect." Eve watched Abigail root around in the cooler for several minutes before pulling out the bottle and wiping off the water. She pulled off the wrapper and removed the top. "Hand me your glass." Eve handed over her glass and then Abigail's. "This time, I will make the toast."

"Only fair since I did the last one."

Abigail sat on her knees and that made her even taller than Eve and made her want to stand up so they were closer in height. *Focus Eve,* she told herself.

"Eve, my darling girl. You came into my life like a wrecking ball. Wait that isn't right, that is a Miley song. Let me start over. The first day I met you when Nori introduced you to us, I knew there was something about you I was attracted to. My soul must have known then it met someone it wanted to be with because I haven't been able to stop thinking about you since that day. I knew you weren't looking for love, or me for that matter, but alas somewhere along the line, you decided to give me a chance. I am grateful for this because my life has been blessed and definitely not boring since you have entered it."

Eve opened her mouth to say something, but Abigail held up one finger and then bent over on the side and grabbed something. Was that a ring box? Woah, woah, woah. That better not be what that looked like. This was going way way too fast.

Eve knew her eyes had to be as big as the plates they ate dinner off of, but still Abigail continued. "Calm down, it isn't an engagement ring." Eve's body relaxed and it was only then she realized she must have frozen stiff again.

"Although, I won't rule that out for sometime in the future. No, neither of us are ready for that. This is simply a gift from me to you so you will have something to remember tonight by. I wanted to let you know, my dearest Eve, that my heart has grown fuller with you and I know we show each other in many ways how we feel, but I did all of this not only to show you I care about you, but to tell you I love you. Not the 'hey I love you, girl,' but the 'gut-wrenching, soul-pulling, completely life-altering love.'"

Eve sat there speechless. She had no words to say. Abigail opened the box and sat down crisscrossed. There on a chain was a little telescope. It was beautiful. Not as beautiful as the woman in front of her, but pretty.

"Come on now, don't cry. This was supposed to be a toast to my amazing girl and the love I have for her. Are you going to take the gift or do I need to politely clean up everything and go because this is too much?"

Eve threw herself at Abigail and tackled her onto the ground giving her a big, long kiss. She sat up, straddled Abigail, and looked down at the kind woman underneath her. "Of course, I am going to take it. And..."

Eve paused for a moment, perhaps a moment too long because Abigail grinned up at her before saying, "You don't have to say it back. Wait until you are ready. This is about me professing how I feel, not about making you say or do something you aren't prepared for."

"No, I want to say, you are right. I had no intentions of ever being in a relationship and never with a female. But, you and the rest of our friends have unlocked my heart and broke down some of the walls I had erected. I fell for you when you took such great and tender care of me when I was sick. Since then, my feelings for you have only grown stronger. So, yes, my Abby, I am taking your gift and your love and giving you my love in return. I love you, too!"

"You are such a precious person. I think it is really time to enjoy that drink and celebrate. What do you say? That and chocolate?"

"I will be sad on the day that I say no to chocolate."

"Yeah, I think we both will. Hop up then so we can indulge in some sweets or else, I am going to pull you down and find something else sweet to snack on."

Eve could feel her face heat up; however, she rolled off of Abigail and crawled over to where, magically, her drink hadn't spilled. Abigail's, though, was empty. "Uh-oh, I will need to wash your blanket."

"Nah. I have to wash it anyway from the dirt carpet we are laying upon."

Eve was done waiting, she grabbed the container and opened the lid to find it full of two slices of chocolate cake on one half and then the other was covered in brownies and truffles. Not waiting a minute, she snatched up one of the truffles and bit into it. Rich chocolate goodness cracked open to showcase a chocolate mousse with a little bit of caramel in the center. "Heaven! There is no better word to describe this. Here, try this other half." Eve thrust the piece out to Abigail while grabbing another one.

"You know we can have our own."

"Yeah, but there is no telling how many different kinds there are, and if we share, we can sample more."

"I can't beat the logic." Abigail took the piece from her fingers. A few seconds later, Eve heard sounds coming from across the blanket. "You are right. And the cooler didn't cause the caramel to harden too much."

"I think we need to sample a couple more and then dive into the cake."

Abigail giggled, "You know, you are acting like you haven't eaten in days. Either that or are stranded on an island and you are figuring out to ration food or split up job duties."

Eve glanced up and then back down. "You might be right. I can get a little weird and hyper with food in small batches. Sorry."

"Hun, don't be sorry. It was cute and I was teasing you."

"I know." Eve shrugged it off. She knew that sometimes her pattern with how she ate things was seen by others as peculiar. Heck it was to her at times, too. "This time you pick one."

"I am going to close my eyes and grab one." Eve held the container out for Abigail to grab a random truffle. Instead of opening her eyes to eat it, she kept them closed and bit into it. "Mmm. this one has coconut in it and something else, maybe almond flavoring." Abigail opened her eyes and then held the truffle up to Eve's mouth, "Taste."

So, Eve opened her mouth while keeping her eyes on Abigail's and slowly wrapped her lips around the treat and Abigail's fingers. She chewed slowly and her voice came out a little huskier than she intended. "You are right, very tasty. I love coconut."

Eve saw Abigail swallow, causing the corner of Eve's mouth to raise in pride.

"Umm." Abigail cleared her throat, "You ready for the cake? Are we splitting a piece of cake or each having our own? I mean, I am willing to split a piece, but I think one of them had a big A on the top."

"We are definitely each having our own piece." Eve thought she would have to take the truffles back to her room and the two of them could have fun eating them later. "You know how much I love this cake."

"Yeah, and you got me hooked on it. It looks like it might be a little different tonight, though."

Bending over, Eve studied the various layers and realized that Abigail was correct. "Oh, he put a few different fillings in there. That one looks like peanut butter or caramel mousse. We will have to see if we can figure out what they are. Good thing neither of us has many allergies."

"True. Hand me a plate from the basket and we can use it to put the cake on."

Eve dug through the picnic basket and pulled out four paper plates, she put two of each together to give more strength and handed them to Abigail. Once she had the chocolate goodness back in her little hands, she licked her fork clean and cut off the first bite. Each time she ate the cake, it was like experiencing it all over again for the first time.

In an effort to keep their conversation light, and honestly, she was curious, Eve asked, "What are your plans for the summer? I am not sure if we have talked about what everyone in our group is doing."

"You are right. We haven't. I assumed it would be about the same as we did last year or over winter break, which is probably why it hasn't come up."

"And?"

"And what? Oh, my plans. Yeah, I am going back home. One of my high school teachers who helped to develop my interest in chemistry teaches at camps aimed at elementary and middle-school aged students. So, I assist him in doing that part time. Plus, I will help out around the house. I usually see if I can pick up a part-time job or something so I don't go broke during the summer."

"That sounds like it would be a lot of fun. Do you like working with kids? Are you wanting to go into teaching?"

Abigail shook her head even as she managed to put another forkful of cake into her mouth. "No. I do not want to go into teaching. That isn't where my passion lies. But, during the summer for short periods of time, I enjoy it. It may be something I continue down the road volunteering when I can manage it or bringing more STEM-based opportunities to kids and showing them what is out there, especially for girls."

"I think both it and you are wonderful. I would have loved something like that as a kid. I look forward to hearing all about the camps." And she realized they wouldn't be together for the summer. That made her sad. She wondered if Abigail would forget about her.

Surely not, it wasn't like they couldn't talk and video chat. After all Jess and Nori were separated during the school year and they were making it work.

"Earth to Eve, where did you go?"

"Sorry, I suddenly thought about the fact that I wouldn't be seeing you for over three months."

"You know..." Abigail started and then paused as if gathering her words up and then began again a little slower, "You could always come back with me and stay with me for the summer as my guest."

"Oh I couldn't do that. First off, I think I would be too anxious to stay with you and your family. Plus, I would have to find a job. Mostly, though, I am taking some summer classes."

"You are?"

"Yeah. I found out that I can stay in a dorm they have open for summer classes. Then I can continue to work at Michelangelo's when not studying. Since I don't have an apartment or anywhere to go, I figured this was the best option for me. There is a small gap of time between the end of Spring term and the Summer one, but I think I might take off and go on a vacation. I have never done that. I have saved up."

"What if you came and saw me for a couple of those days and maybe Nori for a couple of days. If not at the beginning, then at the end of summer before Fall classes begin?"

"I think I could swing that. I hadn't thought about what I was going to do during that time period. I know they kick everyone off campus. I know I can't afford to go on two away vacation trips, but maybe if I could visit you both and stay at your house that would work. I could do some chores or help out to pay for housing."

The glare that Abigail shot her was very telling. "I didn't say how about you come work off some imaginary debt. You will be my guest and you will be treated as such. I will show you around, we can hang out and have some fun. I have absolutely no doubt that Nori will feel the same way. I know you maybe aren't as fully comfortable, but you could even go visit Mel and Kat. In fact, maybe we should all do an exploration of everyone's home. This is a great idea. I am going to make it happen."

"I think I might have let free a monster," Eve teased.

"A monster that is going to ensure you have lots of fun. A Fun Monster. Muahhahha."

"I think that is more mad scientist. Oh that fits you. Yes, Abby the Mad Scientist. Very fitting with your studies and all."

"Smartass."

"That would make me Eve, the Wandering Warrior."

"Wait a minute, yours sounds cooler than mine."

"Tough. Let's see, Nori's would be what?" Eve tapped her chin with her fork and belatedly realized she just put chocolate all over it.

Abigail laughed and handed over a napkin, "Here. And I think that it should be Nori, the Calculating Chicken."

Eve was swallowing her cake and choked on it. When she was able to speak again, she asked, "What?"

"You know she is a mother hen and takes care of everyone, but I wanted a little alliteration so went with chicken."

"I think we need to change that."

Abigail threw her arms up. "Fine. What do you have?"

"Nori, the lover of Pi."

That time Abigail busted out a belly laugh and ended up falling over on her side. In between her bouts of laughter, she asked, "You… know that… Professor… Edison… goes by… Pi… to her friends… right?"

"Yep. That is why I chose it. The one thing I remember vividly from the first day I met Nori was her shrieking over me having a class with Professor Edison."

"That is a winner."

"So, the score is Eve - 3, Abigail - 0."

"We were keeping score?"

Eve leaned in close and whispered, "Always."

Abigail just shook her head and both of them finished their cake.

As soon as their stomachs were full again with chocolatey goodness, they laid back and simply watched the stars twinkle above them. It was relaxing and kept Eve from thinking too much about what awaited her back in her room. After another hour, Eve was beginning to feel a sugar crash coming and sat up before she fell asleep in her meditative state.

"I am starting to get sleepy. I hate to end this wonderful night, but I think we better pack up and head back."

"I agree."

Eve began to stack the plates and put them on top of the insulated bag with the rest of the dishes. She made sure to wrap up the glasses so they wouldn't knock together and break. Then she turned off all the candles and then immediately turned a couple of the brighter ones back on to help illuminate everything.

The ones that were turned off, Abigail grabbed and put into the box followed by the rest of the items until everything was stacked up. Using the lantern, Eve carried the vase of flowers, the picnic basket, and the bag from Michelangelo's while Abigail pulled the cooler with the box on top and carried the blanket in her other arm with the flashlight on her phone turned on to help see.

Once they closed the gate behind them, Abigail was able to hit her car unlock button and it triggered the headlights on the car to come on. That helped them get the rest of the way to the vehicle safely. Eve loaded up the backseat while Abigail drained the melted ice. When they were in the car, Abigail grabbed her phone.

"Do you need directions to get us back?" Eve teased.

"No, I have to text and let Doug know that I am done. If I don't, I might be hunted down."

"We don't want that to happen. I might have to use my backpack to defend you. It is still full of books."

Her girlfriend laughed at her as she placed her phone in the console. Soon they were on their way back to Eve's dorm. It didn't take very long to drive over there, but Eve was still appreciative that she didn't have to walk it. She was exhausted after the long day. Tomorrow at least she could sleep in.

When they arrived at the dorm, despite Eve telling her that she didn't need to, Abigail walked Eve to her dorm room and helped to carry something up. "Do you want to come in for a bit?"

Abigail stepped into the room, but stayed near the door. "I want to stay, but I think it would be better if I left."

"Are you sure?" Eve didn't want her girlfriend to leave that night.

"Not really."

Grabbing Abigail's hand, she tugged her close and then wrapped her arms around her waist. "Then stay with me tonight and we can pretend we are still on our date."

"You sure?"

Eve raised up on tiptoes and breathed one word against Abigail's lips before silencing any conversation with a kiss, "Yes."

Epilogue

EVE

It was the day after everyone had finished their finals and they were having a packing party. Everyone decided to rent a storage unit to keep the majority of their things in while they were on summer holiday. It actually came about because Eve needed a place to keep her stuff until the summer session started and Logan asked about renting a unit for a month. That got them all talking and instead of the smallest unit, they bumped it up to a bigger size and split the cost. They were talking and thought maybe Nori, Abigail, and Eve would get a two bedroom apartment next semester and share it. They were going to look at the costs of both and decide what was the better deal.

Eve was all in favor of that because it would mean no more horrible roommates. There was even talk of maybe getting a three or four bedroom house instead to rent and seeing if a few others they knew would be interested in splitting it. Abigail mentioned Alex since she was a great roommate to have in the dorms.

When she brought up Alex's name, Eve didn't miss the look that crossed Melissa's face. She had a feeling that there would be no shortage of excitement with Alex in the mix and she would be voting a huge yes to having her move in.

In the meantime, they were boxing everything up and moving it over. Eve already said she was taking the front of the unit because she would be accessing it in the near future. Everyone agreed that was smart.

Once they had everything packed up in storage, they headed over for pizza to celebrate surviving the semester. Alex, Garrison, Ford, and about four or five others were joining them so it was going to be a big group with lots of fun.

Eve was sad to see everyone depart for the summer, but she knew they would all be back together in just a few months and everyone would keep in contact until then. Eve felt Abigail grab her hand and squeeze. Who would have thought that the first day when she was lost and struggling to find her class, it would all lead to great friends and falling in love for the first time?

ABOUT THE AUTHOR

RK Phillips is a quirky, nerdy, number loving person that finds inspiration in her dreams. She currently resides in Texas, but originally from Oklahoma where she has spent the majority of her life. By day she is an accountant, but after work her right brain is freed. Imagination and creativity come out to play in her writing, crafting, and sleeping dream world. Some of her favorite things are books, movies, numbers, and tigers, not necessarily in that order. She loves hearing from people! So, send her an email or connect with her on Facebook.

rkphillipsauthor@gmail.com

fb.com/rk.phillips.148

Made in the USA
Middletown, DE
30 June 2023

34258743R00159